SHATTERED PORTRAIT

Carey Maytham

ISBN: 978-1-4669-3395-8 (sc)
ISBN: 978-1-4669-3396-5 (e)

Trafford rev. 04/27/2012

 www.trafford.com

North America & international
toll-free: 1 888 232 4444 (USA & Canada)
phone: 250 383 6864 ♦ fax: 812 355 4082

CHAPTER ONE

"What's the time Elize?"

A mumbling sound came from the other side of the bed at five in the morning on an ice cold day in their chalet in the woods outside Boulougne. Elize and her husband had nothing to depend on for survival and warmth but the little wooden chalet type cottage that Maurice had built himself in that summer seven or eight years ago before hardship had struck his painting circle of clients and he was having to eke out a living for the time being. He was doing an almost fraudulent commission of artwork that was a copy of a famous Giotto Madonna, ordered by the Compte of the nearby castle.

Maurice had been wandering in the grounds of the edifice and had come upon the Count surveying the damage done to the moat of the castle by the recent melting of heavy snowfalls in the area. The Count had discovered that Maurice was an artist. Ever on the lookout for a subject to paint he had inquired about the Count's family. He knew a little about them from the odd bit of gossip that he had unearthed in the local village tavern where he had spent many idle hours on the hunt for

1

subjects to use to flaunt his artistic prowess and also the coffers of the little cottage in the woods.

"Elize get up. You never want to be the one who stokes the fire in the living room first in the morning. He nudged her almost violently in the early icy hours. The windows of the bedroom that also served as a studio when he was awake were thickly coated at the edge with snow and he could see snow flakes falling in the dim light of day, so dim that he could hardly see very far outside.

He could hear the wind gently soughing amongst the pine trees outside as he lay there Elize still breathing deeply as she slept on. He heard the two children stirring. They would be hungry. He was determined not to have to be the one to stoke up last night's fire in the grate and now nearly pushed Elize out of bed.

"Elize—the fire! We must have some warmth in the place. Go and wake Grandmêre and the children and put some oats on to boil for breakfast."

Maurice had heard the only cock in their barnyard crowing. As usual it annoyed him because somehow the urgency of the day's fare seeped into his consciousness. It was not only the cock that had awoken him although it was the most irritating on this frozen morning, but also the rest of the poultry. They had a habit of wakening him every day.

The mooing of their cow urgent to have her udders tapped gave a superficial soothing to what Maurice felt as he was fully awake now. It would be another hard winter's day of eking out a living with his painting. He tried to fight against the angry feelings that it was arousing in him as he lay there. Elize had still not moved.

Why should he have to support his mother, wife and two children? All of them? A grating voice came from the small room next door. It was the old lady the only person on earth that Elize had any fear of. So Grandmêre was awake. That meant that they would all have to get up to face the initial chaos of the day. Grandmêre's sharp cackle of a voice sounded through the door. Elize who feared her sharp tongue sat up suddenly as she heard the sound.

With the general sulkiness of the morning's rising she stumbled sleepily into the children's room regardless of how she looked hair wispy and nightdress crumpled.

"Angèle, Paule!" She shook them going from one bed to the other in the cold of the morning.

"Is breakfast ready?" This was Paule.

"No you idiot—Grandmêre has only just woken us as usual. Your father is of his habit still in bed. He should set the example in the household and rise first."

"Then I'm going to stay in bed some more too," said the eight-year-old Paule.

"You are a naughty boy," chided his mother continuing "Angèle you'll get up to go and milk our cow won't you little girl?"

"Yes mother" came a sleepy but willing voice from under the coverlet that her mother had patiently stitched in the time when Maurice was out painting. This was when they had seen better days and life had seemed more fruitful. The little girl pattered off to the bathroom and not to be outdone at the prospect of a new day Paule leapt out of bed too. Then there was the usual argument over the use of the bathroom only to be quelled by Maurice's sudden awakened presence.

"Off you go Angèle—you are quiet this morning. You seem to be the only one who wants to get up on these frosty mornings!"

"Oh! me too mama" came the words from little brown-eyed Paule. Angèle was already dressed and struggling with the rusty latch on the kitchen door leading out to the barnyard. A reluctant Maurice followed her to supervise the milking of their only cow. This was because Elize was trying to prepare breakfast for the five of them with little Paule dancing around the stove like a Red Indian.

"Quietly now Paule or I will spill this hot water that I am boiling for our oats. Go and see how Angèle is getting on with the milking outside you naughty boy."

She had just noticed that he was not wearing his warm parka.

"Go and put on your warm clothes."

She thought to herself, it is just as well that I keep a steady eye on these two. Just then in came Angèle trying to carry the huge bucket of milk with Maurice trying to take it out of her hands without slopping the full container of fresh creamy milk. Grandmêre entered the room and shrieked at Angèle when she saw what was happening.

"Let go child! Maurice can't you take it from her?"

"No, no, papa let me carry it I must, mamma said so," The little girl said in high squeaky voice. This was yet another example of the way Grandmêre was interfering in the lives of the family. Maurice shrugged and whipped the bucket out of the child's hands. She began stamping her feet and letting out a string of angry words in her tiny girl's voice. As usual taking upon herself all the chores and tasks of the day Elize tried to soothe the situation by calling them all to breakfast. It was seven o' clock by the time the fire was stoked and they had all had their porridge. This was all they could afford to eat in the bleak mid-winter. A cautious knock on the door came to their ears. Both children yelled:

"Its Lazlé. Lazlé has come to take us to school. I'll let him in," cried Angèle."

"No I will," argued Paule and roughly pushed his sister away from the door that opened anyway and a dwarfed hunchback figure, clearly a cripple appeared brushing the snowflakes off his frame before he entered.

As Lazlé the hunchbacked cripple made his way through the deep midwinter snow his long boots sinking down into the muddy terrain, he thought as he usually did on this walk of the poor Elize, for whom he had a deep and growing affection. He in his warm-hearted way felt increasingly angry with Maurice because of the way he was treating his wife.

He and Maurice had come to know one another in the village tavern Maurice always interested and willing to meet someone new there. The grotesque shape of Lazlé's body had fascinated him over the years that their friendship had formed. Maurice in his enquiring way had found out much about the unfortunate man who it seemed had a twin brother, Anzlé. Lazlé heard about Elize and had upon their meeting doted on her.

He saw a little into the cruel way that she was being treated by Grandmêre and Maurice. They has made a complete skivy of the poor girl and the two children being quite young were thoughtless as regards the humbling and tiring tasks that Elize had to do to keep a roof over their heads.

Maurice was becoming increasingly manipulative of Elize as he knew she had nowhere else to live and took advantage of his poor wife at the slightest opportunity. All this while he for a large part of the day had to paint for a living.

Lazlé sighed. He was nearly at the little chalet and had as usual remembered the way there by the way the trees were growing in the forest. As ever in his lonely life with his mother on the outskirts of the village he looked forward to being part of the domestic scene. From the outside it looked so cosy but Lazlé knew through his own pain and suffering from his wartime paratrooping accident that had reduced him to his poor crippled state, that this was not so. Both he and Elize were suffering.

No, he was aware that beneath the apparent domesticity simmered arrogance and selfishness on Maurice's part and pain and increasing anguish on Elize's. Her mother-in-law did nothing to make life brighter for Elize whose own parents, who had lived in the village had died only a few years ago. This had left her penniless but for what her husband could eke out by way of an artist's living. Her mother and father had at first thought that he would become a well-known painter but towards the end of their lives they had become sadly disillusioned by Maurice.

Lazlé had left his mother's little cottage on the outskirts of the forest in the depths of which Maurice had built his little chalet those ten years ago when he was courting Elize. Both came from prominent members of the little community outside the large central town of Boulougne. Maurice's father was a professor at the University while Elize's mother was a government employee who had lost her husband a victim of the Second World War.

Initially while a young man searching cannily for a life partner to mother children that was instinctual to them both he had shown the first signs of his manipulative nature as he grew older becoming obsessively so. Elize had no father so it had been easy to worm his way into Madame Groze's ménage. It had been easy to court Elize too because she was a single daughter having only brothers to complete the family.

Elize had a gently rounded almost heavily sulky face and who by virtue of the family circumstances knew very little other than the domesticity of running a home. Lazlé's thoughts as he ploughed his way through the deep snowdrifts were of Elize. Upon meeting Maurice in the local village tavern he had immediately summed up his rather money grasping nature that lay beneath an outwardly cultural façade.

Lazlé had known Elize's father during the war years both having fought as paratroopers in the French underground Resistance movement. Raymonde, Elize's father had died on one day of landing in a war-torn area nearby the village where he had grown up. Lazlé pondered this as he neared the chalet. He had been lucky he supposed to come out of the fray alive.

Little animals put their furry faces out of their burrows beneath the heavy snow. They were disturbed, these sensitive little creatures a hedgehog then a squirrel. Stoats and weasels slunk rapidly out of sight also as he walked.

But then would it have been better if he had died like his best friend Raymonde rather than having been left alive in his awkwardly crippled state? His whole left shoulder had been pulled down, a shriveled arm nearly reaching his knee on his left side there having been the stump of a tree impeding his fall. Nothing could be done to repair his crippled state and bravely he managed to move from one place to another and use his right hand as he did now to knock on the chalet door, eager to see Elize as he was every day.

Soon the little wooden chalet was within sight. The animals in the barnyard were active. Angèle must have milked the cow for the animal was mooing contentedly. He thought to himself—all so seemingly peaceful and loving on the surface. He knew that the tensions beneath the apparent orderliness of the day-to-day activities at the chalet simmered fleeting though ever-present hostile feelings.

As someone who had suffered greatly and he had, Lazlé could sum up the relationships, each between the other from the outside looking in. Elize he knew was treated as a servant by her husband who for little input on his side expected his wife to clean, cook and wash as well as see to the children. All this was with no end or reward in sight.

A lot of the time Maurice was desperate for work and became irritable with so little to do. He idled away the time and would not help around the chalet. Lazlé could see this trying as he did when he had walked the children to school to give Elize some assistance at her tasks. It was Lazlé who emptied the slops, who cleaned the barnyard, washed down the chalet floors and slaughtered the occasional chicken for the pot.

He felt so much for the poor Elize who had no father to step in to request Maurice and his mother to lighten Elize's tasks. Observant though Maurice should have been as an artist he did not notice the supportiveness that was growing between Lazlé and his wife. Lazlé noticed too the way Grandmêre despised the replacement of Maurice's sympathies from her to his wife. Maurice was nevertheless becoming harder and harder on poor Elize.

Then there were the children. They, it was obvious to Lazlé just took everything Elize did for them for granted.

He had collected them that morning for school. Elize upon opening the door to him that morning had given Lazlé her usual rare smile and would wish them all merrily on their way when they were ready, saying: "Do you reading and writing well today. Lazlé will fetch you again at one o'clock. I will have baked some bread by then and churned the butter." He began to chide the children as they waited to leave the surrounds of the chalet.

Lazlé had a rather highly toned voice partly because he had been through so much pain when his injury had first happened after one of many parachute jumps. Elize as a loving woman and mother understood this and their two voices resonated softly as they spoke. Lazlé had knocked on the chalet door and had it opened for him. Elize's voice was low with the ongoing pain her overworked back gave her.

She did not want Maurice to know this because he showed her no sympathy and regarded her as a chattel and a maidservant, more and more as the days went on and the children grew older. Elize would never admit it to him as his teasing at first during their marriage had been humorous and salty but now was becoming quite unkind. She did not want to provoke herself into loosing her temper as she seldom did.

"Elize," Lazlé as usual summoned up his quite painful grin pulling his head up to face her "How is the family today? Are the children ready yet? Have we time to say a few words to one another while they pack their school books into their knapsacks?"

Her low peasant brogue fell sweetly and soothingly onto his hearing.

"As usual their books of reading and writing and drawing became quite untidily left around while I was chopping the vegetables for the stew last night. That was a meaty bird you slaughtered yesterday Lazlé. Make yourself at home while you wait, do."

Maurice's now almost grating voice was heard from their bedroom-cum-studio upstairs. Lazlé had noticed that with his concentration focused on his visual arts, he did not always hear too clearly and had only then realized that he and Elize were passing the time of day while they waited for the two children to stop squabbling over their books and find their parkas, jerseys, mittens and long snow boots that had not been put away on the day before. Maurice's slightly rasping voice came down to Lazlé and Elize.

"Are you fighting again you two? What is it now?"

Angèle was squealing—"He took my mitten yesterday and now I've lost it."

Maurice said bad temperedly:

"Your Grandmother has knitted you both several pairs of mittens."

Grandmêre's voice came shrilly to everyone's ears.

"Do you need more mittens? You know you just have to tell me Elize."

Elize shivered with the cold air coming in at the door and at the sound of her mother-in-law's cackling voice. She confided softly in Lazlé:

"You know that Grandmêre just wants some more to do that is easy like knitting so she and Maurice can comment while I am busy." She sighed

Maurice sauntered down the stairs but his face was pinched with cold. He had heard Elize's last words and questioned sarcastically:

"Well what are you doing Elize—passing the time of day with our hired hand when there's work to be done for both of you?"

Lazlé could only just stop himself asking what Maurice was going to be busy with that day. The words that came out from Maurice then made he and Elize feel a little foolish with their humble tasks.

Maurice boasted:

"Count Alois of the chateau has employed me yesterday to do a portrait of his beautiful wife Claudine, using and copying a famous portrait by the master Renaissance artist Giotto that he owns. I am at the moment or for today anyway, doing preliminary sketches from memory to get my hand in at my painting. You know that I have been unemployed for a couple of months now. This will be a real boost for the household coffers.

"Elize!" He spoke sharply. "Is breakfast ready" I must get started at first light. I must tell you that under no circumstances must the two children be allowed in to the studio where I am working during the day. They are not to upset what I am doing in there. The door of the room must be kept locked do you understand?" Elize assented.

"Anything you say Maurice. Here is your plate of porridge and yours Lazlé. She sighed again inwardly. Now she would have to rely on stoking the fire in the grate for the moment to keep warm. She would not be able to snatch a little rest under the blanket as she did when Maurice was out working or looking for work. This would have been while Grandmêre was taking her nap and the children were not yet back with Lazlé from school.

Silence reigned as the four adults and the children breakfasted. As usual Grandmêre croaked at Lazlé:

"Our chopped wood pile in the box of firewood is getting low Lazlé. You will have to go out later this morning when it is a little warmer to cut more for the grate. You will have to break up a lot more than you did last time. If the weather sets in badly as it seems it is going to we might even be snowed in. It has happened before."

Her voice was creaky and her forecast for the weather scared Elize who said:

"Come now Grandmêre it will surely not be as bad as all that."

The ever thoughtful Lazlé said:

"When I return from seeing the children to school I will start today's work by sweeping down the floors so Elize can tidy the house."

"Yes," quavered Grandmêre spitefully as she watched Elize clear the dishes and start washing up. "There is never enough to keep Elize busy. Hurry with the dishes Elize I need you to help me to the bathroom." Ever willing Elize nearly broke a cup trying to be ready to help Grandmêre. The old lady had been sitting as close to the fire as she could and when Elize came over to assist her and she helped the old lady up the blanket she had over her fell to the floor onto some sparks that had fallen from the fire. As she bent to shake out the rug the sparks fell dead into cinders and Elize felt the momentary comfort and warmth of the fire that even now needed stoking up with the long iron poker kept for the purpose.

Lazlé had slipped out straight after breakfast and later appeared at the front door with a sack over his good shoulder containing Elize knew some chopped firewood. Coming out of the bathroom where it was warm Grandmêre screeched at Lazlé:

"Shut the front door Elize—I'll be down with influenza if you let that frosty air in here right after I have bathed." Elize sighed and hurried Lazlé to lay out the chopped wood to dry.

She would have to ask Lazlé to keep the old woman occupied so that she could manage to bath herself. She settled Grandmêre in the rocking chair near the fire again. Lazlé had used some of the spare wood dried from the last time he had cut some to stoke up the flames. There was now to Grandmêre's intense satisfaction a roaring blaze in the grate. She watched Elize begin the dusting so that Lazlé could sweep the floor before lunch.

The cat a pet of the two children appeared hungry as usual and Elize left off what she was doing to see if there was any chopped fish to feed the animal. She knew it would not leave her alone otherwise as she was the only one who fed it. Grandmêre looked on in delight as the cat, a mild irritation to Elize with its demands, lapped its morning milk. Then Lazlé had the upper hand in the little domestic situation.

Everyone would have to move. The floor had not been swept for a week. The old lady squawked in horror at having to leave her warm spot by the fire.

"Lazlé you are making a thorough nuisance of yourself. This room does not need sweeping for at least another week or two. You ought to be cleaning out the barnyard by this time of day." He replied gruffly but assertively:

"I'll be doing that after lunch." Maurice's harsh voice came down the stairs

"Isn't it about time you got the chicken stew onto the boil, Elize? I brought back some potatoes from the village yesterday had you forgotten? They should be peeled by now."

A tingling sense of righteous anger ran down Elize's spine. Yes she had felt much for Maurice when they had first met, admiration for his art and fascination for his enigmatic personality. She found herself continually curious as to what he was thinking when he was not conversing. And he did not talk much she found. She thought that he must be very intelligent, another facet of his nature that attracted her to him. He had tremendous drive as well.

It was he who rather unkindly started the day off for them all by pushing Elize out of bed. She found it so difficult to wake in the morning. His rasping voice scared the children into getting up and ready for school. The only one he was slightly gentler with was his old mother who when awake sat all day on the old rocking chair with a patchwork rug that she had knitted spread across her lap. Elize thought as she called up to him shortly that she was cooking up the stew, why is Maurice's attitude towards me so callous? As he descended the wooden stairway she asked him while trying to control herself:

"Why do you have to be so impatient Maurice? You know that there'll always be something in the pot. Tomorrow Lazlé has told me that he is hunting a hare for us. He has found a spot in the woods where there is a whole family of hares taking cover from the snow."

Half humorously at this news from the kitchen Maurice quipped:

"There'll be a mess to clean up once Lazlé has finished cutting it up. You can be sure of that and I am not dirtying my hands with it. Don't get any blood on the floor—quite likely if I know the two of you." Elize replied:

"No of course not I'll be ever so careful not to stain the table or floor in the kitchen."

He smirked unseen to her. He could always put Elize in her place. She always took him so seriously. The time for laughter that they had at the beginning of their marriage seemed to have vanished and in its place was left just a necessity of communication regarding the children and his mother. Lazlé he hardly deigned to speak to. He did not realize that the crippled man saw right through him in the domestic life at the chalet. Also from his brother Anzlé, Lazlé knew much about Maurice the artist. Right at this time they were all becoming crotchety because Elize was about to dish up the chicken stew. She supposed that she should be grateful that Maurice had brought home the potatoes as there was not too much chicken left over from yesterday.

There was ever increasing tension in the chalet while Maurice was at home. Usually Maurice the artist was out seeking materials in the form of willing subjects people, especially women who were ready to act as models for him. To all who knew him the fact that he sought out the females of the species to work with gave them the impression that he was somewhat of a womanizer. Deep below the surface of this impression given was an impatience with the opposite sex with their titivating, dressing up and endless conversations.

Maurice without lusting after his subjects wanted to have the pride in creating for as long a time in the future, a picture that anyone would want to gain pleasure from. These were done in charcoal or better still a colored sketch. He wanted to take the credit, not them his subjects. It just so happened that he, a man and an arrogant one at that found women the most fascinating subjects to draw.

Elize found herself persecuted by his constant search for a perfect figure to capture on paper. He was an unusually attractive man with glowing sharp piercing eyes forever in use and changing in appearance. When they had first married he had seemed to her someone who would make an adorable husband. For both of them the reality of children had changed all that.

Somehow he had managed mostly by using his own married state, to avoid entanglement with any of the women he used as models. These women only wanted to gratify their own egos and vanity. At the time of being married for ten years or so Maurice had become a little world weary in his profession and had grown greedy wanting to make his way in the world.

To start with he had in passing by the edge of the woods become companionable with the Count of the castle whom he found was resident and owner of the chateau. The Count came from a long generation of aristocracy in these parts and had inherited his wealth. He used his chateau as a viewing venue for the public and tourists who might be interested in the old building. It was an ideal spot Maurice could see for touting for business for himself.

Count Alois Bonpierre it seemed was a lusty old fellow who was married for the second time to a beautiful woman about ten years younger than himself. It was unclear to Maurice where they had met. This did not really matter but the Count always trying to be one up on the next man, at Maurice's promptings agreed to ask his wife if she would model for the artist. Count Bonpierre responded explosively:

"My wife—model for you? Do you do portraits or nudes?" Maurice was quick with his reply."

"I have found from shall we say experience—yes from what other people like it will depend on both your and her feelings. The women feel more strongly about it when they meet me."

He paused realizing how egotistical this statement would have sounded on his home ground to Lazlé or Elize.

He was dependant on both these two people for his bread and butter. Being persuaded thus to think in this vein, he remembered that their cow had been given to Elize by her mother and Lazlé saw to it that there was always a fresh batch of baby chickens in the roost ready to be raised to be slaughtered for the pot. This last was done by Lazlé every week. He also attended to a small vegetable patch at the end of the barnyard. His situation was most humble in comparison to the elite Count and his wife Claudine.

Curious as ever Maurice passed a little more of the time of the day with the Count who did not seem to have anything in particular to occupy himself with at that moment. After a while Alois did assent to Maurice's request. Maurice wanted to know a little about the Count's first wife seeing as Count Alois had some time back mentioned that Claudine had a predecessor. Alois was about to launch into the tale of his first wife when to Maurice's annoyance one of the castle's robust looking yokel farm workers appeared on the scene wanting information about some task that the Count had set him to that morning.

"Sorry sir," the lackey ventured "but Baptiste needs a pair of hedge clippers to help me with the trimming of the castle's hedge borders.

"Tiens," exclaimed the Count—"don't ask me ask the head gardener."

The man left totally downhearted as Maurice skeptically could see. He thought to himself. It must give a person quite a feeling of power to be the owner of such a large and important estate as the castle.

"We were interrupted and rudely too," continued Alois much to Maurice's feeling of importance at the interest being taken in himself by such an important personage.

"Yes Claudine will most certainly model for you if I ask it of her. You must just tell me what she must or must not wear."

Here again Maurice simpered inwardly at the Count's somewhat chauvinistic attitude. Alois continued again:

"It will be rather an unusual assignment if I agree to it."

The Count continued in a rather high-handed manner as regards his wife whom Maurice had only heard about through passing conversations with Lazlé.

"I have rather an unusual request to make though I do agree to let you do her portrait. I will in just a while explain if you have the time Mr. Barbier." At this opportunity Maurice smirked inwardly.

It looked as if his cajoling of this important personage would pay off in the form of a commission. Why should he think of himself as a failed painter? Matters artistically for him were looking up in this conversation. Maurice had found it best to take matters slowly when arranging for an assignment to do a portrait. He answered covertly but appeared as he hoped interested in what the Count wanted to say. He was a man in his fifties so was apt often to think and speak a little more slowly than the up and coming generation.

"You will perceive when I let you into the secret of the manner in which I would like my portrait of Claudine done that this will not be granting you the usual sort of assignment that you might receive."

Count Alois was about to take Maurice into his confidence the artist could see. The ageing man took in a deep breath and said hoarsely to Maurice:

"You understand my man that I am the proud owner of an old master portrait that of the Renaissance artist Giotto." He drew in his breath again. "It is a Giotto

Madonna. Priceless, Mr. Barbier priceless. That is priceless to me. The picture is mine. And do you know why it is mine, why I chose it? I was visiting the Louvre a few years ago and I found myself standing before this very portrait almost as wonderful to me as the sight of the Mona Lisa. Suddenly something connected in my brain. The Giotto Madonna had the most unbelievable likeness to my wife. I could not believe my eyes. I knew then that I just had to own that portrait."

Awkwardly he coughed and stumbled out the words:

"You may not know Maurice—I may call you by your first name?" Maurice was impressed and sharply answered in the affirmative, one up in the conversation with this question of the Count's.

"Well I will admit to being quite a wealthy man as well as an art collector in a small way. I knew I could afford to buy my Giotto with the agreement of the gallery's board of trustees. And I did."

CHAPTER TWO

Now what I want in a commission from you my dear Maurice is a portrait of my wife wearing a dress that I choose for her based on my Giotto Madonna that I will let you see. I have it under wraps in my study at the castle. There is an uncanny likeness between my wife and the picture of the Madonna. In the picture the countenance has an air of composure and grace to a greater extent than I see in my wife but an air of graciousness that I would like to see in her more often.

I thought that if I could find this state of loveliness in my wife it would make her more attractive and make me love her more by making her realize her potentiality of beauty in maturity. To me she is young she is only forty-five years old. I think it would change her sense of self-worth if she could see such a portrait of herself. It might make her love me more to know that I her husband thinks of her in such a way. She seems to have lost something of the attraction for me that she had at first but I am at a loss to know why."

Maurice smiled to himself. Through his conversations with Lazlé he had found out that Claudine was having a love affair with his brother. His brother and he although they lived separately were the remaining brothers in a family whose parents had died. Lazlé and his brother Anzlé were twins and about the same age as Claudine and they had met one day while she and the Count had dropped into the local village tavern one evening and the brothers had been there.

Maurice and Lazlé were acquainted as Lazlé out of the goodness of his heart helped out at Maurice's chalet. Lazlé was an old friend of Elize's from her childhood. They had known one another from a young age. Maurice was now a go-between with Anzlé and Claudine much to the artist's sick pride but Maurice was using the situation to his own ends. This was because it would be remunerative to himself to paint the portrait that the Count was asking him to do.

He knew why Claudine was losing her affection towards the Count and was intending to use the situation to his own ends. He and Claudine were a similar type of person. They would come to know one another now that Maurice would be painting her portrait. The Count finished the conversation by arranging a dinner party for Maurice at the castle within the next week. Maurice declined to bring his wife with him although Claudine would be there.

Maurice spotted Lazlé approaching them with the two children tow. He had just returned from the schoolhouse on the edge of the village and was walking them home. Here was yet another opportunity for Maurice. He had just about as much as he could take from the rather blustery and bombastic Count whom he judged to be in his early fifties. He made an excuse saying:

"And here are the two apples of my eye my two children and my chalet help Lazlé."

The Count, a selfish man by nature was only vaguely aware of Lazlé's existence. He remembered that Lazlé was Anzlé's twin brother. Anzlé he was quietly sceptical about, as he had rather vainly noticed the attention he, Anzlé paid to Claudine his wife. He wanted Claudine under his thumb and of course this caused her to rebel with what was in any event a second marriage. Anzlé was the target of her deeper affections that were quite welcome too.

Anzlé was in the tourist business in the village near the chateau and depended on Count Alois Bonpierre for much of his income. The castle was a tourist haven for visitors from all over the world and Alois and his wife met many fascinating people while living at the chateau.

Anzlé had angled for Claudine's favor Alois unknowing of it. The couple met regularly far into the wood in their affair during summer. They had thought themselves to be unseen in their love making on the soft green grass deep in the forest. Maurice, ever perceptive had come across the couple. He was immediately envious of the two feeling that he and his wife now had a humdrum existence with all romance rapidly disappearing. Elize he knew even found more time for Lazlé than for him during the days at the chalet.

Elize hardly had time to visit her ailing aunt in the village, who was her only surviving relative.

Only sometimes when Maurice was busy at the castle these days could she persuade Lazlé to see to the work at the chalet in the mornings. Usually she got the sharp edge of her mother-in-law's tongue for doing this but Lazlé who was willing to wait on Grandmêre hand and foot pacified the old lady. He was however always relieved when Elize returned in time to make lunch. Nothing was said of Maurice's observations of Lazlé's twin and his lover Claudine when the artist arrived back at the chalet in the early afternoon.

Lazlé was aware of the many occurrences in the village and chateau. He found his appearance of a dwarf in his crippled state made him unselfish and sensitive and he only wished to help people. He felt a great love for human nature in accepting him in the ugly state his war experiences had left him in. He did not even feel jealous of his brother in whose likeness his had been born.

Lazlé often tried to imagine what life would have been like had he not had the paratroop accident. The fall haunted him. He had landed on his side as trained in the army but had at the time a sudden fear that all would not be well in his reaching the ground and had let his body go slack instead of tensing up as he should have done. The result had been injury to the whole of his left side a squashing of bones in his shoulder, arm, side and leg, dwarfing him in a way that the doctors had been unable to repair surgically.

People in the village behaved sympathetically towards him and at first paid him attention but he had now come to be accepted in the awkward shape that the war had left him in. He had been left for dead when it had happened but had managed to crawl to a nearby village where he had been helped by a kind person to a hospital nearby.

Lazlé had the strong willpower of a trained paratrooper and had found work domestically in several of the houses in the village where there were young families. He was now working for Maurice and Elize. He was tremendously fond of Elize and together while Maurice was out painting at the chateau the two set about putting the chalet to rights. The two children left no little bit of havoc in the afternoons after school.

Elize did not like working in the barnyard as she found it too messy. Lazlé was only too happy to pander to her wishes that he clean it out every few days. He forked the chicken and cow manure into the vegetable patch that he also tended.

So day by day Maurice grew craftier and more selfish of his creature comforts. He expected total luxury and comfort from Elize that she with her good-natured heart was always ready to provide. Not yet having become a typical worn out and bad tempered housewife she, only one of many of Maurice's imaginary amours, led a conjugal life with her husband.

All the time Grandmêre looked onto the proceedings in the cottage with a crafty eye when she was not at her knitting seated always in her rocking chair by the fire that Lazlé stoked every now and again. All was quiet in the woods outside and every now and again the click click of Grandmêr's knitting needles could be heard.

Grandmêre kept a beady eye on Elize. She was certainly dominated by her mother-in-law who kept the girl hard at work in the chalet and made Elize fetch and carry for her. The old lady found it hard to get around and Elize in her youth and innocence did not realize that she was being manipulated by Maurice's mother.

The artist's wife's only outlet for her emotions that were gradually being shattered by the cruelty of her husband and her mother-in-law was the comforting presence of Lazlé. Maurice thought of himself as being highly observant and noticing of much that went on around him but in fact Lazlé by virtue of his disfigurement and the humility that he was suffering because of it was by far the more perspicacious of the two. In her own quaint way Elize took advantage of this part of Lazlé's nature.

Maurice was absent from the chalet now with his commission to paint a portrait of Claudine the Count's wife. There was only the old lady to monitor Elize's activities. She and Lazlé made excuses to be outside either to milk the cow or feed the chickens or to see to the vegetable patch that Maurice had ordered Lazlé to create and tend in the barnyard. Carrots, beets and spinach grew plentifully under the cripple's careful eye during the months when the chalet was not snowed in.

Maurice took on a new arrogance with his assignation to paint the Countess Claudine's portrait. He took out the normal stresses and strains of being an artist on his wife. His mother noticed this and wallowed in the apparent masculinity of the attitude that her son was taking towards his wife. Lazlé was also aware of it when Maurice came in during the late afternoon.

Maurice found Lazlé a willing confidante to his tales about the day spent in Claudine's presence. Elize was not good enough for his relating of the day's events at the chateau. He hurried her on to get his mother washed and clad in her nightwear while he talked over the day with Lazlé. Lazlé absorbed all this with a willing ear anxious for news of Claudine's relationship with his brother Anzlé.

Anzlé took a somewhat superior attitude towards his disfigured twin brother as he was having great success in his tourist business. Lazlé took his brother's rejection of him manfully enough but was worried about his brother's affair with Claudine having come across them making love in the woods while on one of his solitary hunts for hares for Elize's pot at the chalet. He could not see a happy ending for this relationship. Count Alois Bonpierre was a powerful man in the community and would cut his wife off without a penny should the affair be uncovered.

All these adult affairs Lazlé was grateful that he was not really part of. His parachute mishap at the end of the war had caused him to be physically deformed and therefore rejected by the community that he lived in. He managed to live a life apart from the folk who came and went in the forest near the castle and in the village nearby. He walked and hunted in the woods to his heart's content finding pleasure and solace in nature during the summer months and in winter wandered over the mysterious snowy patches between the trees and silently watched the scurryings of the little furry animals there to and fro as they sought the sustenance of mice and rats during the winter months.

Lazlé had a hunting pistol that he kept oiled and polished and he was able to bag a fair number of hares for Elize's cooking pot that winter. He sensed her gratitude when she saw him coming to the door of the chalet having heard his boots crunching in the snow as he approached, the animal's lifeless body slung over his shoulder.

The children on holiday now in mid-winter shrieked in delight at the sight of the dead hare. They knew that Lazlé would spend some of the morning shaving and skinning the animal. Then their mother would cut it up and together with some green vegetables that she would ask Lazlé to pick for her from the vegetable patch, and put together with plenty of seasoning, a delicious stew for them all. This would be a wonderful change from her chicken dishes that were usually served up.

Lazlé helped Elize with Angèle and Paule. Being Maurice's children they were quite a handful and needed to be watched continually. It was surprising, Elize realized the dangers to children that there were in what was a supposedly safe chalet to live in. The kitchen utensils with the remains of Lazlé's shaving of the hare, the razor blades and the log fire in the grate had constantly to be watched and cleared.

Also Maurice's temper was driven to breaking point if the studio-loft where he touched up his paintings was disturbed by Angèle or Paule. So it was up to Lazlé and Elize to keep the two energetic children entertained downstairs. Elize liked them to go for walks in the woods with Lazlé to get them out of the chalet so that she could tidy and clean and set the furniture to rights. Lazlé was only too pleased to oblige and supervise the two on a foray into to forest. He enjoyed the children's company their newness to life giving him fresh insight into what they saw in his beloved wood.

"Elize," shouted Maurice shortly after reaching the chalet one day, "I am in the loft and the sawdust on the floor seems to be all churned up. You know that I like it spread evenly on the floor so as to create a sweet-scented atmosphere while I am painting. The bed looks as if the children have been bouncing up and down on it as well as on our armchair. There is a most terrible disarray in here. Please come Elize."

"Those children again. The naughty pair. It is the holiday season, you know that Maurice," she said in self defense.

Maurice had been out that morning and she was having a long conversation with Lazlé. They had heard the children shouting with a great commotion but had put it down to the enthusiasm of the holidays. Grandmère tapped her cane stick crossly but could do nothing without someone moving her from her rocker near the fire. This

Lazlé and her daughter-in-law did not seem to be prepared to do for her.

The couple, comforting one another in a conversation went into the farmyard garden for a while before Elize started cooking. Lazlé had been ordered by Maurice to kill, pluck and clean a chicken for the cooking pot. Elize ventured:

"What is wrong with Maurice these days do you think? Whenever I start talking about the children or Grandmêre he takes a very high-handed attitude and interrupts me at every phrase of communication that I might make towards him. Ever since the count offered him the commission of painting the portrait of his wife he has become more and more arrogant. I can scarcely get a word through to him! I almost get the impression that I am not even wanted here at all. But he likes my cooking he says. So Lazlé the sooner that you can bag us another hare I would be glad." Lazlé responded:

"Elize you know that I love hunting in the woods." Elize especially knew this and Lazlé spoke confidentially to her. "I have something to tell you Elize. My brother and the Count's wife are having an affair of the heart. I came upon them towards the end of last summer, almost Autumn it was, lying together on the soft grass deep in the wood. There I suppose they thought they would not be discovered. I tried to keep out of their hearing and sight but they are obviously lovers and it would have been just embarrassing to have disturbed them. I stood in the shadows watching them quite horrified that it was my own twin brother who was one of the actors in the scenario. He looks down on me in my unfortunate crippled state so that we scarcely communicate, even see one another. He has always been a womanizing dilettante much to my embarrassment. I was the quieter and more thoughtful one even before incurring my injury."

"Oh!" said Elize, 'There's Grandmère calling me, I can hear her rasping voice. It must mean that Maurice is back and complaining about something."

She was only too right. She heard Maurice shouting.

"Elize—Elize! What has been going on in the bedroom today? You know that I told you that you were not to let the children into the upstairs room where I have left my painting! Have you seen what they have done? They haven't a care at all about what their father is working at. Look at the sawdust. It is floating all over the room. It is in the bed—the bed will have to be shaken out completely. And see here—there are fragments of sawdust sticking to my practice portrait of Claudine that I am working on. I will give them such a beating. When did they create this havoc?"

Elize answered him slyly.

"They are trying to have some fun now that they are on holiday. They must have jumped up and down on the bed in here and scattered the sawdust around the room." She looked afraid, and thought how to calm her husband.

"Some fun?" He said. "Elize if this happens again I'll beat the living daylights out of them."

Maurice, typically the artist was fuming with anger. Elize tried to quieten the situation, saying:

"If you give them a telling off I am sure that they won't attempt such a prank again."

She looked at the painting.

"There's not too much sawdust stuck to the picture, it was dry this morning I could see." Maurice was furiously scraping off the few flecks of the dust that were spoiling his work of art as far as he was concerned. He muttered:

"I was an idiot to bring the painting down to the chalet but was getting so involved with working on it that I thought I could put in a few hours at work here in the evenings."

He was very cross and Elize was forced to take the blame in this domestic upset as she had been many times over. To Maurice's delight she was becoming cowed and harassed. He had to have a scapegoat in his relatively unimportant standing in the little community.

Grandmêre's shrill voice added to the commotion. They gritted their teeth at her harsh inquiry:

"What is happening upstairs Maurice? You know I can't get up the stairs to help." "Help!" Muttered Maurice grimly scratching off the last of the sawdust particles that he imagined were adhering to the practically dry painting. Meanwhile Elize had unobtrusively escaped the clutches of the old woman, taken hold of the broom and rushed upstairs to the bedroom-loft.

She opened the window letting in an icy blast that added to Maurice's discomfiture. She had shaken out the bedclothes that were full of sawdust. While Maurice was standing this way and that staring and peering at his work of art from all angles Elize did a lightning fast job of sweeping clean the remaining sawdust in the loft. She had crept down the stairs to avoid more of Maurice's wrath.

The old woman was just waiting to hear Elize's cowed version of what had just happened upstairs. In a cupboard in the upstairs room Maurice kept some of his painting equipment that had fortunately not been interfered with by the children. The disturbance of half an hour ago had caused his artistic nature to flare as it always did in such circumstances and had caused no little grief for the tired and harassed Elize. Alone now in the loft that Elize had left in a semblance of order he stared arrogantly at his painting.

Claudine's fiery amber eyes matching the gold colored dress that she was wearing for the sitting stared back at him. He thought to himself: so different from Elize's cloudy placid blue eyes. Claudine's tawny long hair scraped up into an untidy pile on her head—evocative, yes. His deeper artistic thoughts got the better of him.

Whose passion was she trying to evoke? Certainly not the Count's her husband's. He was surely long past a physical relationship of any telling with his beautiful and to him, young wife. Maurice adjudged the Count to be getting on for his sixtieth year, while Claudine must only be nearer to forty-five years of age.

Claudine had glanced at him sensuously continually during the creation of her portrait. Maurice did not return the glances his mind being on attempting to succeed in mixing in the likeness of the Giotto Madonna into Claudine's portrait as the Count had ordered.

Although she was keen to see what he had created so far Maurice had refused to allow it fearing recrimination from Alois should Claudine tell him of any criticism that she might have of the developing picture. And as he came down to earth standing in front of his work his thought train told him that the Count was uncreative, a superficial person lacking artistic feeling anyway.

His thoughts about Claudine and husband Alois drummed on in his head as usual to his own ends. What could he gain from the situation? Certainly the Count was paying him handsomely for each sitting. But what more could he gain for his own ends? Then he thought desperately and gloomily whether there was anything more forthcoming from the Count from the commitment to finish the painting of Claudine. If so what would he do with it? Elize and he were not an ambitious couple socially so there would be nothing to be gained from that quarter.

Even though the Count was paying him well for the portrait where would that get him other than to lift him out of the doldrums of the mediocrity of his reputation as an artist in the little community. There must be something more to be got out from his continual exposure to the beautiful Claudine.

Suddenly he snapped his fingers together. That was it! He would have a flirtation—even as he thought of it, an affair with the beautiful woman Claudine. It would add spice to his life, make it really worth living. His artistic techniques would enable him to do this quite easily. He began to calculate. He had already noticed in the few sittings he had with her that she was quite intrigued with what he was doing in fact quite fascinated by his own self. This would count towards the ends he had just decided upon.

It was not unusual for the subjects especially the female ones to be over-interested in what he was creating on canvas as after all it was their likeness that he was portraying. He was always doing a complimentary shaping of the head or a seductive coloring of shadow to a cheekbone all to his own ends. Mostly though he was cynically not really too taken with his subjects finding them on the whole quite mundane. Count Alois on the other hand for all his pomposity had chosen a most unusually and intriguingly beautiful wife.

She was an enigmatic woman and Maurice thought that the first few steps would be to get to know something of her background story that was before she had met her current husband. Egotistically looking around the little loft-bedroom that Elize had carefully tidied he considered. This was no place to work. He would cover the canvas and take it back to the chateau. The situation there had become a little too tense that was why he had decided to work a while at the chalet. The reason behind this was that the Count and his new wife even in all their luxury were continually at loggerheads. No, he would take his work back to the large room at the top, at the back of the castle where the light was best.

Maurice had quite enough of domesticity for the day.

Knowing that it would upset Elize he stalked through the chalet with a grim expression on his face. He walked out of the front door carrying the painting without saying a word to her or his mother. Baiting her knowing the effect her son's behavior was having on her, as this was how her late husband had also behaved she remarked spitefully:

"Gone again has he? I know just how it feels dear. He always manages to make it seem as if he has gone for good. But he never does maybe more's the pity for you. I tell you Elize he has nowhere else to go but here. Underneath all the bluster Maurice is an unhappy man. I know that he takes devilish pleasure in chastising you Elize, but without his home and you and I, Lazlé and the two children the world that he is king of would shatter. There is no doubt that he is a man with tremendous fantasies and imagination because of the type of work that he does. But at the end of the day it is you that matters Elize even if he does not show it any more." She finished with a dry cackle of laughter.

Elize stirred the rabbit stew beginning now to wonder when Lazlé and the children would be back. Soon in the distance she heard the playful shouts of glee of Angèle and Paule and the fatherly tones of Lazlé's pleasant voice. She thought for an instant how much pleasanter it would be to live with someone like Lazlé, quiet, unassuming and thoughtful. The children came sprinting in and made straight for the kitchen.

Elize called through to them—"be careful now the stove is dangerous. It is boiling our supper and is hot."

The children then stood back as she dished lunch for the five of them and kept back a portion to warm up for Maurice's supper Over the meal the old lady entertained herself with her two grandchildren.

Lazlé said in a low voice to Elize:

"I saw them in the distance again Anzlé my brother and the Count's wife in one another's arms, a distance away on our path in the forest. The children did not see them and I called them to take a different route to school."

As he spoke the old lady cocked her hearing aid sensing the glee of some gossip. Lazlé, seeing her interest stopped his conversation with Elize at this point only to continue while helping her with the enormous amount of washing up over from lunch. He intimated to Elize now a dear friend of his:

"Anzlé is playing fast and loose with Claudine. Soon they will be seen by the woodcutters and other folk gathering mushrooms and spring flowers and gossip will be rife throughout the village. It will come to the Count's ears what they are doing."

"Yes," said Elize knowingly. "People in those sort of relationships are never very careful about being seen. It is as if they throw all care to the winds. At the time it does not seem to matter who sees them, if anyone at all. Only afterwards do they think to rue the day that they were espied. I suppose many of the folk who frequent the wood would not recognize them lying on the grass."

Lazle remarked hotly:

"I am so embarrassed about my brother's amorous escapade. He knows that he is walking like a cat on hot bricks as far as the Count is concerned. For all his bluster Count Alois is a shrewd man. He is very proud and boastful about his marriage relationship with the somewhat younger Claudine. He is approaching his sixties and Claudine must only be in her mid forties. If the Count Bonpierre finds out about this he will have no hesitation in naming Anzlé as co-respondent in yet another divorce suite for Claudine.

You see he likes to keep Claudine in his clutches, and that she fights against with him. I know all this from the odd comments that Anzlé has dropped when we have been together on various family occasions. He does not go into the romantic side of matters with me though. He does not know that I have seen the two of them together and have recognized them."

Meanwhile Maurice glad to have some spare time while walking to the chateau was carrying the rather ungainly portrait that he was working on. The sun was out and the wood was abounding in crocuses, bluebells and other spring flowers. The golden rays lighting up the soft green grass did nothing to lighten Maurice's slowly hardening nature.

Calculatingly he wondered if Claudine would be waiting for him in the light-filled north facing room at the back of the castle. Of course she would he thought angry at his doubting. Wasn't he the most important person in her life? Was he not showing in his painting of her, the wondrous likeness to the exquisite Madonna of a world-famous painter of yester year, many centuries ago when women were highly adulated religiously?

He would most certainly put her high in his women's beauty ratings, as he was portraying her as a classic figure for the sake of her husband. Maurice, when he painted his female subjects could not help ferreting his way while he was busy with them, into their little foibles and feelings about their own looks. This gave him a sense of egotistical pleasure in his work

The sun had been up for some hours. He glanced outside into the sky. All he had each day was two hours with Claudine. Maurice by virtue of his calling in life was committed to taking a profound interest in the seasons when light and shadow had to be considered in his paintings. It was early spring and winter was passing although there were still thick blankets of snow that the village woke up to in the mornings.

That day of profound observance of his model had passed like any other. He was as usual attracted to his subject but more so than usual today he felt. As he put his paints together and washed out his brushes in the convenient basin at the back of the room he sensed that Claudine was still there. The gentle aroma of one of her milder than usual cigarettes came wafting over to him. He had heard her open the stiff lattis window and the early spring breeze blew the wisps of smoke inwards while also letting in small gusts of woodland air. She spoke:

"It's coming on well surely my portrait?" He replied gruffly feeling very much the humble painter in the presence of the Countess even though rumor had it that she had clawed her way up in society. He knew suddenly that they had much in common. That was it. She had confided in him one day that winter that she was one of a family of eight children who had lived in the poorer districts of the city of Paris

Likewise Maurice had told her that although unlike her being an only child his parents had also been of very humble origins His mother even though all she had known in her life was motherhood had ambitions for her son.

Against her husband's will she had befriended an aged artist well known in the village. She had begged the old man to give Maurice lessons offering the few household management coins that she had to spare in payment. The eccentric old man had accepted Maurice as a pupil and his mother was thrilled when old Monsieur Alain pronounced to her that he found the young Maurice to be quite talented.

Claudine on the other hand told of the constant grabbing and fighting to survive that she had experienced as a child. It was all her poor mother could do to keep Claudine and her brothers and sisters off the streets. A TV producer had noticed the entrancing seventeen-year-old waif sitting in a doorway with some other urchins and had made a brief career for her. This had only been a transitory period in her life and she had been let down. But she had by then seen better things in life

As Maurice slid his brush this way and that, up and down and round and about he tried ever more accurately and skillfully to encompass both Claudine's actual likeness and the similarity to the beautiful new wife that Count Alois had explained painstakingly that he wanted to see from his possession, the Giotto Madonna. It was a difficult task as Maurice was finding. He had seen this immediately such an observant an artist was he. It was obvious to all that she was a ravishing woman. Secretly Maurice looked down on the Count's ability of observation

There were though details in both Claudine and the Giotto portrait that escaped the vision of both Claudine and her husband. Again the Count had raised Maurice's ego to unrealistic heights when he had commissioned him to emulate the famous Giotto Madonna. He had told Maurice that unless he could make a sizeable profit for the work he had been asked to portray the Count would be forced to sell the Giotto work to maintain repair work to the chateau.

Contemplating on this level of fineness required in the work that he was doing his heart surged with what was for him a feeling of genuine pride. This was just one of many sittings that he was working on though during all of the sessions his imagination ran riot. He found that this happened to him every time he took on a new model. Often the manual nature of his work left him gaps of time for imagining the circumstances of his subject. He was a devious man and in this portrait as in others he did not want Claudine to know of his sly interest in her. Count Alois had confided in him that his and Claudine's was a second marriage.

Alois had also told Maurice that her first husband had been a prominent businessman who had divorced her in favor of what to him had been a more interesting woman. Her first husband had become infatuated by musical culture and his second choice of a wife after Claudine had been an opera singer. Claudine for all her charm no longer intrigued him.

She had vindictively bounced back. Moving in upper crust circles as she did and with her wealth and beauty the somewhat older Count had been an easy catch. When Alois, charmed with his new wife had arranged for her portrait to be painted, vain as she was this sent her senses sky rocketing with ambition. Her new husband had told her of his prized possession the Giotto Madonna and how it reminded him of her.

On his way to a sitting of Claudine's at the castle Maurice's idle mind began to picture his model. He could see her in his mind's eye in quite acute detail. He had painted many women during the time he had been following his artistic profession but to him she was the most enigmatic. Experienced now in the way women moved and the expressions on their faces he could sum up without being told the kind of life they had lived. From the mobility of her face the subtle lines that he saw he immediately etched onto his canvas carefully as this was a delicate part of his presentation.

The lines around her lips spoke of luxury and being spoilt. Also he could see that she had been a gourmet and was either an expert cook herself or had been in the habit of enjoying others' delicacies for much of her adult life. He was also aware of a sulkiness that he ascribed to her divorce and its aftermath before she had married Count Alois in the between marriages period. She was a strong personality but he saw perseverance for personal gain marked in her as her moods changed gently while her thoughts came and went.

There was little interchange of conversation. Maurice had placed the valuable Giotto to one side of his model without Claudine noticing of it. He thought astutely that he would not tell her what her husband had observed in her likeness to the Madonna not knowing that Alois had told her about it. Claudine was not, Maurice had summed up, an overly educated person more someone pursuing short term gains in her life.

In fact he thought to himself while busy on the soothing repetition of painting in the backdrop of the picture, that she had probably come from quite a poor Parisian background and had ambitions of being a social climber. She was clearly a classically good looking woman. Maurice had noticed as with many of the models that he had painted that Claudine was becoming gradually more and more aware of him especially as he was creating a likeness of herself that was most flattering.

She was a cunning woman. Just as he could see so much into what she aspired to in glamour, she was slowly observing the sort of person that he was. She had met many men in her life. She could see that he was not obviously good looking or the kind of man that her past socialite acquaintances would have considered attractive but that there was a definite charm about him

Chapter Three

Maurice was greeted gruffly by two guards at the entrance to the chateau. They gestured to him to go on up knowing his business. Down the long cool stone corridor he walked and up the back stairs to the room that had been set aside for him to be used as a studio while fulfilling his commission of painting the glamorous Claudine. He walked into the room head down in a brown study.

He sensed rather than saw Claudine at first. She was attired in the customary gold lamée dress agreed on by the Count, Maurice and herself. The gold flecks in the tight-fitting dress glittered in the sunlight entering in from the side window. She spent a lot of time out of doors and her golden tan and glistening tawny hair made Maurice see her as a glowing sunlit icon. The warmth of the scene gave him the encouragement to begin. He felt so unlike what he had experienced on leaving the chalet that morning. His mood suited hers. He could see the enigmatic full smile on her face. It was a smile that only a man could tell meant that she had more than one lover, if Count Alois could be considered as such.

Well anyway thought Maurice to himself it was well known in the village that she had been a wealthy divorcée upon marrying the Count. Count Bonpierre was overly fond and proud of his chateau. He had bought the portrait of the Madonna in better times. Claudine on a visit to the chateau before their marriage had happened to caste her eyes over it, and the Count upon looking first at the portrait and then at Claudine had been struck by the likeness between the two

Claudine was overwhelmed at his reaction and being somewhat of a social climber had quickly accepted Count Alois' proposal of marriage to her. He was in a position of having lost his beloved first wife in a riding accident a few years ago. Little did Alois know of her morals and social ambitions. She seemed to him just the person to fill the role of Countess especially with the monetary support that he was bound to give to her.

Still in a surly egotistical mood Maurice did not bother even to utter a good morning to his model. She had just finished smoking a cigarette he noticed and had stubbed it out shaking her hair back from her forehead. At the same time she stretched her body in relaxation for she knew Maurice to be a hard taskmaster in allowing breaks in posture while he was busy painting.

Later Maurice was feeling a little more cheerful than usual as it was a Friday. "Well that's it for this week." As far as he was concerned any kind of activity even his beloved painting was well, just work. He had not noticed Claudine move, but looking over his shoulder, he heard her say:

"Mmm—the portrait is coming along well Maurice! But I can see that you have a long way to go with it!"

Maurice tensed. He had not realized that she was that observant about his work. True the basic likeness of

Claudine was there but the detail—his mind went straight back to his studies with old Monsieur Alain—there was just so much detail to pursue.

Her eyes—their glances were so constantly fleeting that he was finding it difficult to get a permanent still effect on his canvas. He had bade her farewell and such thoughts preoccupied him as he walked slowly through the woods. It appeared that there had been a heavy snowfall the night before that had been continuing on and off throughout the day, with the sun shining only a little that morning. The flakes were constantly settling as he left the chateau after his two hours with Claudine. He strode through the snow that reached above his ankles. He kicked at it bad temperedly with his heavy boots.

He had left the painting that he was working on facing away from the window so that the light would not fade what he had done so far while he was away for the weekend. He walked more quickly as the snow became less deep when he approached the chalet, the only home he knew. He spotted Lazlé and Elize from a distance.

They seemed to be closely involved in conversation. He thought to himself quite egotistically, Lazlé and Elize—what a couple. These high and mighty thoughts came to him because of his association with the Count and Claudine who were by far superior in his eyes than his humble dwelling and all who were involved with him there. He had a stab of uncertainty. Quite where did he fit in? Was he of more importance up at the castle or did he hold sway in his little kingdom with Angèle and Paule, Grandmère, Elize and Lazlé?

Sometimes he thought nobody noticed him in his comings and goings. He must make his curt and surly presence felt. As he had foretold to himself Lazlé and Elize had scarcely noticed him nearing them. This was part of what Monsieur Alain his old mentor had taught him. An artist should never make his approach or presence too obvious. But he was curious to know what they were talking about. Coming upon them suddenly they both looked up with a start. Maurice chided harshly:

"So this is how you while away the hours Elize! I would have thought housework was more important, and that the barnyard should be more than enough to keep you busy Lazlé!"

These last words were uttered almost threateningly. This started up an attitude of grumbling and bad temper that lasted the whole weekend. Elize tried to talk him out of it. She knew that he went scouting around the village for future models to paint. At the present he was relying for their meager income on what the Count was paying him weekly for as long as he was busy on Claudine's likeness to the Giotto Madonna.

Both Maurice and the Count had kept it quiet from Claudine that Maurice was using the Giotto picture as a basis for the commissioned work. Maurice had put it to one side slightly behind his model. She did not notice his unobtrusive quick glances to the right at her back.

The Madonna in her portrait was placed slightly to the right of a fairly large window looking out over a river and some somber countryside. The picture was also lit up by a brass chandelier to the left so it must have been a time of late afternoon when it was being painted. The colors in the masterpiece that Maurice was copying from the famous work of art were rich and lit up by the soft glowing light of the Italian countryside. Maurice was not going to let Claudine into the Count's secret intention just yet.

As many of the Renaissance Madonnas the lady in the portrait did not look as lively as her modern counterpart but was of course of a far more religious appearance. This aspect of the picture Alois had told Maurice that he wished his wife to be aware of when the picture was complete. Alois hoped that she would be so enchanted with her own portrait when it was done that she would behave a little more demurely as in the finished work. Count Alois was a man from a previous generation and did find his wife at times a trifle simpering and pouting.

Maurice understood the type of connubial life that she must have lead until the present. He found it difficult though to put the two aspects of what he was aiming at in the picture together. The long drawn out domestic weekend full of children, Lazlé, Grandmère and his long suffering wife not to mention the sounds from the little farm enclosure was thankfully over.

Life to Maurice was the ever-changing romantic world of his models and their lovers and husbands. He involved himself totally in these and it kept his ego on a high level of emotion. His mind was totally on his work and only as he ploughed through the snow on his way to work did he let his thoughts wander. Always flickering in his mind's eye was Claudine's visage and that of the Madonna that he was emulating.

He thought then on that walk to the chateau that he would try and put painting out of his mind. He had a workable method of doing this. His old father had raised his son to be highly aware of the animal and bird life around and above him when walking through the forest.

It had clearly been snowing heavily again that morning but the fall had stopped shortly before he had left the chalet. So he looked around and upwards as he plodded along. The sky through the lacework of leafless pine and beech tree branches was an iron gray pall over the forest. Along the horizon were the surrounding hills. The village, chateau and forest lay in a little valley that made the weather even icier as it was low down away from the plateau.

The sun powerful as ever pierced the horizon to the east with an eerie red glow flooding the green hillsides of out of season vines with a strange light. Snow hung everywhere and bit by bit dripped off its heavy weight from the branches of the trees. The whole scene about him made him feel empty and cold. Life—he thought snugly in his parka—there was much left though that made it worthwhile being alive.

He thought to himself a little crossly of his nagging old mother. Then he realized that he could not have this constant flow of the different stages of his portrait haunting him day and night. Wasn't it enough that Claudine was continually praising his work to her husband? He need not be that much of a perfectionist.

There were woodland animals to sharpen his eye. Nothing but gray, brown and blacks were the shapes around him otherwise. What should he look for first? It was fairly early in the morning still only about nine a.m. That was it—the owls of the forest would just be settling down in a convenient crook of the tree branches to sleep for the day. He had often noticed them but now he felt it an urgency to set eyes on one or two as he needed to blot out temporarily from his over active mind Claudine's portrait and that of the Giotto Madonna. Their place in his imagination was so strong that the vibrant colors flashed in his brain making him stumble. Then on looking up he heard the wing of an owl fluttering on being disturbed by his rather clumsy progress along the snow bound path.

Yes, he had come upon it in the same tree that it always came to rest in, to sleep during the day. What a diversion in his thoughts to have seen the great bird. It must have fluttered down in its awkward way onto the tree branch after hunting for prey during the night. He must have disturbed it in its morning slumber though he passed by often and knew that it was used to him. He looked at it closely once again and picked out the flecks of black, gray and white feather colors of the bird all tucked neatly away in it's sleep.

He saw again the unusual features of the bird of prey it's ears cocked alertly above it's head. At his approach one eye opened halfway and Maurice fascinated by its presence immediately stood still. He had disturbed the owl but knew that it would not fly away being in all probability sated in appetite by a field mouse caught during the night. His father had told him that owls had nightime hunting vision.

All this he was relieved to realize had taken his mind of his searching in his mind more of the story behind Claudine's life that he was becoming more than preoccupied with. He had stopped in his tracks upon seeing the owl having quietly walked on along the same path that he followed every morning to the chateau.

It was a Monday and he had risen from his bed rather more readily than usual having been wearied by the cloying domesticity of the weekend. He was at that time something of a nine days wonder to his children whom he did not often see with his portrait painting taking him away from them.

He worked in the afternoons during the week on a picture that he had done from memory of the portrait that he was working on at the chateau. For some reason the Count only allowed Maurice a couple of hours alone with Claudine. This was not enough for Maurice and he drew in important lines and nuances into his practice sketch in the afternoons at the chalet. This kept him busy and away from being under Elize's feet as she busied herself with the children's games and homework. Also she added to her stew vegetables that she chopped as Lazlé brought them in to her from the barnyard garden patch just outside the kitchen window.

Maurice sat correcting his practice working portrait of Claudine. He was occasionally frustrated not being able always to remember every detail of his original portrait. He also pondered over the likeness that Alois had seen in his Madonna masterpiece.

He could not put his finger on the similarity. The Count was a strange man as far as Maurice was concerned. He was all bluster and pomp when it came to dealing with his staff at the chateau or passing the time of day with the odd villager who was wont to take a short cut through the chateau grounds on into the wood and on to the snowbound villages on the other side. Underneath all the Count's show of pomposity that was to give others a sense of his importance, Maurice had detected a canny man. This even though Alois was approaching his late middle age.

He liked the older aristocrat as he felt that they had similar personalities both hiding an introverted judgmental and profound nature. For them towards others life seemed to flow on easily enough but underneath there was an almost cold hearted and calculating way of thinking.

Idly but coming up short as he was fast approaching the chateau he wondered if the Count had summed up his own nature and Maurice's in their similarity. On this occasion while tramping through the snowbound forest along the path he knew now almost by heart, he wondered why Alois had chosen the humble Claudine for a wife. He must have known about her background that she was from an impoverished Parisian domicile. Maybe he had relied specifically on her classic good looks. If he did know about her background he must have been struck that someone as lovely as she had come from such a lowly family.

From the little about herself that she had so let out to Maurice it seemed that she did not have any ties with the family of her youth. The Count probably deemed himself too haughty for this as he was an aristocrat. He would not want anything to do with Claudine's parents, brothers and sisters. Certainly she had made sure that they did not seek her out.

As he still had some way to walk on his way to the chateau that day he played a game that his father had taught him. This was to pass the time as he trod through the snow. It was to distinguish in the fresh snow the recently formed footprints of the little animals of the forest. The foxes he could tell left four marks, each set of double prints quite far apart from one another the fox being quite a large animal. Then there were several other little creatures for him to try to identify from the signs they left in the newly fallen snow. His father an amateur woodcutter in the forest had brought him up to recognize the telltale marks of stoats and weasels in the newly fallen snow. He could also see the hare's reminders of it's leaping from one spot to another in search of greenery in the form of grass and plants on which it fed. The otter's trail he also recognized immediately.

There was a little stream with a makeshift wooden bridge crossing it. This rivulet was still iced over. The season was passing gradually from winter into spring. He noticed several rough holes in the ice covering of the stream and guessed that the otters in the vicinity had scraped away the surface so as to prey on the little water animals in the water flowing underneath where he supposed there were also frogs and minnows. The stream was not that small so there must be a variety of little fish perhaps also salmon.

He became entranced by the snowy wilderness and tried to imagine the wood as it looked in summer with the woodland freshness of earth and pine. The bark of the trees was still damp and gave off a distinctive woody scent. The frost hung heavily on the branches forming a delightful lace work against the iron gray sky. The melting snow washed away against the roots of the trees baring their tough wooden trunks to the spring air.

He was nearing the chateau now and had forgotten already the suffocating domesticity that he had left behind at the chalet the only home he knew. He reflected on the picnics that he and Elize had enjoyed with the children when they were still little. Elize had chosen the spot in the forest where they had decided to build the chalet and with Lazlé's help as well as his father's supplying the wood they had built the chalet themselves.

He must hurry now. The day was lighting up becoming just right for the painting of Claudine's portrait. He emerged from the wood and passed onto the melting snow on the lawns surrounding the chateau. He assumed his pose of a working artist. The guards at the moat's bridge knew him and he entered the great castle with nothing but a surly nod of his head. He made his way along the freezing passages and stairways to the bleakly sunlit room at the back high up that he was using as a studio.

He had passed through the silent wilderness of the wood and on his way encountered another woodcutter of the village known to him a friend of his father's. The villagers certainly knew how to make use of nature around them in order to earn their living. The old woodsman had spent his life working in the forest that was thick with trees chopping wood that could be used for patching up holes in walls or for furniture or even in the gardens of the houses in the village.

There was a continual need of timber from the three or four varieties of trees found in the forest. The most popular were pine and oak and there was a furniture craftsman who had premises in the village so the ones who chopped the wood were popular and useful men in the community. Walking up the stairs to the studio these thoughts were still with him.

He arrived and rubbed his hands together to warm them to be ready to handle his pen and paintbrushes and pots of paint. This he did every time he came into the slightly cosier studio that he had been permitted to use by Count Alois. All during the winter months he had to be careful of his colored paints screwing the lids on carefully and he wrapped them in cloth so as not to let them ice up in the chilly room in the tower of the castle where he was working.

He bent down slowly to scan the levels of paint left in the containers also to see which were empty. He noticed that four or five of the colors would need replacing. Yes, he thought carefully to himself going through the color spectrum in his mind. The dark brown, pale blue, bright yellow and pale cream were all finished. He cursed to himself. Should he put off his visit into Boulougne town to purchase replacements of the colors that were emptying slowly as he worked?

He quickly totted up in his head what Elize would need from their savings for their meals for the rest of the month. Certainly she and Lazlé ran the chalet market garden and barnyard quite economically enough. He really could not complain as the lucrative amount paid to him in the community for the portraits and other design work that he had branched into was always enough for a trip into Boulougne for a day with a meal at midday at his favorite bistro. He turned to face Claudine who had softly entered and was as usual ready for him.

He had turned slowly from checking his painting materials and saw the lovely sight of Claudine fresh in looks as the morning outside. She spoke first as was usual in their relationship. Maurice had found in the long silences necessary when busy painting his models that when he let up to wipe his brow the women always started conversing. This was somewhat irritating as he needed every moment in their presence to look critically at his work to begin again to make the subtle changes on the canvas that were so necessary to the artist.

So perspicacious was he that he noticed acutely every light change and every time that she moved even slightly. He knew from past experience that his models were wont to feel slightly cramped and uncomfortable from sitting in one position for more than one hour and Claudine's appointment with him had been arranged for two hours. After one hour was up Maurice became tetchy at the slow progress that his work was making. He thought to himself that to hurry would just spoil the whole effect. He walked over to the Giotto Madonna to absorb more closely the atmosphere of the portrait that he was supposed to be transferring to his own painting. He stood back to observe it.

Claudine said:

"Why are you continually looking at that old picture?"

She was not educated enough to know that it was a famous portrait. Maurice realized this. He explained:

"You know that this old work of art was bought from a famous art gallery in Paris by your husband in wealthier days when he was younger. He told me that he saw a likeness to his second wife formerly a Parisian street urchin that was yourself. I will let you into the intrigue. Count Alois wants me to get the likeness of the Madonna in the old painting into my work that I am doing of you. You see the tourists are not coming so often to view and admire this chateau. Money is slow in coming in from the French Government to subsidize the running of the chateau and he hopes to sell the Giotto Madonna for near on the fortune that he paid for the picture. It will be a while before this can be arranged though."

At this confidentiality Claudine drew deeply on her cigarette and asked naively:

"Does that mean I will be famous too?"

Maurice answered:

"The Count and I will see that my portrait of you will be hung in a prominent place in the hallway of the chateau so that visitors and many tourists can see and admire it."

Maurice in his masculinity became quiet and sulky again. He knew that at present he would never make it in an affair with Claudine nor actually did he really want this. There were too many irons in the fire for him. Every model that he painted seemed attractive to him physically but he knew he would never make a first move. But Claudine! It would set up a web of intrigue that he would delight in. He would then succeed in putting himself higher amorously speaking than either the Count, or as Lazlé had told him than Anzlé with whom she was having an affair of the heart.

Being an artist Maurice tolerated free love as was the fashion of the time and did not care about the morals of his unfortunate wife Elize. He knew that she would be heartbroken if she knew that he had seduced another woman, more especially Claudine. He did not think about the fact that by doing this he would be throwing away domesticity, his wife and family.

The act of seduction was at the back of his mind still and as he had assembled all he was taking with him to return home he slowly and calculatingly gave her a full glance. His looking took the upper hand with her visually just as she was finishing the last of her cigarette. So absorbed in the last puff of smoke was she that she hardly noticed his slightly greedy stare. Then Maurice walked arrogantly out of the studio.

The long passages with their gray stonework dampened his mood and he noticed that there had been another heavy snowfall while he had been occupied with his painting that morning. He entered the wood on the way home to the chalet and his mood changed sharply. He became aware of his isolation in the dead silence of the forest.

The only sound was the slow dripping of melting snow from the branches of the trees falling onto the thick snow on the ground below. Again his thoughts took him back to his childhood when he and his father made expeditions into the forest to cut wood to sell in the village. He became acutely aware once more of the little animal tracks as the snow melted into them causing them to be obliterated forever. There were stoats and weasels about he could tell. They would flee at the sound of the crunching of his heavy boots on the melting snow.

Once he caught sight of the brown redness of a fox disappearing into the undergrowth. These animals would never harm him. Then he knew he was on the right path as he came to the tree with the enormous owl perched in it. He looked behind him as he passed by and saw again the lingering yellow blinking of the great bird's eye.

The owl gave him an eerie feeling. He thought back to his learning days—he had practiced his art drawing an owl surely. That was right—his father had told him that an owl was a symbol of wisdom hadn't he? The bird's huge eyes and the massive wink it had given cheered him somewhat in the icy weather. He quickened his step.

Hadn't Lazlé told him on his way out of the chalet that morning that he had snared a hare the day before and skinned and deboned the dead animal to Elize's liking so she could cook a rabbit stew today? As always Elize cooked a fine meal hot as hades over their coal stove in the kitchen. It was just what he felt like on this day towards the end of spring while it was still so cold and with frozen snow everywhere sometimes melting and causing little rivulets to be avoided while walking home.

Home? For once he was looking forward to the warmth and domesticity of his cosy chalet. So he should he meditated on the final stretch on his way back. He and Lazlé had built the dwelling together some years back while the two children were toddlers. Before that the little family had been housed with his mother and father. Then his father had died shortly after they had finished building the little chalet in the wood and for all his selfishness

Maurice had felt obliged to invite his now ageing mother to set up house with the new family.

He knew that the old lady worked on Elize's nerves. Everything Elize did was commented on and criticized. The older woman had a sharp tongue. Lazlé came and went shepherding the children to and from school that was one of his duties at the chalet. Maurice was only able to pay Lazlé a pittance for the work that he did in the barnyard and vegetable garden. Fortunately Lazlé shared a small cottage with his twin brother that gave him a roof over his head.

Anzlé was something of a businessman in the small village community as he owned a restuarant and a small general dealer's shop. The brothers kept themselves so busy that they scarcely saw one another. The fact that Lazlé was a cripple from his paratroop experiences had forced them apart somewhat. Lazlé had always been the gentler of the two. Anzlé was somewhat of a ladies man.

Maurice tramped along the muddy lane down to the forest where the branches overhead dripped down now and again in the warming sunlight. Large areas of green tufts of grass had sprung up during the weekend's sunshine he noticed. The gentle northern spring was upon Boulougne and the surrounds of the Cathedral, the chateau and the famous woods.

The sunlight filtered through the leaves just budding on the branches of the trees. There was a fresh scent of foliage abounding and even the surly Maurice felt a surge of new life enter his being. Sometimes in the forest were large patches of grass and spring flowers daffodils, snowdrops and bluebells.

As he exercised his vision to the utmost to keep him aware of the sights and situations around him he kept turning his head. Suddenly to the far right of him he saw a couple lying on what was surely dampish grass. They were partially hidden by the trunk of a large oak tree but as he screwed up his eyes to peer at the two he got a clear glimpse of them.

It was midday. They were so engrossed that they paid no heed to anyone in their foolishness. He could see immediately that the woman was Claudine. She must have changed into an old summer dress and come down to the forest to meet—who was it with her? He recognized the man but could not put a name to him at first. He recognized the voluptuousness of his model Claudine's figure. It was obvious that the two were having an affair. The Count, Maurice felt sure was quite past being able to bed his new wife and she must have felt physically frustrated. He could see her lover's profile now and it seemed vaguely familiar to him. It was someone he knew who had an almost identical face. Suddenly he realized who the man was. It was Lazlé's twin Anzlé.

He would hurry along and not disturb them. He did not want to involve himself with Claudine or her lover at this particular time. Best to set the pace for home not upsetting their alliance. As he tramped on he heard in the quietness of the woods children's voices and saw Lazlé with his two young approaching from the other direction. They were all on their way back to the chalet

On another day when the spring season was truly making itself felt with warmer days of sunshine Maurice was making his way across the chateau lawns newly grown green when he came across the Count outside surveying his property. With his mind on his painting that he would be doing that morning he did not feel in the mood for light banter just then.

The portrait was in its final stages. Maurice found that not only when he was actually painting in the makeshift home studio that he used but also in his paid time, his mind and imagination had to be wholly focused on what he was creating. This called for intricate thought and visual imagination. Not realizing the mind of an artist the Count greeted Maurice:

"And good morning my man. I have not set eyes on you let alone spoken with you for a number of weeks. How goes it with the portrait of Claudine?" Maurice answered:

"To tell the truth my mind and very being are entirely absorbed even to this point in time with the painting of your enchanting wife."

Maurice was coming out of a rather introverted state of mind that had been dwelling on the details of the picture that he would work on that morning. The blustery nature that was the Count's made Maurice feel less isolated in his calling in life. Here was someone who wanted a conversation with him. He usually worked silence with one or two remarks to his model about posture or subtle changes in their posing. He said in a gruff voice mostly from the chill of the morning speaking from inside his parka:

"The picture will be finished in a matter of a month more. I have sketched out the basic visage of Claudine and have fortunately attained a likeness both of her and the Giotto Madonna in my work." Flatteringly he said to Count Alois:

"How clever of you to pick out the likeness in the face of Claudine and the Madonna."

The Count cleared his throat proudly. He said:

"There was no doubt about it when I saw the Giotto study hanging in that gallery. I paid a fortune for that work of art."

Maurice had been thrilled to be working from the famous picture in the Count's collection of artworks and had spent hours trying to catch the atmosphere given out by the well-loved Madonna in her picture.

Chapter Four

Playfully for that was part of his nature when his usually surly spirits were lifted he told Claudine when ready to start work for the morning something of the intrigue behind her portrait.

"I'll spare a few minutes to tell you more about what I have been commissioned to do by Count Alois. You have surely noticed the old picture in its frame that I have positioned in the studio slightly to the right of where you are posing on that old armchair upholstered in green fabric?

"Yes I have often wondered why it is this room that you are using as a studio. I have often admired it wishing that I could have looked so pure and beautiful as the lady in that portrait," answered Claudine. Maurice responded slyly knowing something of her promiscuity as he wanted her to understand that he knew a little of her amorous adventures.

"In the early Renaissance period of art the Madonnas, many of them led very chaste lives that is within their marriages. What I want to do is let you into Alois' and my secret. Alois when he saw the Giotto Madonna for the first time (Giotto was the painter of the old portrait) fell in love with it because as he told me it reminded him so much of you his wife. I can see your voluptuousness"—here Claudine pouted, "but Count Alois being an older man can only see the purity in you and what is more connects your looks with the portrait.

He was so charmed by it that he was persuaded to buy it for a vast sum of money. He told me how much he paid for it but I'm not going to repeat the amount. What he did compare in the Giotto was you and your looks, Claudine. He asked me a lowly artist to do a painting of you using what Giotto brought out in the loveliness of the Madonna picture.

That is why perhaps you have noticed I slide my vision frequently to the right fully to capture the mood of the Giotto Madonna and transfer it into my own painting. It is not easy for Giotto was a famous and excellent painter and his observance of detail was immense. Do you see a likeness of the Madonna in my portrait of you so far?"

She rose slowly from her position on the armchair where she had been posing for Maurice. He said:

"As a woman you will be very aware of every last detail in your facial appearance. I see that you wear heavy make-up."

She broke in:

"Yes I do don make-up only heavily when my husband and I have a late social evening. Then I have to be up early to help supervise the kitchen staff and to play hostess to Alois' tourist visitors and also to friends of his. He has many such amongst the nobility of the country.

As usual the fact of his doing the portraiture of a model brought forth much of the story of her life. This aspect of his work intrigued him. He had formed many female relationships thus and to all intents and purposes would seem to many to be something of a womanizer. He did not think of himself in this way. Life as an artist was just getting to know one intriguing model to the next. The women he painted seemed ultra-real to him the subtle colors of their hair, eyes and lips almost tempting him physically during the time he spent with each one.

Claudine though seemed to be a super-model to him and he was beginning to be absolutely captivated by her. He felt egotistical about the fact that the Count, something of an art connoisseur as he was discovering had chosen him for this task. Claudine broke the silence as he peered this way and that unobtrusively at the Giotto Madonna.

"That Alois should have chosen that old picture as a likeness to myself! I find it most flattering indeed. He has told me last evening in fact that he wishes to see the progress on the work you are doing. The gauze veil that you cover my picture with we will lift tomorrow morning when he comes up to the studio. I see that you have positioned me at precisely the same angle that the painter Giotto has done with his Madonna. I had not noticed that before."

Maurice smiled craftily to himself. In a studio it was he who had to be observant not the models. In fact he had found his models to be quite introverted, most of them. They seemed to go off into a dream-like trance while holding the pose he gave them while being painted. Claudine he admitted to himself was a little more of an exception to this rule.

The artist had passed Count Alois several times on his way up to the studio every day. The Count was usually taking a breath of fresh air while overseeing the lawns and gardens of the chateau. When that was done and the gardener and workers had reported to him Alois moved off to find out what was happening on the small farm that he had introduced in the nether regions of the chateau grounds.

Today Alois had something to communicate to Maurice who had as usual shot him a questioning look for some chat on his way up to the portrait room. He said that he would be coming up to the studio to view the progress Maurice had made on the picture. He intimated:

"I would like to see particularly the likeness of my dear Claudine to my much loved Giotto Madonna. This masterpiece quite haunts me and fills my imagination as does Claudine herself. The chateau is undergoing a risky time financially and this is the last time I will be using the famous picture sadly before selling it. That is using it to all intents and purposes as a basis for the likeness in your own work of art, Maurice."

Maurice felt flattered that the Count who was known to be an art connoisseur should put him in the same bracket as the talented though now historical Renaissance painter Giotto. Maurice reiterated:

"It is just as well that you warned me that you are coming up to the studio. It upsets me when Claudine is disturbed. It is better usually that she does not speak while I am busy with my painting. She begins to talk and gesticulate otherwise, a typical Frenchwoman. Then she does not stay still and hold her pose for me. I will warn her that you are visiting the studio so that she will not get too excitable. She is a very emotional person I have found." Alois answered:

"But this is what makes my wife so charming and entertaining. I never can have enough of her."

Maurice turned on his heel and walked on up to the chateau over the drawbridge and on into the rather chilly interior of the chateau. On reaching the studio he found Claudine as usual ready for him. He addressed her curtly:

"Your husband will be coming in to view the progress that I have made on your portrait Claudine. I do not want to be interrupted so can you not react to his presence with too much movement." She answered:

"That won't intimidate me too much."

Maurice to his own ends thought favorably to himself that she did not sound too overjoyed to be seeing Alois at this time.

He was coming to know Claudine better and better. Both painter and model had in common the fact that they had to claw their way up in society, she having succeeded further than Maurice thus far with her marriage to Count Alois a member of the French nobility. The artist had observed the nobleman, covertly trying to sum up for himself Alois' knowledge of his wife's activities during the days he spent overseeing the estate of the chateau. Clearly he only had need of Claudine on social occasions such as lunches, dinners or cocktail parties to entertain friends, or to publicise the chateau to tourists who would pay to admire it's beauty and it's gardens in the surrounds.

Maurice adjudged the Count s entering that phase of manhood when physical desire was emptying itself. He had chosen to make the divorcée his wife supposedly some years ago when his male ego and physical prowess was on the point of waning. So he now made use of her in these other social ways. Claudine had made reference to Maurice that she found the Count rather boring, pompous and overbearing.

To what did she owe the voluptuousness he quite literally had to paint out in her portrait? He was afraid for her that the Count might notice and complain. Was it to those full lips, cheeky upturn of the nose and face and half closed eyes looking slyly at the viewer. Many times he had been on the point of asking her outright if she had a lover. He could do it jokingly he thought but considered again that she might take it wrongly from him and be angry. This would certainly spoil a day's painting, a mood swing away from the usual self-satisfied pose that she usually held for him.

They heard a cough from the stone stairway leading to the studio. Alois was making his way up to see the proceedings in the artwork Maurice was doing. He had promised to do this on one of his meetings with Maurice when the artist was on his way to paint Claudine. The two heard his gruff words.

"Hallo, hallo. And how is my dear wife today? On form for her picture?"

Jokingly he addressed Maurice:

"I hope her self-control in posing is good enough for you today Maurice. I know she likes a cigarette or two during the morning. Sharply Claudine interdicted:

"Maurice allows me one when he rests up for a few minutes during the painting, don't you Maurice?"

Maurice was flattered at her deference to him. He observed from her statement that she was afraid of her husband. Cannily he thought then, knew in fact that she must have another relationship apart from the one with the Count.

Alois ageing now and with a full social schedule with the business of managing the financial running of his chateau, had walked into the makeshift studio shuffling slightly. As he approached the two pictures he gave a grunt of satisfaction. Obviously he had taken a strong liking to the Giotto when he had first seen it not having been with his wife at the time of viewing the valuable portrait initially. It must have opened up in his mind a longing for Claudine and must have made a big impression on him. Being a wealthy man he had made an offer it.

He had to discuss the buying of the work with the curator of the little portrait museum in Paris where he had found it hanging. The curator had set up a meeting of the Board of Trustees of the gallery and it was agreed that the high buying price that was being offered by the Count indeed warranted the sale as the money could be used to buy other works of art for the gallery.

He looked quizzically at Claudine whilst peering out of the corner of his eye at Maurice who was staring languidly at his painting. He was actually thinking at the time that he needed more paint supplies especially a four or five color variation of yellows and golds and pale creams.

Suddenly Claudine seemed like a flashing firework to him, he had involved himself so deeply in her portrait. The feeling subsided as he became aware that Count Alois was addressing him somewhat tersely.

"How long have you been working on her picture Maurice? It seems an age. You have been coming up to the chateau for weeks now."

Alois looked at Claudine frowning. Maurice became a little frightened at his attitude. Was his portrait of her not up to Alois' expectations? He had a good reputation as the village artist.

"The work needs another three weeks or so of putting the finishing touches to it."

Alois snapped:

"Yes I can see that after looking closely at what you have achieved so far. Hmm. I do so catch that likeness to my Giotto Madonna. Her eyes—yes you have captured that sultry look about the Giotto lady. Her lips curl just as the other work of art. You have her hair just right too with the gold coloring. The neck perhaps that needs a little working on?"

"Yes. Yes, yes," answered Maurice. "But this will all only come in time."

The Count stood looking at the newly worked on portrait then at his wife after casting a practiced eye onto his Giotto.

"Yes I think it's coming on Maurice. I knew if I gave you a chance you would work on the likeness. She really looks quite stunning captured in paint for ever."

Maurice thought to himself that the Count was quite a pompous old goat to have run after and fallen for such a shallow character as Claudine. She was sweet enough superficially. Maurice considered that Alois had overlooked the calculating social climbing part of her nature. He wondered too if Alois was in for a big social fall when the true part of Claudine's nature came alive for him. This all showed what an observant person Maurice was.

"You have attained a brilliant likeness, my man!" Continued Alois eulogizing now. Maurice felt flattered enough as the Count he knew from many conversations with the older man was quite a connoisseur of the current art world. Maurice could not understand why such an intelligent man should overlook his wife's faults such as were apparent to the artist.

It must all be to do with Alois' ego and social standing. To have a young and beautiful wife manipulative in her socializing was quite enough for the Count. The three grew quieter and after a minute or two Alois said gruffly:

"Well I'll take my leave now Claudine—Maurice you must get on with the painting. It is coming along excellently. I am quite satisfied so far and will look in next week to see the progress made by then."

Maurice breathed a sigh of relief as he watched Count Alois leave the room. He and Claudine heard him shuffling down the staircase outside the studio. Then it was back to painting for Maurice. Claudine resumed her pose and quiet now her thoughts fell onto the affair she was having with the rich banker Anzlé Laban. Maurice had been right in noticing her promiscuity and voluptuousness in his observations of her in his work as a painter. He always managed to get close to his models, almost under their skins.

Claudine thought to herself that Anzlé was becoming too demanding of her and she was finding him almost boring. The here and now was important to her. In her presence was a man who was really playing up to her looks and her beauty. Was that not more enticing? Anzlé had been on her mind and in her thoughts all these weeks while she had been having her portrait painted at the Count's behest. She looked at the artist Maurice with newly opened eyes. He immediately noticed her change in mood and knew that it was to do with him. It was typical behavior of his model subjects. This was different though.

From an artist's point of view she was just another woman. They all, his models had their story of why they were having their portraits done. It was usually a man, husband, father or lover who instigated the wish for a likeness on canvas of a girl or woman. In this case Maurice put himself outside of his artist's guise and knew what an incredibly lovely woman Claudine was. She was over forty years of age but looked as if she was twenty-five. This is what having luxury and wealth could do for you. He thought wistfully about Elize what a poor hard worked wife she was to him. Almost reading his thoughts Claudine slyly struck up a conversation with Maurice.

"I really know so little about you Maurice where you live if you are married, have children and of whom else you do portraits."

Maurice kept his surprise at her questioning to himself. He felt chuffed that this beautiful woman should be taking an interest in him. He said:

"It just shows how little self esteem I really have that I should feel so flattered at your interest in me really only a humble artist. In my own world I am the most important of all. Yes Claudine I have a little chalet in the woods adjoining the chateau that a friend of mine Lazlé Laban who is a war time cripple helped me to build just after I married."

He noticed that she gave a start at the mention of the name Laban. This was unlike her and the observant artist wondered why. She had whipped out a cigarette from a gold case. This was obviously to be their mid morning break. Claudine felt that she knew Maurice well even though she was only aware of very little about him. Two matters had suddenly bothered her that was the reason she had lit up a cigarette.

"Your wife, she is alive then?" She breathed out the smoke. He stood there quite an unusually attractive man she suddenly thought. He looked down at the rough floor boarding in this little used forgotten room at the top of the chateau. He raised his head and looked sideways at

Claudine. As an artist he found it difficult to look anyone straight in the eye.

"Yes." He paused. "I am married. My wife hardly notices me she is so busy in our chalet. We have two young children."

Claudine looked surprised. To have a child had never come her way. She was not a maternal type of woman preferring to maintain as she thought her beautiful body. She had missed out on what makes a woman truly lovely. The mystery of having a child did make her curious and she was prompted to ask Maurice about it. She said:

"You do not look the paternal sort of man at all Maurice. I imagine a father to be really stunningly good looking, totally in love with his wife and devoted to his children."

This brought Maurice up short. He felt slightly insulted at her summing up of the sort of person she thought that he should be. He had her interest in him nevertheless that was unusual in a reaction to him as an artist. He would nurture this curiosity of hers about him. It would be a break through in what he had always thought about himself. That was that he was a person with looks and personality only noticeable by a rarely observant female. He felt that Claudine with her finely chiseled features and sensitivity of person was one of few such people. As he put down the brush he was working with to have a break from painting, she queried as she slowly took out another cigarette from her gold case:

"What is it like to be a father of a family?"

The question made the part of him that existed in that other world from being an artist, feel fulfilled as a man but he was yearning for something more in life. Was it fame and adulation as a painter of portraits? He answered:

"It is no idyllic dream to be a father of a family. The children are constantly under my feet and my mother who lives with us is constantly sparring with Elize my wife. There does not seem to be a place for me in the domestic situation. It seems that my role in life is out of the home at work. And work for me is scanty." Claudine responded:

"I can see that your work must take you from one portrait and relationship with a model to the next. The villages around Boulougne are filled with interesting people. You must have no loss of fascinating faces to paint. How do you go about finding and settling with someone whose face takes your fancy to express on canvas?"

The answer to this was just as close to Maurice's heart as was the art of painting itself. At this stage in their relationship he vowed not to let this curious woman into his secret. He fobbed off her question and began to take the upper hand in the conversation and ask her more about herself. Then he changed his mind to answer her query.

"Well Claudine that is one of my greatest secrets. I suppose it lies in the fact that I am a man and you a woman. You have probably noticed how gregarious men are. We males will talk to just anybody. We are adventurous and ultimately the warrior sex. I am one of those men."

Claudine looked intrigued but Maurice realized that she was just another female who would never understand how the male ego functioned. He continued:

"Though as an artist I am a bit of a loner. I like to sit back in a pub or bistro and ponder deeply on the particular model whose portrait I have been asked to do, how her brain functions. Usually I throw up my hands in despair. I will never completely understand a woman's mentality, the way she thinks."

Claudine as he had thought she would pouted and fluttered her eyelids in satisfaction. He imagined that he would never know about her relationship with Anzlé, Lazlé the cripple's twin brother. She did not realize that although he did not know everything about a woman he knew more than most. She had told him much over the weeks about her feelings about Count Alois that her husband was such a poor lover that she was being driven away from him.

She had not told him the truth that she had been thrown into another man's arms by her husband's poor libido. Somehow Maurice had known such feelings would come out. This was always the effect on a woman having their portrait done had. But how to answer her question as to how he tracked down his subjects? He began after some minutes of silence doing some brushwork:

"You see if I am alone in a café or bistro and I see a face, one that stands out for me either in beauty or just interesting or one with intriguing features I immediately have a compulsion to record it on canvas. It is a part of my life the part with which I aim to make myself famous with in a small way.

So what do I do? Simple. I approach my hoped for subject pretending to pass the time of day. When I say I am an artist and would like to paint their portrait they fall for it every time.

I must tell you these meetings are few and far between because each one takes a few months to complete. Often a woman is busy with domestic, shopping, children or even employment duties. But Claudine once I have made up my mind I keep the image of her face in my mind for as long as it takes to paint her likeness. These models are always willing to make time for me." Maurice suddenly exclaimed:

"I can see that only a little painting is going to be achieved by me this morning." He paused then went on: "Why am I letting out all my secrets of being an artist to you Claudine?" A haughty expression came over her countenance. She had found in her adulthood of the last ten years or so that she had the ability of letting people confide in her. Somehow people trusted the enquiring though gentle, voluptuous but self-controlled person that she was.

"Oh!" She said. "I find people who come to know me often confide in me. It must mean that am a trustworthy person."

As she drew on a cigarette she had lit a look of guilt only visible to Maurice flooded her face. Maurice took advantage of the moment sure now that she was not all that she seemed. He put his head down pretending to do some intricate brushwork then suddenly looked up from his work and said raspingly:

"Is it men or women who believe in your trustworthiness?"

He was feeling vulnerable that he had allowed long closed facts about himself to come out into the ears of this enchanting woman. Maurice was prodding her as a character somehow insisting to himself that he must know more about her. So far the inquisitive though guarded tactics he had used with his other models had come to fruition in Claudine. He quickly thought to himself. So people find this woman superficially trustworthy. I have observed her carefully and detect a flaw in this superficial facet of her personality. So he asked again carefully:

"Is it women or men who find you so beguiling Claudine?"

Maurice was intrigued now coming to the root of the person that he suspected that Claudine was. He aligned this thought in his own mind to this very similar nature of hers. That was a bold front covering a tragic weakness. This toughness he knew was necessary for them both to make their way in life. If then they had this similarity of nature they could form a friendship outside of portrait painting where both of them had to be in the studio at the Count's behest.

Claudine though fobbed him off somehow sensing his curiosity in her private life. She felt an empathy so far with Maurice but like a thunderbolt realized that if she let out anything concerning her relationship with Anzlé, Maurice's handyman's twin brother, her position at the Chateau would be axed by her husband. Count Alois was one she knew who took pride in his social position with her, the glamorous Claudine as his wife.

She had to tell someone and she felt Maurice had much experience with women. He must have, having painted so many models. She wondered if he did nudes as well. An intellectual conversation ensued as the subject was a sensitive one. She lit a cigarette signaling that it was time for a rest from Maurice's painting work. She would begin the confiding process by asking him about his life. After all she really knew nothing about it. She ventured a question:

"I know that you live in a chalet. Where is it, Maurice?" He answered quickly:

"Deep in the forest beyond the castle grounds. I walk here from there every day during the week in snowfall, rain or sunshine. In winter it is lonely and mysterious in the Bois de Boulougne with snow-hung tracery over the bare branches of the trees at that time of year.

There are little animals scurrying about in the undergrowth and in winter their different footprints' patterns form on the smooth lying snow. My father taught me to identify them by the little beasts' different paw marks in the heaps of white snow. But why am I telling you all this Claudine? These experiences are deeply embedded in my consciousness."

He was playing into her hands. She responded:

"Maybe it's because you see beyond just what I look like. I am a real person you know. Not just another Madonna being painted for Alois' pleasure."

She said this almost pitifully that was unlike her. It was not as if she wanted sympathy only she did need Maurice's attention. But he was used to this, almost promiscuity from his models. It was his calling however for he had to delve deep into his models' lives and experiences to create the all-embracing mood for the portraits.

Then came the reverberating question from Claudine for whom Maurice was developing more than merely an interest:

"Are you married Maurice?"

He found that the question stunned him. Was he going to let out all the details of his personal life to this woman? He knew that she, like him was of humble origins. He was eager not to be the first to betray to her all that was dear to him. He suddenly felt a deep sense of guilt. At least for all his lack of appreciation of the home Elize had made for him he could tell Claudine, yes, he was married.

Claudine looked up, her entrancing nose in the air. This painter fellow was one up on her. He was married and it seemed had been for some time. He talked of two children of school going age. He had said to her:

"My oldest child a boy is ten years old my younger child six. You do not have children Claudine?" She answered:

"That I should have been that lucky Maurice. No I was divorced, let down in a business situation to do with television actressing in Paris. My act flopped and I found myself as penniless as I had been before my ex-producer husband picked me up off the streets, as homeless as when I was a street urchin all those years ago. Yes I had ten years of marriage but my husband twice married before, a hardened man towards women took me about Paris restaurants and bistros, television and acting studios at a pace that I could hardly bear and I finally found myself divorced and in a psychiatric home.

In this last institution I found my level in life. I realized my true origins and my place in society but I still had ambitions. After coming out of a home for mental breakdowns I was forced, impecuniously to return to my alcoholic parents in the poorer parts of Paris. My father was a butcher but had a weakness for drink. My mother was not quite as bad but was worn out with eight children of which I was the youngest. I had hardly known my parents because my older sisters and brothers had seen to my growing years at school and all that went with it.

After my marriage came to pieces by a stroke of luck I happened to find myself passing the time of day with Count Alois in a small gallery of art in Paris into which I had wandered one Saturday afternoon. I was now nearly thirty years of age and the Count, twenty years older than myself at that stage courted and married me after two years. Underneath all his pomposity he was quite an advocate of what was then called "free love."

Growing bored as was typical of a man at all her woman's talk, Maurice who had been working at the portrait while she was talking put down his brushes and said:

"I am impressed Claudine at your dogged persistence for survival and from what you tell me, a start of humble origins into quite a classy existence. I can understand what life has been for you, a struggle as it has been for me too. But there are the bright spots the little social successes that make it all worth living for—you in your aristocratic social environment and I in the way of making a name for myself as an artist. You and I have a lot in common definitely."

He looked at her curiously as she had glanced away from him out of the window seemingly to judge the weather. He misjudged her facial action as she had not children to hang out washing for as did Elize. So he said thinking that she might have heard some story about he and Elize:

"And what do you know about my life other than that I have told you?"

He had hardly told her anything apart from the fact that he was a married man. Sparring now she admitted:

"I know that your wife's name is Elize." She held her breath.

Maurice gave a start. He did not want too much of his domestic squabbles spread around the village. As a child he had to bear too much of the result of the gossip about his poor father and sharp-tongued mother. The fact that everyone in the village knew others' business and the state of their purses had made him feel very cowed especially as a teenager and these facts had made him isolate himself and his family by building their dwelling place, the little wooden chalet in the depth of the adjoining woods. He responded quietly and nervously. He felt that his name was at stake.

"And how do you know that?" She replied:

"You have a handyman called Lazlé don't you?"

Not losing any of the tension that he felt about keeping his activities innocent though they were of his family secret, he countered:

"Well that is so but tell me I am curious to know how you have come across this information."

Her whole body started shaking and she grabbed at a nearby glass of water and gulped it down her hand quivering. Maurice thought, was she a drinker of alcohol too? She had never told him anything about that. He questioned:

"Do you need a little wine Claudine?" "No," she answered. "I must confide in you why I am reacting this way about Lazlé." Then it all came gushing out:

"Lazlé has a brother called Anzlé to whom before Lazlé became disfigured in the war time he was an identical twin. They were and Anzlé still is, most good looking and charming men. Anzlé is a wealthy banker whom I met on one of my husband's social occasions. I fell for him and he for me. The long and short of it Maurice is that Anzlé and I are having an affair." Tears filled her eyes. She confided: "I feel sure that you will keep this to yourself."

CHAPTER FIVE

Her face puckered and Maurice who found this state of affairs quite common amongst his female clients put down his painting brush with a kind of mocking sympathetic expression coming over his countenance. To take the situation forward he asked the obvious question knowing the answer before she even spoke. Anzlé has me absolutely dangling as if on a thread from his finger. He has complete and absolute control over me physically. I can do nothing to ease of out of the relationship as he teases me saying that he will tell Count Alois my husband about our activities. She jerked her lissom body towards Maurice and said biting her lip:

"You will not tell Alois Maurice I know you won't. Say you will not Maurice. I know I can trust you." He replied:

"How did you come to be in this situation Claudine? Of course the whole matter has not to do with me so of course I will repeat nothing of what you have told me. I only hope the Count will suspect nothing either of your affair or that you and I are simpatico."

Maurice felt a surge of the worst part of his nature that of manipulation. If she could keep the secret of herself and Anzlé then he could gradually ease her into more promiscuous poses, good for his artistic eye to practice but the pictures could be sold to Anzlé who was a wealthy businessman. Maurice felt a twinge of guilt at what he proposed to do, but took the bull by the horns and put his question:

"Will you pose for me?"

At her sudden suction of breath in fright she uttered hoarsely fumbling for a cigarette in her gold container. He went on tersely for he could hear footsteps, the Count was shuffling up the stairs. He said quickly:

"The sketches will be for Anzlé to purchase. I am sure both you and he will enjoy the experience, that I am planning towards the beginning of summer when it is warmer." She said demurely if that was possible: "But where . . . ."

Hearing the old door to the studio being pushed open with a creak he slyly picked up his painting brush and as the Count's head appeared from behind the door Maurice appeared to be busy on the golden brown subtlety of Claudine's left cheekbone. Claudine had resumed her pose and composure very fast. Underneath her pulses were racing. Count Alois suspected nothing concerning his wife's confession to Maurice nor about Maurice's trickery at attaining more business for himself and his family in his bribery of Claudine. She was the picture of innocence and butter would not melt in Maurice's mouth as the Count said curiously:

"I thought I heard a commotion up here." Maurice said:

"Oh no nothing untoward." Alois looked suspicious and said:

"Just climbed the stirs to look in on you and your artwork, Maurice. Also I wanted to make sure Claudine is not becoming too bored with her constant posing that is necessary for your painting, Maurice."

The younger two spoke together. Just as Maurice said: "All is going fine," he could see that she felt guilty though her husband did not pick it up. She said: "I'm quite alright Alois. You know I smoke so when I do get bored or uncomfortable I talk a little to Maurice. He also needs a break from his work now and again. He is here for nearly three hours every morning. My portrait is taking a long time. Maurice told me why the lovely old painting stands to one side of the armchair where I am posing. What do you think Alois?"

This last was said with a sudden burst of confidence. She went on:

"I can see a distinct similarity to the Madonna in the picture in what Maurice is doing with my likeness."

The Count nodded tersely as if he had the feeling something was not quite right but was not intending to question it. He had a full day with the managing of the chateau and the surrounding estate and after sizing up the work Maurice had done so far he said curtly:

"Well I'll leave you to it."

After he left Maurice was not long more with Claudine that morning. He was anxious to speak to Lazlé about his twin brother's amorous dalliance with Claudine. He wanted to be sure that Anzlé was taking precautions and that the whole affair was being conducted covertly enough. That was, secretly enough so that Alois would never find out. He wondered where the two met now and after arriving back at the chalet cornered Lazlé in the barnyard out of earshot of Elize and his mother. Elize diligently though care-worn was sweeping the floor of the living area having lifted the large mat that covered the entrance. It was not unusual for Maurice and Lazlé to be in conversation for she knew that the faithful handyman at the chalet would let her into the subject of the conversation later.

She also knew that Grandmêre would not leave her alone until she had heard what it was all about as the only control over her son she had was by manipulating her daughter-in-law. Outside Lazlé was looking stumped for words but managed to speak:

"This I cannot believe. Since the last war we two brothers have grown apart. Anzlé has become egotistical, and yes I will say it even of my own brother, a womanizer. I on the other hand have grown quiet and humble owing to my disfigurement after the parachute accident I had. But I must say Anzlé is being very daring and precocious to have seduced the Count's wife. Thank goodness that he is not married."

The next morning it all came pouring out from Claudine into Maurice's ears. It was a hot summer day when she and Alois at odds with one another because of the uncomfortable heat had decided to patronize a well-known little bistro on the outskirts of the village for a meal and something cool to drink, followed by a capuchino coffee.

The bistro was quiet at the time, the lunchtime clients having returned to their workplaces for the afternoon. Claudine told Maurice about that day:

"Alois was behaving like a crusty old man. Nothing I could do or say could please him. In the end as the meal progressed and he ate sparingly I gave up trying to be a dutiful wife and partner. I involved myself and I will say flirtaciously with a couple of tourists sitting opposite us. This was not unusual as Alois liked to chat to strangers in the village hoping for their interest in visiting the chateau for a fee. The poor old man must really have been feeling his age for on this occasion he took no notice of my convivialities and just sat there drinking his coffee with some bon-bons supplied by the owner who by this time had come up to our table to make himself acquainted with us.

He must have noticed what poor spirits Count Alois was in. Alois just stared right through him. The owner told me his name was Anzlé. What a handsome man! He told me as we chatted that he had several financial interests in the village and that as it was such a lovely day had decided to put in some work at the bistro we had chosen for our meal.

"Where do you live?" I asked fascinated by the interest the handsome man was showing in me. I had forgotten that I also was an attractive woman what with the fantasies that he was creating in my mind. Then as he left the table he gave me a card with his name and telephone number on it."

Maurice interjected sharply:

"Show me that card—you must have it with you. I want to know this man's name. It is vaguely familiar to me."

Maurice found himself for the first time with one of his models jealous and curious. Here was intrigue he could follow up for his own ends. He was surprised at the spontaneity of his own query. He had to see who it was who had an interest in Claudine. She delved into her carry bag and found the card for him. The surname stood out on the card. It was Cordier the same as Lazlé's second name. This must be Lazlé's twin brother that Elize had told him about. Maurice thought to himself: yes apart from his disfigurement Lazlé was a fine specimen of a man as his brother Anzlé must be

He began to wonder then. How close were the brothers? Would it be possible that Anzlé Cordier had confided in his twin brother about his love affair with the Countess Claudine? If so could Lazlé have told Elize about it? He relaxed though with the kindly thought of his wife. She was a hard worker and it was unlikely that word of mouth gossip would go any further than her as she was housebound during the day and the family did not make night time outings.

Then he rethought his whole current situation giving a start when he remembered that he had manipulatively asked Claudine to pose for him nude to make herself a classic artist's model. She had more or less agreed but the time and the venue they had not decided on. He began to wonder would his and Claudine's arrangement filter through to Elize and worse still to his mother? Both Elize and Grandmêre would react antagonistically if they knew about the new posing plan. Elize would be sulky though self-sacrificing and Grandmêre would be very prim about it typical of someone of the older generation. As far as Maurice was concerned their attitude would seem to be narrow mindedness. Not that they could do anything to stop it.

Maurice had a double-edged intention in his request to paint a nude of Claudine. The first was to make some money from selling the pictures to Anzlé Cordier whom he knew would be able to pay him handsomely for three or four picture positions.

The other was a very real male interest in the golden haired Claudine's body. As he thought about it he could have kicked himself for falling to his wish to see her naked although it was an artist's prerogative. Then a third thought struck him. He could bribe her for his own ends, the details of it as yet unsure to him as yet by the fact that Anzlé would know his lover had been exposed to the artist. And if the story of the nude paintings and the person who had commissioned them became known Alois would then have ample proof of his beautiful wife's infidelity.

But Maurice had made up his mind and found himself caught in a net of intrigue. He and Claudine had agreed on her posing for him the next day and after settling in at the castle studio he enquired of her:

"Where do you suppose the safest place would be to do the nudes?"

For a moment it seemed as if he would have nowhere to work. Claudine answered:

Anzlé has agreed to my posing for you for a remuneration. His farm on the outskirts of the village has a large barn that gets plenty of light. It also has soft straw scattered on the floor. I am sure he will let us use it for your painting purposes. Alois will not miss me for a few hours during the day. He is always busy with the estate. Should I talk to Anzlé about the proposed sketches?"

"No," answered Maurice. "I have found that in such situations as yours it is better that I myself approach the future owner of the sketches. I am going to make sure that he pays me a good price for them. I am taking a risk of upsetting Count Alois by doing this." Maurice was enjoying the intrigue that he was imposing between himself and Claudine. She interrupted sharply:

"You won't tell him will you Maurice?" He shook his head.

This was just the reaction he had hoped for from her. It would mean that he had the upper hand in the situation. So Claudine arranged for the three of them who were involved in the clandestine arrangement to meet in one of Anzlé's bistros in the village one afternoon later in the week.

When they met, the handsome dark-eyed man soon saw the woman with whom he was having an affair as he strode confidently into the bistro. She was as full of puzzles as a little monkey was his friend Claudine. What could she be up to this time? Anzlé was not surprised or even jealous to see her sitting at a table with yet another male who had a curiously interesting countenance. Maurice realized by looking at Claudine that this was her lover. He fixed Anzlé with a penetrating stare of interest more than intending to put him off his guard. Claudine lifted her lips to his kiss of greeting. Maurice looked away at this gesture. With a little embarrassment the two men were introduced by Claudine who stifled her mirth as she said to Maurice:

"This is Anzlé, Lazlé's twin brother."

"Oh!" said Anzlé somewhat haughtily, "so you are Lazlé's employer." Maurice answered:

"He is not so much employed by me as being a helping hand at the chalet. He is a friend to my wife who is housebound all day with my children being at school. I intend to ask him if he will help me to carry my canvasses, easel paints and brushes to the barn where Claudine tells me you might offer to give me a venue to paint."

Maurice realized now that Elize would have to be let into the arrangement as Lazlé would be bound to tell her what was transpiring between the chateau, village and Anzlé's farm barn. Finding himself leading the arrangement he said:

"It is important that nothing is said to Count Alois of the sketching as he might smell a rat. He need not necessarily be told why I am doing the sketches or whom they are for but he might blame me for what he could consider his wife's promiscuity. Upon Anzlé being told of what was being organized the three of them agreed that the whole matter be kept as quiet and unnoticed as possible. Maurice was nearly satisfied with his portrait of Claudine, with the Count's requested veneer of similarity to the Giotto Madonna. Every time he worked on Claudine's portrait that was less and less as the weeks flew by his cynical nature became keener to begin sketching her nude. In a way this was typical of his attitude to women in the years spanning his career up until the present. Why should it be he Maurice who always had to take the back seat in the adulation of his portraits by the men who commissioned them? Was he not equally important?

But no. It was always such comments as "her eyes are so blue and clear" and "what an ivory smooth brow she has" and "the hollows in her cheeks are so appealing."

Always it was the portrait's likeness itself that was admired each time while the dark penetrating eyes of Maurice looked on in the situation from the side-lines. Yes it did make him feel good even egotistical, to have his work admired thus but seldom did he receive compliments as he felt due to him.

He arranged with Lazlé to transport his painting apparatus, his bottles of color in their varying states of fullness, his easel, some canvasses, and brushes out of the chateau where he had been painting. Lazlé was smitten with guilt upon being told when all of Maurice's apparatus had been transferred, what Maurice would be working at. As a man even though he was disfigured he felt pain on behalf of his now beloved dear friend Elize, Maurice's wife. He was at a loss to know how to help her as she suffered sorely at the verbal attacks of both her husband and mother-in-law.

Through all this Elize kept up a burning feminine love for Maurice who knew that it was she on whom he ultimately relied on for his standing in the community. He did not want it to be the talk of the town what he intended to paint for a price for Anzlé, and he and Lazlé made a surrepticious getaway from the chateau along the country lanes to the barn. He made sure it took place during mid-morning when most of the village folk were taken up with their usual activities so as not to be seen by any curious locals.

Maurice had arranged for a meeting with Claudine on the following day, the artist and model agreeing that they would arrange the posing from day to day at a time when Claudine knew she would not be needed by her husband. It was now approaching summer when the weather made it more comfortable for Claudine's nude posing with the warmth of the season. The barn with its farmyard associations was also sheltered and cosy although Maurice wondered, slightly amused how his model would find it sitting on the somewhat spiky straw.

Lazlé who had to carry most of the load of Maurice's artist's utensils awkward though it was for him in his crippled state, with relief dumped them unceremoniously on the straw alongside the wall of the barn. The hay scattered and fell as they opened the door and entered. Lazlé said manfully to Maurice:

"You do not often paint nudes do you Maurice?"

"No,' he replied," "only when they are the object of my special interest. This woman the Countess has used her wits to elbow her way up in society. She had a setback having been chosen to do television work and was abandoned by the business entrepreneurs to just as her parents had left her in the gutter. Then Count Alois found that she took his fancy though both of them were older than most. They in their way fell in love and married both flaunting the Catholic Church as their belief. I think that they make an ideal couple. In my own estimation I do not regard either of them as being overly intelligent but both have the wit to survive especially socially. That is the most important asset of nobility to know the diplomatic word when it is needed and to be discreet. The Count has managed so far to be quite secretive almost with regards to his wife's origins. She apparently is completely out of touch with her numerous brothers and sisters and alcoholic parents."

Lazlé who as usual was the listener in such conversations, said:

"Well I must be on my way. Elize will be getting anxious about the children whom I have to escort from school. Do remember me to the Countess Claudine if she knows of me. I am anxious to meet her."

Little did he know of his brother's secret that early summer's afternoon as he took a different shortcut through the now grassy surface under the trees of the forest. He took with him as always his trusty cane and struck the ground slightly irritably with it as he walked. By virtue of his disfigurement his head was bowed down. It was an effort for him to move his head from left to right but as he walked he saw in the far right of his vision two figures lying together in a patch of sunlight under a beech tree.

The leaves made patterns on their bodies that he could now see were in a state of half nakedness. He stopped in his tracks embarrassed and hoping that he had not been seen. He was right, he had not been noticed. They were engrossed in their lovemaking. The man suddenly looked vaguely familiar. As he watched covertly he was horrified to see that the two persons he had come upon were his twin brother Anzlé and a woman who could only be the Countess Claudine.

He was still quite far away from the couple but it was only too clear to him who they were. He and Anzlé were identical twins so to Lazlé it seemed as if he were seeing himself in their position. He pulled himself up—yes, like himself except that he had been dwarfed and disfigured by his wartime experiences. It was an old habit putting himself in Anzlé's shoes but the gentle spirit that he had developed since the frightful fighting separated him totally from his much-loved brother. He had a friendly relationship with the Countess who graciously passed the time of day with Lazlé every time they passed one another when Lazlé was escorting Maurice's children to and from school.

She realized that she had been seen in the amorous entwines of his brother. Gentle character though he was he vowed that he would chide his brother for his actions. He would not go so far as to say he would spell out Anzlé's activities to the Count but he would certainly warn him of what could happen if perchance through one of the passing local peasants the affair should come to the Count's knowledge. This was quite likely to happen.

These lovers had thrown care to the winds thinking they would not be seen. That evening the brothers met in the house they had shared since their parents had died. Lazlé daringly took the bull by the horns:

"I saw you and Claudine this morning in the woods."

Anzlé's expression did not change. He tried to avoid the subject pretending that he thought Lazlé had seen he and Claudine walking together in the forest. He was not going to admit his and Claudine's infidelity to anyone, but Lazlé persisted:

"Shame on you Anzlé. What would our father have said to you had he known about this? I know women find you attractive but with Claudine! I am horrified. You already have a reputation as a womanizer. Anzlé retorted:

"Stay out of my life brother. If you say anything to Alois Maurice will hear about it and your livelihood depends on your work at the chalet. You will miss Elize if that were to happen." He said this quite unkindly.

Lazlé hung his head. He had spoken before now of the cruel manner in which Elize was treated by Maurice and his mother. The argument was getting them nowhere and they were quits. After settling themselves with a brandy to drink they retired to bed at odds with one another both thinking how they could preserve a their somewhat parlous relationship. Anzlé was the more cannily minded of the two

Maurice went on his way now that Claudine's portrait was finished and he was awaiting instructions as to what to do with it. Count Alois had hinted that he might try and sell it to a New York gallery. While Alois was delaying about this Maurice finally tracked down Claudine and Anzlé at one of the bistros in the village. They did not seem to mind him joining them at first but when Maurice told Claudine's lover of the permission she had granted to him to paint nudes of her his brow clouded and he took an aggressive attitude towards Maurice. So she said to Anzlé

"But darling you said you would love me forever if you had paintings of me." He answered:

"I was only being frivolous you must have know that Claudine"

She was persuading him though and she could sense Maurice's encouragement in the way he stared at her with his dark unfathomable eyes. She was almost winning now and Anzle was being forced to give in. She went on:

"I told Maurice that I would pose for him in your barn. The paints, brushes and easel are already there. I'm sorry Anzlé if you misunderstood. The paintings I arranged with Maurice are to be nudes. I took you at your word you know. It is now just a question of how much you are going to pay for the pictures that Maurice will do."

Maurice now came up with some verbal support in the manipulating way that was his lot in situations like these. It was a gentle handling of Anzlé as Maurice was not certain what Alois' reaction would be. It was in such situations that he realized the very special role in society that he played as an artist. It was one, more surely in the pictures that he planned to do where he must not get carried away in as a man in the presence of a beautiful woman who was gracing him with her body to sketch. Maurice then tried to urge Anzlé on to making an offer for the projected pictures, but also continued:

"I certainly hope that this arrangement does not come to the Count' ears. He will surely want to know why I am doing this."

Claudine's ego was being gradually inflated now typical of the situation that she was used to finding herself in. She also had the interest though in different ways, of these three men, her husband, her lover and this strange artist who was showing all this attention towards her. She did not know but it was for Maurice's own ends.

The two of them Claudine and Maurice arranged to meet at the picturesque though dilapidated old barn that stood on Anzlé's farm. It was occasionally used to stable horses and if the weather was very bad, the few cows that he owned. They greeted one another at the appointed time ten o'clock on a summer morning early during the week. Anzlé had let Maurice have the keys to the barn. Claudine knew what Maurice had persuaded Anzlé to let him do a few poses for him to sketch. The object of the exercise was not only to fill Maurice's purse. He had become fascinated by this one time street waif who had clawed her way up in society on her own. He had also for an artist become entirely enamored of her looks, quite fascinated in fact.

From what he had seen having been in her company for a couple of months while painting her portrait in the mode of the Giotto Madonna picture owned by the Count, she also had a lovely body. Maurice was surprised at himself at becoming so interested in the Countess but thought that this kind of feeling came over all men at one or other time in their lives.

Maurice ushered her into the warm almost steamy barn. He walked quickly over to a spot where bright sunlight from an overhead fanlight beamed onto the rough wooden floor covered with straw. Maurice who was quite familiar with Claudine's nature knew that if she had to shed her clothing she would want to be warm. He knew that she hated the cold a feeling going back to her poverty-stricken days on the Paris streets when she hardly had enough to wear. He thought to himself grimly that she had enough clothing now. He knew that at the Count's expense she made more than an occasional journey to visit the haute couture shops in Paris, the world of the belle monde where famous people purchased fashion wear. Maurice said:

"I think this is a good spot to start. The sun will keep you warm and there is a rich interplay of shadow and light right here."

As she undressed slowly and pensively she smelt the recent presence of chicken, horses and cows. She ventured:

"We won't be disturbed, I hope?"

"No" said Maurice. "I have made sure with Anzlé that his few laborers have been told to keep away from this barn in the mornings for the next few weeks."

Maurice controlled himself at the sight of her naked body. He said answering her questioning look:

"I think I'll have you curled up facing the sunlight. Then I can have a shadow in the background and your body will be highlighted by the sun's rays."

Claudine spoke while Maurice was setting up his easel and putting his painting jars and brushes in some sort of order, and said:

"What a wonderful sunny and airy space for you to work in Maurice. But for the straw that is a little spiky when my body touches it I will be able to relax thoroughly to make your sketching easier."

She drew herself up like a cat sitting on a sunny doorstop. She felt a wave of intimacy as Maurice finished arranging his paints and equipment of bottles and walked slowly and thoughtfully up to her reclining body free now from the trappings of her clothing. He bent his knees so as to come down to her level and show her exactly how he wished her to lie.

"Yes," he said that will be good—one leg lying over the other in a bent position. Rest your head on a crooked arm! Thighs raised up." His deep brown eyes bored through her but she had no knowledge of what the artist in him was experiencing at the sight of her beautiful body. He gently touched her hips and she responded easily.

"Just a little forward here. Feet stretched out and left arm lying alongside your breasts."

Suddenly the intimacy of the scene hit her like a knife cutting through her body. Yes Maurice was an attractive man in a rough peasant way. She gave a start. Nothing like Anzlé's handsome slickness though. Strange she had never noticed before what an attractive man Maurice was. Even more attractive, yes than Anzlé.

But it would never do for her to let on that she felt this way. Perhaps it was just a fact that Anzlé had been persuaded by Maurice to paint his lover for a handsome fee. She cowered a little at the thought that if Alois found out he would be enraged. She broke the silence as she watched Maurice walk back to his paints. It was almost a plea to be let out of their situation. She said sharply:

"Oh! Maurice, Anzlé is bribing his brother who saw he and I making love in the woods. He told me that if Lazlé who does not approve of our affair at all, does not keep it quiet and not tell Elize or my husband about our activities, he will see that Lazlé loses his employment with you, Maurice. It is beginning to work on my nerves being the focal point of four men, you, the Count and the twin brothers."

Maurice stared at her curiously. Soon after Elize and Lazlé found themselves talking together.

"Oh! Elize!" Said Lazlé. My brother told me that he and Claudine are lovers. He admitted to me that their affair had been continuing for a few months already. The bad part about it is that it is that it is only Maurice and I who know about it. He saw the lovers in the forest and now has Claudine under his thumb as regards Alois. He will do a nude of Claudine. If Alois stumbles on the secret that I am telling you my job will be at stake. I will be heartbroken if this happens it would mean I would not be able to see you every day."

Elize felt her stomach ache with jealousy that Maurice was painting nudes. She knew that he had only done this while training as an artist and had not done it in his professional life as yet. She realized that the Countess Claudine must really have taken Maurice's fancy.

She felt pierced through with hurt that he should do this. Would she even admit to Maurice that she knew about the intrigue? She questioned Lazlé standing in front of her a picture of remorse for her sake she knew.

"Do you think that I should tell him, challenge him that I know Claudine's posing? Make an issue of it? I did not think something like this could happen when I married Maurice. I did know he was an artist though, I suppose," she continued bitterly, "that we should be grateful for the extra income but what a price that is for me to pay. I know I would never do posing like that myself. But then I am married to an artist." She finished with a puzzled look on her face. Lazlé said:

"I will speak to Anzlé my brother." I am the only family he has left in the world and he will surely take my view of the situation seriously. From what I can understand the troublemaker is the Countess Claudine. She seems to have a hold on quite a few men including her own husband.

What do you think he would do if he knew, Elize?" She said: "I cannot say but I hope for her sake that he never finds out. Considering my hold on my husband I find it a dangerous situation for Maurice to be in. It could upset our marriage and I have to consider the children. I might have to hire myself out as a charlady. Oh! Lazlé!"

She put her hands to her head and shut her eyes in horror at the thought. Lazlé put an arm around the young woman whom he had come to regard as a friend. They were together many hours of the day. Lazlé knew how cruelly Maurice treated the poor Elize. He supposed that Maurice thought that Elize would be even more in love with him if he treated her harshly. Lazlé knew this was not the case and that Maurice and his mother were making Elize just miserable. Lazlé said:

"It is the end of the day now and I must go. I will try to edge my brother out of the liaison with Claudine for it is causing trouble in three households. The Count does not know anything about the situation between Maurice, Claudine and Lazlé. I fear for Claudine's status as the Countess should Alois find out about what she and Maurice are doing. If it were to be judged it is to all intents and purposes quite above board with Maurice being an artist who earns his living by painting and sketching models."

Head bowed Lazlé closed the door on the little chalet for the night. Elize stooped down to pick up a child's toy from the floor and called Grandmêre to eat supper. The old lady said shrilly:

"Where can Maurice be Elize? He is never as late as this usually." Elize answered despairingly:

"I really don't know Grandmêre. Let us and the children begin our evening meal."

Meanwhile on that sunny afternoon in Anzlé's farm barn Maurice had yet another day of sketching and painting this time at Anzlé's request. Although the twin brother had been persuaded to pay for the drawing by Maurice, quite a handsome fee, Anzlé had rather pushed Maurice into the work and Maurice had been only too pleased to agree.

That afternoon they had to have frequent pauses both for Claudine to have a break with a cigarette and Maurice to rest his arm from working all afternoon at his easel. He said to Claudine:

"What time is Alois expecting you back?"

"Oh!' she said, "I told him that I was doing my usual shopping in Boulougne. He will not inquire where I am this afternoon. He knows too that I rest in my room when I return to the chateau as I find the town life quite exhausting. So we can be here until the sun sets." Maurice walked from side to side of his painting criticizing what he had produced. As the shadows in the barn grew longer he realized that it was growing late and that he would have to hurry to get back to the chalet for Elize's evening meal.

Maurice slowly packed his brushes and paints, easel and bottles into a large canvas haversack that he slung around his shoulder. Claudine said:

"Evening is drawing on. My goodness—it's quite dark all of a sudden." They went out into the country lanes Maurice having latched the door of Anzlé's barn. Maurice addressed her:

"It is quite safe for you to walk along here back to the castle but I will accompany you. It would seem strange to see the Countess walking alone here. People might talk and we don't want that."

As they ambled along each throwing in the odd bit of conversation Claudine had the thought that Maurice might take her hand. She would have welcomed this from him as a friend as she had become very fond of him. But she also had deeper motives. She felt close to him and she did not want Elize to know about this. She had a passing acquaintance with Maurice's wife.

Maurice had told her that Elize did not mind the fact that Claudine had sat for her portrait for Maurice at Count Alois' request. He said though that she would not feel at all at ease if told about the pictures Maurice had done of Claudine in Anzlé's barn. She said softly and cunningly to Maurice as they walked:

"I would not like Elize to know about my drawings that you did for Anzlé. I hope it will not slip out in any conversation I may have in passing in the village."

At this Maurice gave a start. He said quickly:

"But you wouldn't do that would you Claudine?" Realizing his social position as a humble artist he definitely did not want to loose Elize and the children. Elize was a very sensitive person, and he knew that he could not guarantee her actions should she find out about his drawings of Claudine. He repeated anxiously:

"You wouldn't Claudine would you?"

Claudine shook her head. I was only teasing seeing how you would react. You really do value Elize don't you?"

They had reached the chateau moat and Maurice stood outside for a long time after she had passed over it and entered the chateau. Then on his way back to the chalet his home he encountered Lazlé on his way back to the village. He could just see Lazlé's glowering face in the evening light through the forest trees. Lazlé said:

"So it's you Maurice. Spare me a moment will you. My brother Anzlé has told me about the pictures you have done for him of Claudine. I chided him about that as well as his affair with her. I would not like Elize to be upset about the pictures as she well might be."

Maurice said aggressively:

"So what is Elize to you Lazlé?"

CHAPTER SIX

Maurice gave almost a little skip as he turned on his heel to make his way through the woods back to the chalet. He always felt light hearted when he had finished a commission and now Anzlé's project of a nude Claudine was over. He, as a married man felt curiously free from guilt at having been visually exposed not only to a man's lover but to a Count's wife.

He supposed that this was what being an artist meant—a complete suspension from lust of the flesh towards his models. He saw only the beauty of a curved body and a beautiful head resting on an arm with golden locks falling to the floor. He had asked her to undo her long hair for the drawings.

He wondered how much Anzlé would be willing to pay him for his work. Anzlé owned a smart town house in the community and was well-known as a shrewd businessman. As well as his home and farm that ran at a profit he owned three or four bistros and stores. He was also known though as somewhat of a womanizer. Mothers in the village kept their daughters out of his way.

Tomorrow he would go and find Anzlé in the village and arrange for payment for the drawings.

Meanwhile finishing up in the barn had left him late for his supper. This evening he felt a rush of emotion and love for Elize his wife. She would never get into such a situation amorously as had Claudine. Sometimes, not often because of his surly nature he felt Elize to be a shining star in his life. The children were boisterous but usually under control and Elize cooked the most divine meals for them all. He fobbed off her question as to what had kept him so late and stacked his haversack in a corner against a wall.

The next day he was up early to bait Anzlé before he left for work so that he could gain recompense for Claudine's pictures. It really was becoming quite an intrigue and the two men were soon bartering vociferously. Maurice was saying to Anzlé:

"But that is not enough Monsieur Cordier—I went to a lot of trouble with these pictures." Anzlé countered:

"But you told me that the Count was paying you a mere pittance for the head and bust portrait that you did for him of Claudine." Maurice answered in a low tight voice:

"Yes the Count and I are on good terms. He has told me that if ever I need to borrow money from him I am welcome."

In all his male egotism Anzlé pulled up short. It would not do at all if the story of his affair came to the Count's ears no less the pictures of Claudine that Maurice had done be seen by Alois. Anzlé felt a little strange when Maurice put it to him more or less bluntly that it might not be possible to keep quiet the secret of the poses that the artist had persuaded him to pay for of Claudine.

He felt then that he should offer what for a humble relatively unknown painter like Maurice would be quite a healthy payment. Maurice though had a good idea of how talented he was as an artist and began to hedge and barter with Anzlé. Anzlé did not realize that Maurice was holding out of a higher payment for the artworks but in the circumstances thought it better to offer more for the pictures. He could afford it he knew. He was going to set a condition though. He bartered:

"First Maurice I would most certainly like, indeed I feel it my right to see the three works you have done. How are you storing them?" Maurice answered casually:

"Oh! I have them rolled up like a scroll put away carefully at home somewhere that neither Elize nor the children will dare to look. They fear my fury the three of them. My mother says nothing but her face tells the whole story. I mention this as you will understand that ours is a large family and we need all the financial support we can get. The Count is paying me handsomely for Claudine's head and shoulders portrait."

Anzlé feeling a little cowed that he had never married and had an almost Casanova-like reputation amongst the community, said:

"Well the whole town knows your reputation amongst the local glamorous women."

This was banter from Anzlé being well aware of his own reputation. Then taking an interest in someone with such matters in common to himself he inquired:

"Why do you work so hard at painting Maurice? You never seem to stop. Everyone in the village sees you come and go from this home to the next with your easel and your rucksack and paint bottles clanking over your shoulder."

Maurice felt a sharp pang but one of upliftment at this pointed criticism that he was receiving from Anzlé. Little did he think that it was to veer Maurice's thoughts and ideas away from the Count Alois who might be primed into the knowledge of his wife's posing for Maurice in Anzlé's barn. Thoughtfully Maurice, falling for the bait said:

"I think it is because I aim high in my art. Frankly I would really love to be both popular and famous as an artist. I would like to be recognized and accepted in art circles in Paris or New York. I feel sure I can do this. I have confidence in myself."

The two were silent together as they walked up the street to Anzlé's brick house, a feature of style amongst the little cottages of the village. Anzlé spoke:

"I see you have brought with you the sketches of Claudine's poses. Of course I must see them before I pay you out. I can tell you that I can afford to pay you quite a high price for them if I am duly impressed. How much did you have in mind?"

Maurice mentioned a figure average for the time and money spent at work on them. Anzlé said:

"Here we are this is my house. We will go inside into the drawing room and you can unscroll the three works for me to cast my eyes over to form an opinion of them. As you know," he continued looking a little embarrassed, "and I think you will understand knowing as you do about my relationship with her,"—he became affirmative a typical male.

"I am her lover. She does not want to loose her position socially as Countess and I go along with her naturally also not wanting to upset the intrigue of the affair. It is as if I am getting the better of the Count, an old rival of mine for being one of the leading men in the village. Put the pictures on my couch. We can use two cushions to prop them up. We will do it one at a time.

Maurice did as he was bid and showed the first one a view from the front from above naturally as the artist was looking down on his subject. It was an ochre pastel unmistakably a likeness of Claudine.

"Good—good," said Anzlé. Just like I like to see her. Did she mention me at all when she was posing?"

He did not want his ego deflated in any way Maurice could see. He looked eagerly at the picture and exclaimed:

"Let us see the second. This one I take an immediate fancy to."

Maurice scrolled up the first picture and produced the second in which he had her viewed from the top of her head downwards:

"Origina l—very original," enthused Anzlé. "Again I see you are looking down at her as a model. I would have quite liked a scene of her on some sort of mount but perhaps you can organize that another time."

Maurice was pleased at this offer. It would help to fill the family coffers. He said quietly confident: "And here is the last one that I did. To this one I have added some tones of color as speaking for myself I felt it to be the best of the three."

Anzlé knew that he was being superficial in this imparting of his appreciation of the three pictures. He was an astute man, highly a connoisseur of woman. In Claudine he had found a beauty someone who had pulled herself up from her humble beginnings in life and who had retained both her personality and physical attractiveness in her approaching middle years.

She had thick golden blonde hair and a pair of enticing blue eyes full of questioning and fun. Her nose was charmingly retroussée and she had a skin of tawny ivory. As he knew her lips were luscious. He was not, could not to another man, express all he felt about Claudine especially one who had so intimately been in her naked presence. Even though Claudine by virtue of her social position as Countess had to spend a large amount of her time with her husband Alois she still managed to elude him for sojourns in the quietness of the woody glades of the forest. This was far from the rest of humanity. Perhaps also she would run down the road to Anzlé's brick house where they met. This was what Maurice wanted to know. He said tactfully:

"What does Claudine do usually when she visits you here in your home? I mean does she spend time in the garden out at the back or does she look again and again at your other art works hanging on the walls? Some are quite modern and drawn by quite acclaimed artists I will be in good company when my works are framed and hung here. Anzlé, I think you should hang the gently colored one in your lounge and the other two in your hallway and study." Maurice continued:

"You do not worry about your brother Lazlé's having to live with them? I know this is his home too but he knows about your affair with Claudine. He has told me that he does not approve at all but what can he do to stop you besides telling Elize. He is not on close enough terms with Count Alois that he should tell him about his wife's infidelity. I'll take the pictures away to get them framed if you like. I would recommend simple amber outlines to pick up the golden glow she constantly shows on her skin from these wonderful hot summer days."

Anzlé answered:

"Well I'll leave that decision to you. You are the artistic one in this scenario even though Claudine provides the spectacle for the pictures." Maurice responded:

"Well the payment that you offered for my poses of Claudine will be quite satisfactory for me though if you ask me to do any more portraits or poses of her I will have to ask for substantially more as recompense."

"No," replied Anzlé, "you have captured my love Claudine in the very finest of detail. I can see it would be highly difficult to get any more of a fine representation of my ladylove onto canvas. I would be prepared to pay you extra if you are going to mention to the Count Alois that you have done these drawings for me. I know that you and he are well acquainted since doing Claudine's head and shoulders portrait. Tell me, why is this picture of her that you painted just before you did my drawings of Claudine so mysterious? Claudine says it has an air about it that my pictures do not have. Why is this?"

"For an extra quota of francs I will let you into the secret."

Maurice felt an eagerness to do business with this rival of Alois' in the intrigue that was spreading slowly into his own life. He explained the story to Anzlé:

"You understand that Count Alois is a wealthy man. He has acquired a painting of a Madonna a Renaissance work by the famous artist Giotto. On first setting eyes on it he was emotionally moved as it reminded him of his wife the beautiful Claudine. He told me that he felt that if only she could assume the air of innocence portrayed by this picture he would have a perfect wife. He hoped that I could fuse some of the atmosphere of the Giotto Madonna into my portrait of Claudine.

This I tried to do. Claudine though laughs up her sleeve at the Count's wish but in front of her husband pretends to admire the work for which I can only thank her. Her reaction to the picture was for me responsible for the considerable sum of money that the Count paid me for the work. All in all it seems that the Count is suspicious of his wife's activities although he cannot put his finger on any misbehavior on her part."

Maurice finished his explanation to Anzlé and went ahead with plans for the finishing touches to the displaying of the pictures. There is a little art dealer at the end of the village that you have probably passed by unnoticing of it at all. The owner there has framed several of my pictures as he does a little woodwork on the side.

He will only take a few days to do it and I can pay him out of the recompense that you have given me for the other poses. I think that he will be finished by the end of the week. I will bring the works to your house next Friday afternoon." Anzlé had sat listening to Maurice entranced by this ongoing story of Claudine. He said:

"I'll be looking forward to the delivery of the three pictures then at the end of the week. I am usually at home on a Friday afternoon as am tired of business by then. I must beg you Maurice not to let the Count into knowing that I have poses of Claudine on canvas, nor tell him of our affair of the heart. He would cut Claudine off without a penny if he knew. I am not so sure that I would want to marry her myself as it would be a third marriage for her and I am always on the lookout for someone more reliable and untainted as a possibility for a wife of my own. I would not say that I am a womanizer."

Here Maurice smiled cynically to himself for he knew that the whole village was aware of the Casanova Anzlé was regarded as. He knew Anzlé's standing amongst the beauties of the village women. Of course he did not see himself for the playboy that he was. He had managed to avoid marriage until now. He continued:

"So you will keep both my secrets, Maurice?"

He felt that he had found a friend in the artist. On different levels of association with women they both had much to do with them. This was something he felt that he had in common with Maurice. In fact he quite envied him his professional position whereas he was very much of a dilettante amongst the opposite sex. In answer to his question Maurice felt that he would like to get the better of Anzlé so he said purposely vaguely:

"I'll try not to let the matter come under discussion when I pass the time of day with the Count on my way to and from the village when I have a commission there. I can't guarantee that I'll admit to doing nude poses or not. It might slip into our conversation. You are aware that I have done a head and shoulders portrait of her for Alois."

Anzlé felt that he had to give some repartee to the attitude Maurice was taking to the matter so he remarked:

"I too am on speaking terms with Alois and could very well mention that I am aware that you as an artist have been in exposure to his wife's nude body by sketching poses of her."

The two men were playing Claudine off one against the other. They realized that there were antagonizing each other so parted company until the end of the week. On his way back through the woods to his chalet Maurice thought to himself that he was being involved in more intrigue than he would really like and for once was looking forward to seeing Elize and arriving home.

As he walked his weary way home to the chalet he rejoiced to himself that through the profession he followed even though he found himself involved to a certain extent with the women and their husbands or lovers, he need never be as physically involved in the intrigue of each circumstance as it came up in his life. This was what made his life interesting though he never knew what was coming up next. It was a fact that his various employers always expected him to keep his distance from his models.

He reflected carefully on his position in society especially as regarding Claudine. He admitted to himself that she was by far lovelier than any of the women he had sketched, ever. How could Alois, her husband think that she needed an extra touch of innocence in her portrait so as to emulate the Renaissance Madonna masterpiece that the Count had paid such a high price for? This was merely because it reminded him of his wife. Wasn't she entrancing and beguiling enough?

This thought was obsessing him and it had been so for some time now. Still he had strength of mind enough to let it be just a fantasy and fantasies came easily to Maurice. Thankfully at that moment reality was upon him. He had stumbled on, although quite a distance away, on a grassy verge on this hot summer day, the two lovers idling away the early summer afternoon in one another's arms.

They had not seen him so absorbed were they with each other and he changed his pathway so as not to disturb them. Just earlier that afternoon before visiting the picture framers for Claudine's sketches he had left Anzlés house under a cloud of dissension of Alois' knowing or not knowing about the pictures that Maurice had done in Anzlé's barn.

Again he wondered if Claudine was aware of the bribery that was transpiring around her. What did she think? That was if Anzlé had told her anything about it. The result she must surely know then would be that Alois would divorce her and a further consequence would be that would be that the thrill would then disappear from her affair with Anzlé.

Anzlé had said before now that he would never marry Claudine should the possibility even arise. Maurice, with the chalet home now in view was suddenly thankful for Elize and the children. They were what were real to him, they and his mother the old crotchet. He thus put on his fatherly guise forgetting about his artistic intrigues.

That night realizing his good fortune in having Elize, having a wife a steady partner in life he made love to her. She was an earth mother always ready to succumb to him. Afterwards the whole story about Claudine fell on Elize's ears. Maurice said hoarsely:

"I admit to being intrigued with Claudine. Have you ever seen her?"

"Yes," answered Elize sleepily. "I have seen her wandering alone in the grounds of the chateau. She is a most beautiful woman. Lazlé has confided in me her relationship with his brother. He says he feels most ashamed of Anzlé but Anzlé is wealthy and egotistical and is vying with the Count for a dominant male position in the community."

Maurice said:

"I must be a very weak person not to want that position in society for myself."

Elize answered quickly:

"But you are all I want in a lover and a husband Maurice."

Maurice turned over in the bed. As he fell asleep he thought craftily to himself, but I am that dominant figure in this village. I have entered the lives of all the beautiful women here. They do not realize it but they all have me to thank for the flattery that I have shown them while doing their portraits. In their subconscious I am sure it is me that they think of when realizing their attractiveness and femininity. The village gossip does not allow for me to compose nudes of them. Not like I did for Claudine. How fortunate that no one knew about it.

He began to have doubts. Those last few times he had been finishing off Claudine's likeness to the Madonna of Giotto, the Count had blundered into the makeshift studio. He must have known there was some sort of relationship between Maurice and his wife. Alois did not know the toughness and hardness that was a quality of both Maurice's and Claudine's characters.

Fearing a more intimate relationship between them Alois began to regret the commission that he had given Maurice. He thought of the artist as quicksilver, someone who came and went almost unnoticed to and from the chateau. He was an astute man but Claudine gave nothing away regarding her posing in the barn.

Alois was now certain that his wife was being unfaithful to him but could not put his finger on who it was who had taken her fancy. He also did not dare to accuse her as he did not for the social reason of her being a graceful partner at dinners and functions, want to lose her as a wife. Maurice thought to himself as he drifted off to sleep that he had taken a chance. But no one entering

Anzlé's home would even recognize the signatures on the pictures he had done

Maurice woke early that morning and the shaded light near the bed threw the most delightful shadows across Elize's face that was turned towards him. Sleepily she opened her eyes but he put his fingers over her eyelids and said:

"Sleep a little longer Elize. It's about time I saw to the children's and Grandmêre's breakfast. I want to talk to Lazlé this morning."

He felt a renewed affection for his wife and his male dominance was as he shaved, getting the better of him. He would chide Lazlé over the handyman's apparent deepening friendship with Elize. As an artist he was observant and amidst his visions of the paintings he had done he had noticed off and on that Elize and Lazlé seemed more and more often in conversation with one another. The few times during the day that he spoke to his mother she would wag her finger at Elize and once had said to him:

"They are often together during the day. I am so deaf now that I cannot hear what they are saying but they seem to be intimate."

They finished breakfast that morning. Elize had fallen asleep again There was a knock at the door. In the silence of the morning with the children quiet after the meal, Maurice heard Lazlé say:

"Elize? Are the children ready? It's me Lazlé."

Maurice, pulling his mouth down in quite a nasty chuckle swung open the door almost shouting at the man.

"I'll put it to you Lazlé. Why are you being so familiar with my wife? My mother tells me you speak together a lot. You are clearly a confidante of Elize's."

Lazlé, dwarfed though he was, felt his hackles rising. It was bad enough that this was not Maurice's usual treatment of Elize. He would defend himself by stating what was obvious.

"I have to talk to her about the children and my work in the barnyard and garden. It's a question of when to feed the animals and when to water the plants, the vegetables and flowers. We are thinking of putting in two or three fruit trees."

Lazlé shrugged his shoulders in a defeated gesture. He looked up at Maurice in a movement Maurice hated, pitying the poor man so much. Maurice said sharply

"It's me who will give orders around here and make suggestions as to how to improve the chalet's surroundings."

He suppressed the guilt he felt at his treatment of the handyman.

"Perhaps your little secret is out now Lazlé. I can understand that Elize would have pity on you." Then Maurice continued: "So does she find you attractive as well as me? I can understand her wanting to give you solace—she is a gentle soul at heart." Then in a rasping voice he changed his tactics. "But no more than that from her. Do you understand my man?"

Lazlé felt his hackles rise with a tingling sensation at the back of his neck. What he was feeling was anger, a man's anger. He felt quite thankful to Maurice for arousing in him a feeling of male egotism, a wanting to fight. This was something he had not sensed since his wartime days. Unlike his identical twin brother he had been the braver of the two but had come off the worse having made an unfortunate parachute drop, one of many. Unluckily there had been a snag in the preparation of the folding of the parachute and he had done a free fall hurtling through the air. Fortunately his landing had been cushioned by the parachute spread and he had not died in the accident.

Alone with Elize a little later, Maurice looked up at her from his seat saying:

"Does Lazlé tell you about his wartime career?"

Elize blushed, something she did seldom. She felt an anger arise in her heart a sensation that she did not want to allow to get out of control. But she did have an aching pity for Lazlé. No one wanted him now. She was the only one who took any notice of him or took any interest in him. And he had been so brave. What could she say in answer to Maurice's probing question? She ventured:

"Yes Maurice. In many ways Lazlé is more of a man than you are. You took backroom employment during the war, hoping to be famous as an artist. You wanted to have time to exercise your painting skills while all the tumult was transpiring. Lazlé did not. He gave his life, his body that was destroyed in the fray. And I can tell you, Maurice he does not want anyone's pity." Taken aback Maurice became the lover, the father of her children.

"Don't be upset." He said. He knew that no one could disturb her like he could. He suddenly felt jealousy eating into him. He thought that he had all women under control, under his thumb. Elize refused to show a tear at the way his charm was upsetting her. Sulkily and angrily she burst out:

"Lazlé is a man's man. You spend most of your time with women."

At this point Maurice put his hand on her shoulder knowing how to get the better of her in this situation. He had to respond.

"I want to let you into a secret." He paused, then continued:

"This is the secret Elize, I want to increase my reputation as an artist. In fact I want to become a painter of some reputation, a good one. Now Alois has given me an opportunity by asking me to do Claudine's portrait. I want to show it to you as I consider you to have a good eye for detail. I have spent three months on the work and evaluate it as my best yet.

I was asked to take into consideration a famous portrait of a Madonna, a Giotto masterpiece. Alois asked me to infuse something of the innocence of the Renaissance Lady into my artwork as he wanted to think of his new wife as coming to him without her history of childhood abuse and neglect on the streets of the poorer districts of Paris. He did not want to think about her disappointment and let down in her previous marriage in the world of TV stardom. He really is infatuated with her."

Elize struck a pose that she knew Maurice would like and said:

"But she is being unfaithful to him. Does he know or suspect this?" Maurice answered bluntly:

"He is getting on to be a doddering old man and she is having an affair." Elize snapped:

"I know. Lazlé told me. It is with his brother. Lazlé is a decent man for all his being a cripple, and is very embarrassed about it." Maurice pretended not to hear what she had said, continuing quite arrogantly:

"I hold the whole situation in my hands. If I tell Alois about the affair and I won't, Claudine will be destroyed socially. So I persuaded her to pose as a nude model for me. She was too afraid to refuse knowing that Alois and I are acquainted and that I might let out her secret."

At this point in their conversation Elize pouted at him, letting out the words:

"I don't think I like that Maurice." He countered:

"Sorry Elize—this comes out because you are an artist's wife."

He was quite serious about this, continuing:

"It does not mean that I too am having an affair with her, no I just find her a subject of beauty, a beauty that a humble artist like myself could never aspire to as a wife." Elize said understandingly though a little tartly:

"I should hope not Maurice. What would become me, and the children then?" Maurice dropped his head and muttered:

"It could never be like that Elize. I do respect our marriage even though Claudine is very beautiful, though in a blousy way. You have the advantage of youth my dear." He flattered his wife, adding:

"And loyalty. She in her social position could make me famous."

In fact I am sure this portrait of Claudine that I have done will be a step up in my career. And this is because Alois has invited both you and I for a mid-morning coffee at the chateau. I understand that he wants to tell me of his impression of the work. He is also curious about you Elize. I think Claudine must have mentioned to him that you and she are on nodding, sometimes chatting terms.

Alois as I call him, can pull many strings throughout the aristocracy of this region and can put my name up to a number of the nobility who lead interesting lives and may even want their own portraits done, or perhaps those of their wives or children. How do you feel about togging yourself out smartly and joining me to see the finished work of art, Elize? I am so proud of it."

Elize responded somewhat hesitantly:

"I suppose I could wear that dress that I bought to wear to your father's funeral—it is the only one I have that is suitable. My others are literally in tatters. They catch onto everything, the furniture, beds and chairs as I do the housework. This particular dress is a three-quarter length and has sleeves. I could wear a white close fitting white vest underneath it for warmth and it would cover my arms. I have a fairly smart pair of boots that I would need to wear for tramping through the forest with you to get to the chateau. I will tie up my long hair tightly so as to look neat for the occasion." Maurice answered:

"Don't go to too much trouble—I know that Claudine won't. And the Count is usually geared up in a riding outfit. Ever since his first wife died in a riding accident he has worn such apparel. It seems that he will never get over it. He was with her when it happened you know."

"Well," said Elize, "I will be keen to meet him. It will be a big event for me. You know that the only time I leave the house is to do shopping in the village."

Then there the party stood with cups of coffee at hand, surrounding Claudine's portrait. Alois was being quite explosive and bombastic in his appreciation of the lovely picture of the Countess that Maurice had created. Alois spoke sharply:

"Bring nearer my Giotto. Yes, the likeness and atmosphere you have captured supremely, Maurice. You know the portrait gallery were reluctant to sell me the Giotto, but I twisted their arms financially.

Since I opened the chateau to tourists my income has increased vastly. It was Claudine's idea too, to let visitors see what historically speaking is mine. Once my dealers have set a price on Maurice's work I will see that it has pride of place in the chateau's hallway."

Addressing Elize he shook her shoulder and blurted out to her his admiration for Maurice's artistic ability:

"Your husband is quite a genius, my girl."

Elize embarrassed at the attention being shown her as Maurice's wife, hung her head but gave a slow voluptuous smile. Claudine's presence hung over the little gathering of admirers as they sipped delicious espresso coffees brought in by a manservant on a tray. There were kitchen quarters nearby the makeshift studio, Maurice knew for he and Claudine had used it while she was sitting for him, to break the monotony. The Count now made an important statement:

"I must tell you all though that I am being forced again by hard times to sell my beloved Giotto Madonna masterpiece."

They all gave a sigh of distress for the sake of Alois' financial position for the Count was well liked in the community. He made sure of that with the attention he gave to all in the area, even to the extent of monetary aid to some of the poorer folk. Then the group dispersed, and went their separate ways.

Claudine, Anzlé and Maurice met that afternoon by prior arrangement at a little vine-covered bistro at the end of the village. Claudine had asked leave of Alois for the afternoon that he had granted. The three were as thick as thieves and just as guilty. Struck with fear at the fact that Alois might find out about the three nudes of his wife that

Maurice had created for Anzlé, the latter begged Claudine and Maurice to keep his secret.

The two smiled at his sudden humility and had some teasing words to say to him:

"It is different now," began Maurice, "sitting in this bistro, to when you and Claudine were lying together on the sweet-smelling grass in the summer shade in the forest."

Anzlé took Claudine's hand. "It would be a huge blow to you, Claudine if Alois knew. But perhaps if you could persuade your husband that if my portrait of you is worth a fraction more than the price he has set for me it would be worth my silence over the matter?"

Maurice said this half jokingly, half seriously. Claudine, seeing Anzlé wincing at the situation stuttered her reply:

"Maurice of course, you know how I value both your friendship and your artistry—I will hint broadly to Alois how I just love the portrait that you did of me and how I see the likeness to the his Giotto Madonna quite clearly. I will also admit to understanding the demeanor that he wishes me to have, just like his picture. He does not want me to behave so promiscuously although he cannot guess why I do so at present."

She glanced from Maurice to Anzlé whose gaze held hers.

CHAPTER SEVEN

The three sat thinking over the situation for a few minutes sipping their espressos. Anzlé thought to himself that he had reason to be jealous of Maurice. The artist must have some sort of affectionate feeling towards Claudine, Anzlé's mistress. Maurice, experienced in reading peoples minds through the expressions playing over their countenances took his chance. He announced:

"I will put a higher price on the three pictures. I would not like to hint to Alois about the work that I have done on the Countess for your erotic pleasure, Anzlé. Anzlé looked slightly antagonistic at these words but wanting to keep the threesome on a friendly basis, hiding any fear he had about the outcome of any such confidence between Maurice and Alois, said lightly:

"Of course I can afford to pay you quite a substantial amount more Maurice, just state your price."

Maurice congratulated himself inwardly on the success of his assertiveness towards Anzlé. There was bickering ensuing amongst the three with matters now drawing to a close in the little scenario in the bistro. Anzlé and Claudine left Maurice in this situation the slightly guilty party in his hinting at bribery. But this was part of his profession as an artist.

He painted, drew and sketched to make a living and he did it in his own way. If he had to push for a higher price in what he considered his work's worth he would do it. Count Alois was a different case. He had paid Maurice handsomely for the portrait of his wife and was highly satisfied with it Maurice knew. He was becoming obsessed with Claudine but was struggling to keep a professional attitude towards the beautiful woman.

Again the immoral situation was driving Lazlé to use Elize as a means of cajoling Maurice into a delicate position as regards his three pictures that he had done of Claudine. Maurice had told Lazlé about his drawings but upon hearing about them Lazlé became furious with Maurice on Elize's behalf. He was aware how she would feel knowing that her husband had exposed himself to the nakedness of another woman.

As far as Elize knew Maurice was only in business for portraits. She would be hurt if she knew and Lazlé in an almost stand up fight with Maurice took Elize's part. This is what the affair between Anzlé and Claudine was doing to them all. It was becoming stifling towards all parties concerned.

Anzlé watched as Claudine left him she crossing the old moat and entering the precincts of the chateau. As she entered the front hallway a laughing sound met her ears. It was Alois. Clearing his throat he said:

"Good to see you Claudine. I was waiting to greet you. You said that you were going for a stroll down to the village. How did you enjoy your outing?"

Alois was not so stupid that he did not see a kind of tightening of her expression on her face. She had immediately tensed, he could see. Now why was this he thought. She answered with the truth as she thought best.

"Yes I had an espresso coffee with Maurice and a friend of his."

"Claudine," said Alois, "why can you not take on the air of amused innocence that Maurice captured in your portrait, that he copied from my Giotto Madonna? I can see that you look the picture of guilt. And what may I ask may someone as beautiful as you feel guilty about?"

Given this standpoint that he was not even suspecting her infidelity, he was far from guessing even from this slightest clue. She shook her head slightly and the locks of her hair fell a little across her face. A sulkiness fell upon her lips as she spoke affectionately as she knew would please him:

"You silly old goat Alois. I have to be out sometimes without you as you know."

Chuckling at her cheeky hauteur Alois could only answer slowly:

"Well the servants all missed you at lunch. I had to substitute Mariette your favorite serving girl for you. Whose else bottom could I pinch without you around?"

Free to do as she pleased as far as Alois was concerned, he doting on her so much she replied almost haughtily:

"But you know that you can trust me Alois."

Her jaw dropped as she told this lie. She knew that she could do as she pleased with her new husband. Secretly she despised him a little as she knew his failing sexuality tied him to her with her always having the upper hand. She gave a little start as the vision of Anzlé came into her mind as she talked to Alois.

Maurice would surely not tell him of their relationship, nor she hoped would Lazlé, with the latter spilling the beans highly unlikely. She was fond of Lazlé who took a very humble stance with the Count and his wife. However Lazlé was yet another of her male acquaintances as she thought, another male admirer. Lazlé would not want to risk losing his place of employment as handyman to Maurice. No, that could never be. Her secret was quite safe.

She would continue to amuse herself with her husband Count Alois. Claudine had tried to find out from him about his previous wife. She knew only too well that he was an imbiber of drink and gathered that Juliette had left him because of this bad habit of his. She could take it no longer. Claudine on the other hand had a tough time growing up and found she could tolerate this aspect of Alois' personality for the moment. It did make the social occasions that they shared most long drawn out and sometimes even Claudine found them scarcely bearable.

She pondered over their three year old marriage. The cocktail parties and dinners they had attended flashed through her memory. Certainly she had been treated with adulation and waited on by their bevy of servants. She had discussed fashion and clothing with her women guests as well as the latest gossip about neighbors' financial standing and amours. She found the aristocracy with whom she and Alois associated to be questionable as far as morals were concerned. Finance was available from the Government of the country and there seemed to be a never-ending flow of it for the privileged.

The nobility though saw to it that their properties were well run and oversaw their staff so that the vineyards and orchards flourished. At social events they were hosting

Claudine flirted quite openly with the male guests. Some of them she found most beguiling. Of course they all fell for her charm of golden looks. Alois found himself sinking deeper and deeper into his drinking as he jealously stood around his wife as she talked vivaciously with his social acquaintances. Claudine found herself beginning to behave morally speaking like those whom she was meeting. On one evening a coquettish woman with whom she was making small talk addressed her.

"You have not got a lover yet? I can see that your husband dotes on you. He is a bit of a fop though I can tell that by talking to him. How do you put up with his heavy drinking?

"Oh, don't you worry," answered Claudine. "I lead him by the nose. He will do anything I suggest. I am enjoying myself tonight so we will be here for some time." She paused.

"Is that what is expected of one in society here?" Amusedly she continued:

"Then I will have to find one don't you agree?"

"Yes," answered the coquette, "only don't steal mine."

"Which one is yours then? So I know?' Whispered Claudine to her new acquaintance who answered:

"Oh! He is standing there on the left near the door. I persuaded my husband who had an attack of gout this evening—too much red meat, you understand—to let him bring me to this gathering." Claudine replied:

"What a dish he looks too. I can see that I will have to hunt down a lover for myself as well."

Claudine knew that Alois was not comprehending any of what she was saying as she had observed that he had taken one or two brandies as well as sherry and wine. Alois came stumbling across to his wife with yet another drink. Claudine frowned slightly as she tried to see what was in his glass. She was a light drinker herself and there were many times on occasions when he had made something of a fool of himself. Claudine was trying to cover up the fact that she actually did have a lover by chatting superficially to the woman who claimed that her lover had brought her to the evening cocktail party.

These were fairly short social occasions evented in turn by the various nobility in the area. These as a matter of course found themselves in and out of one another's homes. They liked to keep in touch with finance, amours and comparing notes in administering their properties. This was as well as discussing politics was concerned. Claudine was eyeing the friendly coquette's lover. She said as Alois nearly spilt some of his drink on her light cotton suit:

"He looks a real smooth one. How original to smoke those long thin cigars. He looks one who could bide his time waiting for you." Claudine answered:

"Yes," he has plenty of time for me too I see!"

Seeing Alois swaying on his feet quite unaware of the two women's conversation Claudine thought. I have a lover too. I was keeping it quiet earlier on as I was afraid that my husband, the silly goose—she blew her cigarette smoke just past Alois' face—might cotton on to the fact of my infidelity. Then I would really be in the soup.

Her new acquaintance looked slightly curious. Alois was standing quite close to Claudine who just fobbed off the coquette's interest. Alois, more interested than she was aware had pricked up his ears. He knew Undine and it was common knowledge in the community that she had a lover spurned by most men in their circle as he was known to be bisexual.

Completely getting the wrong understanding in the conversation he ranted in his drunken state:

"Lover, who's got a lover? I am your lover Claudine." He gave a fruity chuckle. In fact while we are on the subject, let us call it an evening and cheer these folks on their way home. You and I have a date I think"

Claudine had promised to make love to him that evening after the social event. She knew that he had strong forebodings about the loss of his ability at this but always considered himself highly potent when he had been imbibing. Claudine had chosen her time well as she knew how he flopped around in bed quite incompatible to her changing positions. He was a hopeless partner in these situations and it was no wonder Claudine had turned to Anzlé, a far more capable lover. She had met him through Maurice's handyman, Anzlé's twin brother Lazlé.

Although Claudine moved with agility from pose to pose she kept just out of Alois 'reach on the bed and continually kept him fumbling and trying to grasp her body. She was a tease but it only incited him and did not make him any the less determined. Claudine acted this way as she knew she was Alois' second wife and was in a continual state of uncertainty about her marital position.

Sometimes she was sure that Alois saw through her behavior towards him. It was a kind of dejected tolerance of her on his part. After all he had everything to loose socially if it came to the point where Claudine like Juliette his first wife could no longer tolerate his imbibing.

Gradually the couple grew weary of their playing and settled down to sleep. Claudine assured herself of another victory over her husband knowing that by her posing this way and that she was succeeding in keeping his interest in her. She waited until he was snoring and fast asleep and then lit a cigarette. She wondered what Anzlé was doing at that moment. She knew that he was more than half in love with her but both of them had their hands tied by their social circumstances.

Anzlé was an acquaintance of Alois'. He had told Claudine that he did not have much patience with her husband. They were both businessmen with Anzlé being a banker with several satellite monetary interests in the community. He had told Claudine that Alois was unreliable and inaccurate in his business dealings. Anzlé warned her, for her husband's sake that Alois would face bankruptcy if he was not financially more careful.

Claudine was up early the next morning. The day before she had agreed with Alois that they would meet in the morning room in the chateau to see over the chateau accounts. It was the end of the month and Alois was worried now both about his financial and physical failing ambitions. His eyes were drooping and bleary but he gave Claudine a spank on the bottom. He spluttered:

"You had me nicely last night. I can't remember too well but I am sure I was a success in bed."

Claudine just giggled. She was as inadequate as he was about the figure work necessary in the administration of the chateau and its surrounds. She also had a slight hangover from the couple of glasses of sherry she had allowed herself the evening before. They began bickering over the accounts, not being able to agree. Books with black covers lay untidily around the office at the back of the chateau. Alois and Claudine tried hard to get to grips with balancing the books with regard to food, accounts, catering, the dairy and wine farm necessities and water and electricity funds to be paid. Alois complained:

"I am barely awake Claudine. I am feeling my age. Do we need to go the office just yet? I am so enjoying these few cups of coffee that the steward has brought in. Are you having some too? It looks as if he has brought us a few croissants too. Good. This espresso is doing its work. What is the time Claudine?"

She looked at the gold watch that her husband had given her. She answered:

"Just time enough to enjoy our refreshments for the morning. I have a sneaking feeling that the account statements need to be looked at. It is a couple of days before the end of the month and we will be really unpopular if our finances do not balance. Are you ready to go to the office Alois?"

With much humming and hahing Alois pulled himself off the comfortable setee. He remarked once he was up:

"I really must do something to keep myself fit. Dr. Valois says the occasional stroll around the estate is not enough. I must keep more active Claudine. Dr. Valois says my chloresterol level is far too high and that my heart is not in good shape for someone of my age. Claudine answered:

"Well you have been warned Alois. You could easily walk to the village and back every day but you don't do it. That is what Dr. Valois told you to do isn't it?"

"Ho and hum to that Claudine. You know my lazy habits well enough." She chided:

"Come along then Alois. The morning is passing fast. We must look at the balancing."

Claudine had a shrewd interest in seeing to the books of accounts the little she knew about it causing her husband great amusement because she crossed through what the steward of the accounts had spent many hours working at, pretending to know better than he did what was correct and what was not. She knew that she was not at all accurate in her summations of the figures and realized that she caused the accounts steward much grief in giving him extra calculations. He usually had tactfully to put right her errors and that in a way that would not offend her.

Giggling together, Alois fondling her the two made their way from the rather cold office to the warmer cosier front drawing room. There they knew would be an array of drinks set out for them to choose their tipple. After sampling something new in the way of a potent sherry Alois said:

"My girl you are as great at figures as you are in bed."

He chuckled a little nervously for he did not want to put Claudine off in any way. She played her part also anxious not to offend her husband. She desperately needed her social position as the Count's wife albeit his second one for her mere existence and staying alive. Apart from her current situation with Alois she possessed nothing so was very careful to remain attentive to his whims one of which came up at that moment. He repeated:

"You were great in bed last night Claudine. I was good too not so?"

She did not want to displease him so spoke in a low soothing voice:

"But of course Alois you did what you could. I know that you are finding it difficult now but with me around we can have nothing but a successful relationship."

At this he gave her bottom a playful though gentle pinch. Ah! Thought Claudine. I do have the best of both worlds. Pretending to take offence at his sense of fun she said to him:

"But that is how you treat the servants Alois."

"That," he intoned "is how I treat all women in my life."

"So I'm not different to any of them." She responded coyly. Sensing his mistake he said quickly but calmly:

"No Claudine—you are the prime woman in my life. I could not do without you."

All this interplay was before lunch. As the time to eat grew closer she asked to be excused to titivate. This was really for Anzlé's benefit as they had arranged to meet that summer afternoon, blissfully warm outside in the nearby woods. Having imbibed his usual over quota of sherry and wine at the meal she knew that Alois would stumble up to the bedroom to sleep it off.

Then she was free for the afternoon a time that she was giving to her lover Anzlé. The Count was getting on in age in his fifties and she found it easy to pull the wool over his eyes. She did know that she was taking chance after chance in her sojourns with Anzlé. The only ones who knew about their affair were Lazlé his brother and Maurice the artist.

There was no doubt about it. Claudine was keeping two men happy at the same time. How long this would go on she had ceased to think. She was at this time a little worried as Anzlé was becoming more and more pressing in his amorous designs on her.

She took her chance as Alois dismissed her for the afternoon he as usual having imbibed far too much wine. Claudine said:

"I am just going outside to have a breath of fresh air. It has been so stuffy inside both last night and so far today. The heat is intolerable. I think I will walk in the shade of the trees outside."

She did not dare tell him that she was heading for the forest to a spot there where she had arranged to meet Anzlé. She arrived at the venue a little before he did. He surprised her by coming up quietly behind her and masking her eyes from the back of her head with his two sun tanned hands. He spent a lot of time out of doors in the season with his farming commitments. She shrieked:

"Anzlé! It must be you! Let me go!" He answered playfully:

"I must let you go? You surely don't want that do you?"

As he said this she swung round and faced him. They kissed longingly. She ventured:

"There is no one near is there? You must know."

"Not a soul," he answered. He pulled her to him. "Then we can." Again she was smothered with kisses. He inquired:

"When are you going to leave Alois?" She answered:

"He is a dry old stick. I don't know why I put up with him. Most women I talk to on our social occasions tell me they admire me for putting up with his drinking. Sometimes we are held up socially for hours on end. He cannot tolerate people and just starts drinking. It seems unbearable at times for me. I do indulge a little as you know, Anzlé but it is difficult for me to be with him when he is like that. Sometimes I despair of him but dare not make a move to leave. I have nowhere I can go as I am penniless but for him."

Anzlé quipped:

"There is always me." He said this with one of his charmingly rare smiles. She reiterated: "But how can I trust you Anzlé? Wherever I go men let me down. Why is this, you tell me." He answered easily:

"You give in too easily Claudine. It seems to me that they take you and leave you. Am I correct?"

"That is not what I asked you Anzlé. I said: how can I trust you Anzlé? Are you going to leave me too? Are you going to abandon me too?"

They were now sitting on the sweet smelling grass with forest blooms all around them in the shady patch and then they lay down together. They made love for a while. Anzlé suddenly pulled away. He said sharply:

"I have just remembered that I have an appointment with my bankers later this afternoon. I will have to leave you for the time being Claudine." He pulled straight his shirt and rose slowly. She said: "When will I see you again, Anzlé?" He spoke again: "Soon, soon my love." With that she had to be satisfied for the moment.

She stood like a forest nymph dressed in green, hair disheveled and face languid from their lovemaking. She watched him as he made his way out of the forest. He walked along the path that Maurice had made through the woods for his journeys to the chateau or the village wherever he had commitments to do portraits. Indeed as she stood there, along the rough route through the forest where Anzlé had left her in the midsummer afternoon came Maurice.

He was scuffing his feet in the now dried earth as he walked but at first did not sense the presence of someone nearby. On looking up though his eyes fell on the lovely sight of Claudine in all her déshabillé. He knew immediately what had transpired. In an idle mood he was on his way to buy some baguettes to have with the rabbit stew that Elize was preparing for his mother, him and the children. So he thought that he would do a little teasing. He knew that Claudine was aware that he was on familiar terms with the Count. He said looking at her quizzically:

"You have been here for a long time I can see that."

Edging his way into the guilt that he knew that she must feeling at the sight of him he chided her, daringly though:

"I know you were with Anzlé."

"Why state what we all except Alois knows," she broke in. He answered:

"What if I were to let slip a word or two about what his wife engages in when she finds her way out of his presence? Just to whet his appetite of course my dear Claudine." Claudine drew in her breath sharply:

"I thought we were friends Maurice. You wouldn't do that would you?"

"Oh," Maurice answered, "I wouldn't tell him the whole truth. He wouldn't believe me anyway. He is besotted about you Claudine and I don't think that he will let you go even if he was let into the secret. Let's change the subject. Where is my portrait of you hanging? I would like to know what Alois has done with it." She replied:

"He has hung it in the front hallway so visitors and tourist see it directly they walk in."

Maurice's ego was raised by this news. If this was where Alois had put the picture he would be sure to tell all comers to the chateau about the beautiful portrait and of course make sure everyone knew who the artist was. So he continued teasing Claudine gently.

"Alright Claudine. I will use what I know about your affair with Anzlé to get your lover to set a higher price for the nudes that I did of you. You can make this a request from me.

Claudine glared at him and set off home to the chateau saying as she took her leave:

"What it is to have so many men in my life. I can scarcely think clearly."

Slowly and thoughtfully at what Maurice had said to her she walked up to the chateau. She had not thought to pull her dress straight, it was all creased and she had no comb with her to neaten up her hair. Slowly she realize how disheveled she must look. Always on the defensive, Alois if he saw her in such a state would be curious, yes he would question her. She would be able to fob him off though. He was always suspicious of her movements being nearly ten years older than his wife but wanted to keep her as such. She enhanced his position socially as well as personally.

Fortunately there was a slight breeze blowing now that the afternoon was cooling after a hot day. That would explain her untidy hair. How would she vouch for the creased state of her dress? There he was suddenly as she looked up. He greeted her:

"Claudine! You have been away longer than you said you would. What have you been doing my love? What—I know—you have been asleep in the sun I can tell you look so relaxed."

Claudine lowered her head but he did not realize the guilt that she felt at his bumbling words.

"Yes," she said glibly I was walking in the forest quite a way to keep out of the heat and lay down on the grass and fell asleep you are quite right. The wind has started blowing too. Do let me go up to our bedroom to freshen up before drink time."

She brushed past him as he kissed her fondly. As he did so and on the way up to their room she gave a sudden start. She and Anzlé would have to be careful. Maurice was a manipulator that much she had found out by his words to her that afternoon. He was a romantic by nature too though. She did not think that he would let out their secret to her husband. He was simpatico fantisizing in the situation.

She could see Maurice would like to have an affair such as she and Anzlé were indulging in. Both her lover and her husband were prominent and wealthy members in the community where they lived. It would be highly embarrassing, a scandal in fact if Alois was tipped off by one of the servants or farm laborers. She and Anzlé were becoming careless. And she was sure that Alois was not as stupid as he made out. As it was he had forgiven several of her flirtations during their social gatherings

Just yesterday evening there was a cocktail party thrown to promote yet again in collaboration with a tourist agency the nearby hub of local business delegates. As usual Claudine had had no qualms about getting involved with the guests. She was a friendly person and with her own morals such as they were she soon attached herself to a blousy looking fairly young woman who after a couple of sherries as offered round by the servants of the chateau confided in Claudine that it was her lover standing at the exit door of the function room. She whispered hoarsely over a cigarette:

"He is trying to motion me to leave with him. I dare not leave yet as my husband is a financier in banking involved with the Count." Claudine answered glad to have found someone in a like situation to her own. She said:

"If we can wiggle our way over to the Count I will keep him talking—it must be your husband in conversation with mine because he is frowning at you. Does he know about your lover?" The woman answered:

"Not at all—it would cost me my livelihood. I am being manipulated by Henri—he and I slip away when we can. Henri says that if I don't submit to his attentions as I did at first when I fell for his charm her will let out our secret to my husband. Because of this I now find him and his whole attitude quite odious but I feel trapped." Claudine responded:

"I am in a like situation though am being used from more than one quarter. Anzlé is my escort when away from my husband the Count—and don't you dare tell a soul or it will become common knowledge with Anzlé already teasing me saying we must be careful or Alois will find out!

Maurice the artist who lives in the forest is a friend of Alois' and he also is half in earnest of telling Alois about our affair. He won't though as I have the upper hand with him. This is because he has told me about many of his flirtatious involvements with clients whose husbands have commissioned him to do portraits of wives and girlfriends. Maurice is too clever to be caught out though as his wife has control in his family. She cares for Maurice's old mother at their woodland chalet and the old lady manipulates them all. They cannot do without his wife Elize as she looks after the two children. And the handyman at the chalet who is my lover's dwarfed twin brother also knows about it. So I am treading on thin ice in the situation." Claudine felt she had found a friend, for she had held the woman's attention.

The tête-a-tête ended between the two women when Alois and Pierre, Suzette's husband walked over to them deep in conversation. His words to Claudine were slurred from the drink that Claudine had been watching Pierre ply her husband with. Alois greeted his wife:

"Great news. We are going to sell the Giotto Madonna portrait."

Claudine was not really culturally educated and it was nothing to her whether Alois sold the famous portrait or not. So she answered pandering to his excited mood.

"It must be worth a fortune Alois. Do we need the income from it that much?" He replied:

"Not really. Pierre here is willing to find a buyer for us. He is an important financier in this area and has a finger in, shall we say quite a number of pies." Suzette simpered supporting her husband.

"Pierre never fails in a deal. He has American contacts too." Alois responded:

"That's just what we have been discussing, Pierre and I. I happened to mention that we owned a valuable Italian masterpiece of a painting and he immediately told me of a contact that he has in New York. This person is an art dealer working as a curator of a gallery in that city. This man is highly experienced in discerning fake paintings so will verify the authenticity of my Giotto as well as setting a price for it. He has many contacts the United States so will be able to get the highest bid for the picture.

The difficulty is to get my priceless artwork to Mason's gallery in Manhattan. Pierre is too busy to do it for me. Maurice who painted your portrait, Claudine knows a lot about portraiture and art deals although he is relatively young but he has the experience to do the deal for me. I have asked one of the servants to make an appointment for me to see him tomorrow. I am going to ask him if he will take the portrait to New York. I know that he will see to it that the picture is kept absolutely safe under wraps on the journey."

Maurice was ready and waiting to see him the next day. Having been let into Alois' plans he did not show it openly but was thrilled by the importance of the deal he was being asked to undertake. He also savored the break from his family situation that he would have in the United States. The Count approached Maurice again at a meeting. He said:

"I am dead keen on you venturing on this semi-holiday to New York. I told Claudine that I had requested you to supervise with the utmost care the transporting of my Giotto to Gallery Mason in New York. She immediately offered to help you in the transporting of the painting. I agreed that she accompany you as I feel she deserves a break from the chateau regime."

Little did Alois realize that Claudine who had come to know Maurice almost like the back of her hand had of late developed quite a passion for the strange artist's company. For a start she missed his presence now that he had finished his painting of her. The thought of a sojourn with him, a few weeks together far away tickled her senses. Maurice had always kept a cool head with her. As a portraitist of many female subjects he had learnt to categorize them all.

The slot that Claudine fell into was that of a woman of somewhat deceitful easy-going morals. As an idealist and a perfectionist in his art she did not appeal that much to him personally or professionally. What he admired in a woman whose likeness he was asked to emulate were the delicate female touches such as carefully arranged hair and touched up lips. Also he fancied the velvet lace and beribboned clothing of the likenesses of the Flemish portraits of the late seventeenth century. Maurice was a professional man and had his family to think of.

In actual fact he found Claudine by comparison to some of his woman subjects somewhat coarse. Granted she was beautiful enough but voluptuous as Maurice thought, a fallen woman. He knew of her relationship with Anzlé. Alois spoke to the two of them.

"You were not expecting it Maurice but Claudine is keen to accompany you to New York. I have condoned this wish and have booked a flight from Paris to New York in two weeks time. I take it your goodly wife will have no objection to Claudine's accompanying you? It will be a business arrangement. You can both go up to the old studio. I have ordered packing materials of cardboard, cloth and thick paper. You can set about wrapping the Giotto. The cloth you can use to cover the front of the painting."

CHAPTER EIGHT

Claudine murmured to her husband:

"You will not mind me accompanying Maurice to New York then Alois? It will make a wonderful break for me and combine business with pleasure. For it is partly my business what happens to our Giotto Madonna. I almost feel that it is in a way part of me since Maurice used the picture to give its atmosphere to the portrait that he did of me for you, Alois."

"Quite right Claudine," asserted Alois. So you and Maurice can parcel it up immediately so as to be ready to leave with it in two weeks time. When I have booked you both on a flight from Paris to New York I will ask the head steward here to make available the packing materials in the studio. You can set about wrapping it securely sometime today. Perhaps this afternoon would be a good occasion now that we have decided this." Claudine inquired:

"Can Maurice tell me what to do to help wrap it? He has some experience in these matters being an artist. Surely you do Maurice?"

"Yes," he answered. "I have had to parcel several works of mine to be delivered to patrons up and down the country." He questioned Alois. "You did say there is cloth, cardboard and thick paper for our purpose I think? I will lay the cloth after cutting it to size so that it can be wrapped right around the picture. It will prevent any of the existing paintwork of the Madonna from rubbing off.

This will be so that we can tie up the picture in the cloth wrapping with cord from bottom to top and from one side to the other. Only then will we be able to wrap it in thick paper, this underneath the final cardboard wrapping. I would also advise you Alois, to obtain some fermolite packing material to close it up when we are finished. Any shop in the village is bound to have some discarded from ordered shop articles of sale.

There now Claudine I have showed my expertise with you in this matter. You do approve Alois? Then all we have to do is get busy. The task will require two or even three helpers." At this point Maurice looked hopefully at Alois—"to complete." Then Claudine spoke.

"Well first things first. Luncheon will be served in the dining room. Alois, may I extend an invitation to Maurice to join us in our meal?" Alois nodded briefly.

As they left the drawing room ready to mount the stairs on the way to the studio Claudine said to Maurice:

"This will be a tricky task to wrap the valuable Giotto. Alois knows though that you are something of an expert at such a necessity." He answered her:

"How will you feel Claudine, leaving for a break in the routines here at the chateau and flying to New York with me?"

"Oh, I shall be quite excited to go but sometimes I get so blasé about all that Alois gives me that I take it quite for granted. I will enjoy taking the journey with you in particular Maurice. I have always felt at ease in your company and also with you I find there is always something new either to see or do." He replied once they were in the studio.

"Well Alois is the one who has given us this wrapping task this afternoon. Ah, I see he has put the soft cloth and other accoutrements ready for us. It is always awkward doing something like this but once it is finished I will feel that that the precious masterpiece is safe to be handled and transported by myself to the gallery in America where Alois has contacts. He wishes to dispose of the artwork for a large sum of money. He has asked me to take responsibility for all this."

As he talked he was wrapping the cloth around the picture at the back.

"There," he said "the face of the portrait is covered carefully. Now to wrap the stiff paper right around the whole picture. This we can also tie around it with string." He was as good as his word and pulled the cord tightly around the article.

"Then the cardboard," he said. "This will be a good protective measure should the artwork get bumped about in transit on board the 'plane taking us to New York. And lastly we can use the fermolite for securing it. We are ahead of time with this preparation because according to Alois the flight is only booked after another two weeks." Then carefully he said.

"How do you feel about being my business partner Claudine?" She shrugged her shoulders as if not caring one way or another.

"You are not a happy person Claudine I can see that." Maurice said.

"Yes I know," she said. "And why? It is because I have no morals. I admit it, though to you only Maurice. You know about my affair with Anzlé don't you?"

"Yes," he answered, "but I will not let your secret out. We are alone up here in the studio." He paused while sticking the last of the wrapping of the portrait picture with the side of his wrist. "This is the end of an era for us Claudine," he remarked thoughtfully. "All those hours spent by me in putting together both your enchanting likeness and the atmosphere Giotto created in his Madonna."

Maurice was a little sarcastic in the transferring of his thoughts to her verbally. By this he clearly meant to impart to his former model that he did not really think that the figures, one painted most delicately the other almost promiscuously alive, had any likeness one to the other. He thought briefly that Alois had seen a likeness but then he reminisced, love is blind. All this he kept to himself as he did have a weak spot for the Countess and intended to support Alois in allowing Claudine to take the opportunity of a holiday in New York. Then she could be alone with him and if nothing else they could have some fun. So anything Alois said to Claudine in his presence about the forthcoming trip he manipulated his words to say to Alois:

"But I definitely cannot go alone. Claudine would be a great help in this venture. The picture is huge and I will be the one who will have to carry it onto and from the `plane at both ends of the journey. She could then carry the boarding tickets, passports and the license to take the picture out of the country to be sold." Alois responded:

"Also I am sure that the curator of the gallery in New York, Mr. Armand will have a wad of papers to be signed, including cheques. You cannot possibly keep hold of the picture portrait in its state of wrapping as well as all this. Besides, Mr. Armand is bound to want to view the artwork that will mean untying and unwrapping everything you have parceled up here. According to the letter from him that I showed you he is a top class art connoisseur and if you consider Maurice this picture is worth in the bracket of a million of dollars. Mr. Armand will be bound to pick this up." Maurice played along with this information and said:

"Yes, and you found the portrait in a perfect state of repair after all these centuries in the dark little art shop in down town Boulougne. I knew immediately that it was special and you bought it for a song." Alois responded saying:

"Then what we have discussed now can be the arrangements for the journey."

Claudine he noticed looked excited and tried to break into the conversation a couple of times, all enthusiasm fingering the wrapped picture nervously. The daylight was closing in on the three people concerned with the shortly to be sold and valuable and exquisite Madonna portrait. Alois in some way accepted Maurice's and Claudine's fidelity and took his leave of them.

They knew that Alois would be starting his evening drinking session. That left the other two alone. Somehow Alois trusted them and neither artist or model had a deep affection one towards the other anyway although Maurice had seen clearly both into Claudine's personality and her appearance by the sketches he had done of her in Anzlé's barn unbeknown to the Count. This man was still wanting to play the upper hand in his home situation. Maurice had not given two thoughts as to a physical relationship with the Countess.

For a start he knew that she had a lover and as usual with the female subjects of his paintings he was far more interested in coming to know them and the state they found themselves at any particular time that he was involved with them.

This aspect of his nature he was sure that he could further in his relationship with her while they were traveling to America. He had a strange feeling of setting out in an adventure but only had the bare facts of what to expect. These thoughts occupied him after Claudine had left to bath and titivate before dinner. On his way through the chateau he looked into the drawing room where he knew he would find Alois. So on entering he said:

"Ah! You have finished for the day Maurice. I must say that I have every confidence in your experience and knowledge of art. Where was it that you trained as an artist? Oh! You were a student in Paris. That city is an absolute labyrinth of art galleries and seems to be choc-a-bloc full of art students. You must have picked up much knowledge about the subject. You say that my Madonna is a masterpiece of the world famous Renaissance painter Giotto."

Maurice after finishing a glass of wine that Alois had offered said on leaving:

"You do me proud Alois. Yes I do sometimes feel steeped in this activity and the visions it produces both on paper and in the mind. I am sure to be able to fall back on this knowledge and expertise in judging the matter of the worth of the Giotto for Mr. Armand in America. I must leave now. Elize is on tenterhooks to hear the latest news about how the deal is to be structured."

"Right," said Alois as a glamorous Claudine quietly made her presence felt. Maurice glanced empathically at her and then slid out of the drawing room and was soon walking home through the darkening forest. He walked quickly through the forest the trees seeming to close in on him. It was quite safe he knew but the somberness of the night led his thoughts homewards back to the earth mother his wife Elize and the two children as well as his crafty old mother.

As far as he was concerned it was Grandmère who had not only raised him and encouraged his art activities but also was keeping the home together. Elize with her physical proclivities in bed with him was inclined to be lazy and the old lady who was well versed in life especially in her position in the household as Maurice's mother was inclined to tease Elize quite nastily as well as slap her down if she put up any defense.

The two had just had a tiff when Elize's sharp ears heard Maurice's soft footfall on the pathway up to the chalet door that Lazlé had quite recently laid out. She pulled herself up sharply. In situations like this she was never sure if she was going to receive support from her husband or not. Before he was inside she heard him call her surlily.

"Elize are the children in bed—I hope so because I have work matters to discuss with you and Grandmère after we have eaten. Supper is ready I suppose."

Scuffing at the loose rug on the floor Elize answered:

"The answer to both those questions is yes. The children have been asleep for an hour already."

Trying in vain to get the upper hand for the evening Elize said carelessly as if it made no difference to her whether he was at home or not:

"Your place is laid at table as usual. You can sit down if you like. You can wait a few minutes while I dish up." Trying to muster up support even though Lazlé was not with them that evening she volunteered the information:

"Lazlé shot and skinned another hare for us this afternoon. The meat might be a little tough as it was quite fresh when I chopped it up to prepare it for the pot."

Maurice was famished after his afternoon's wrapping of the portrait with Claudine and finalized arrangements for traveling to New York with her according to the Count's wishes. He still had to impart this information to his wife and his mother. He was uncertain as to the reception he would get with his news. That was, from Elize and Grandmêre.

After supper Maurice wiped his mouth smacking his lips after a delicious meal of rabbit stew that Elize had prepared. He thought briefly. She cooks so effortlessly but is so gullible. I'll have to tell her my plans and they are not all bad news at all. He leaned across the table so he would be heard by both women, and began:

"I have news for you Elize, Grandmêre. You won't believe it in our humble circumstances but Count Alois for whom as you know I have been doing a portrait of his wife, has commissioned me to accompany her to New York to sell a valuable artwork that he possesses at present. What do you think about that? He has promised me a substantial percentage of the value of the deal. This is depending on how much I am able to make financially on the deal. Good news, eh, Elize?" Elize pouted. She was a slow thinker but a sound one. She saw Claudine from time to time in the village and had actually passed a few words of the time of the day with the Countess. She adjudged her to be slightly older than herself and a most striking beauty. The image of Claudine came to her mind and while Maurice and Grandmêre were lauding his good fortune, with her down to earth nature she began to wonder about Maurice's and Claudine's relationship.

She knew men as she had come from a family of brothers and just began to wonder about what Maurice might be tempted to do being alone with Claudine, so far away. Hesitantly she asked her husband:

"Why is the Countess accompanying you Maurice?" Answering Maurice said:

"Count Alois would like her presence on the journey to sell the Giotto, in a kind of secretarial capacity. I will handle the artwork it being quite heavy, and Claudine will manage the paperwork concerned." Elize requested one last piece of information feeling thoroughly downhearted at the news Maurice had imparted.

"When will you be leaving, Maurice?" He replied:

"The trip has been booked for two week's time. We will be away for about three weeks."

Claudine felt a little eased at being told this as it would take the double pressure of both her husband and mother-in-law off her. The old lady would not have the iron-fisted support of her son in her rather nasty teasing as Elize buried herself in her daily tasks. She would also have the freedom of at least being able to talk to Lazlé when she felt like it. From what Maurice and the old lady were saying he was going to request the hunchback to stay in the outhouse of the chalet so the little family would be safe in his absence.

Maurice thought he could occupy himself in the last few days before leaving with Claudine for New York by seeing to the packing of suitable clothes for the journey and stay in the great American city. For this he would need Elize's help. He called to her from upstairs. She replied.

"What is it Maurice? I'm coming in a few minutes. I just have a few things to tidy away in the kitchen." Finally he heard her firm step on the wooden stairway that he had built. The sight that met her eyes made her stare in unbelief. Maurice, not the neatest person in the house had pulled all his existing clothes out of the chest of drawers and piled them onto the bed. Elize muttered, knowing that this was the start of a few days of busy sewing.

"What are you doing Maurice?" He answered:

"I have put all my fairly smart shirts that are missing buttons and needing attention at the seam in this pile on the right."

Elize gave a slight groan but soon had out her sewing box and had threaded a needle. Fortunately she had white, gray and black cotton as well as an array of buttons that she had collected since her children had been born. She became busy at stitching sitting on the bed. Maurice said amicably:

"This is when I do really appreciate you as my wife."

She put her head down to the task at hand, shyly now at his admiration. After two days she had his wardrobe shipshape and ironed, standing ready in a new traveling case that he had bought for the journey. Maurice trying to be helpful in the proceedings mentioned:

"I'll put in my toiletries on the evening before we leave. Fortunately this valise I will be using for the journey is made from the skin of some buck or deer so it will not knock up against the picture that is wrapped up carefully. I will have to manage both the case and the wrapped picture on the flight to New York."

Meanwhile in their bedroom in the chateau Claudine was trying to get her clothes in order for the trip. Alois insisted on trying to give her advice. Claudine was finding this a little irritating but she tried not to let her mood show. The woman whom Alois had found on the back streets of Paris knew on which side her bread was buttered though she did find Alois almost childish in his behavior towards her sometimes. She pulled out suits and dresses and finally had a working wardrobe of clothes suitable for the stay. She said to Alois slyly:

"I must say my goodbyes to all my friends in the village the ones I see when I do my shopping every day. They are going to wonder what has become of me while I'm gone. It was such a sudden and hasty decision Alois." She said this a little sullenly knowing that in fact it was Anzlé she would miss in their lovemaking. She waited to confront her lover with the fact that she would be spending three weeks with the attractive artist out of town.

She was sure of Alois' attention toward her but worried that he might find out about her amorous infidelities. Then what might he do? He would not like to be brought down a peg or two by a wife who misbehaved. Then she would only have Anzlé to fall back on and she knew he was against the marriage bond at the present stage of his life. She would have to be careful where she was seen.

"That's fair enough," answered Alois. I am impressed that you are so popular in the community that you have so many friends."

Claudine took her leave. It was late afternoon and she knew Anzlé would be at home, finished with his business dealings for the day. She walked quickly down the side street where Anzlé's house was. She had looked around every so often to make sure nobody from the chateau was watching.

There was no one in sight and the town was quite deserted just before the workers in the village flooded the streets on their way to lunch. She knocked surrepticiously on Anzlé's front door. He opened it a little not expecting her. When he saw who it was he opened it wider and made a sweeping gesture with his hand bidding her enter. The two had a lot in common in their natures both liking to amuse one another.

"Well," he said, "why are you here at this time? I was just preparing my meal. You can't stay can you?"

"No," she replied. "Alois is hosting one of his social drinks evenings." She burst out then: "He has so many facile flirtations, one after the other. I suppose that he does it to try and make me jealous but I just feel insecure because of it. Why I'm here is to say goodbye. I am going on a trip to New York with Maurice for Alois to sell a valuable painting that is a possession of Alois' at the moment."

"With Maurice?" He looked at her in a way only they in their relationship understood. Coyly Claudine answered.

"Well what of it Anzlé? It will make a break and be a holiday for me."

He changed the subject not willing to show her any jealousy that he had. She would be alone with Maurice for three weeks.

"I have given Lazlé my brother some sketches that Maurice did of you from memory. They are under wraps. I had nowhere else to put them. He always speaks so humbly, so admiringly of you. He said he would stack them in the outhouse at the chalet. I wouldn't like Elize to see them as Maurice seems very taken with you Claudine, even if only as a model."

He looked at her quizzically saying.

"There is nothing more in your relationship?" He shook her by her shoulder. "Is there?"

Claudine gave one of her typical half smiles and bade him farewell by replying:

"I'll leave that for you to work out Anzlé. You won't find out anything more than the paintings and sketches he has done of me. You can ask Alois to show you the portrait he did of me in the likeness of a famous painting that Alois owned. He was obsessed with it."

He took her by the shoulder again and said.

"No, it's not goodbye yet. You have a few hours left surely before you leave with Maurice and Alois for the airport. I only meant the sketches of you that I gave to Lazlé as an act of brotherly kindness. They are not there to get your own back on Elize.

Elize is too big-hearted for that. She understands Maurice's calling as an artist. You and Elize are slightly acquainted I think. Anyway she will never find the pictures. They are quite small in size so will easily be overlooked in what Lazlé tells me is a bit of a junk room." This was meant as a friendly flirtation with Claudine one of the last for three weeks. He went on.

"Lazlé tells me that he will sleep in the outhouse for the protection of the family while Maurice is away. I'd better be on my way Claudine. Didn't you say that Alois would be here any minute? He will wonder or jump to conclusions if he sees us hobnobbing together in such a tête-a-tête. Well goodbye Claudine. I will miss you."

After returning to the chateau Claudine turned as she saw the front door open and Alois appear with Maurice. The three of them talked briefly. Alois informed the other two that he had ordered the chauffer to bring the limousine in ten minutes time. Maurice and Claudine had their traveling valises and Maurice was hanging on to the wrapped Giotto portrait for dear life. As Alois' limousine sped down the tarmac Maurice murmured to Claudine from the back seat:

"Are you nervous about the flight Claudine? I didn't ask you if you had ever flown before. Have you?" She replied trying not to let Alois hear.

"Yes when I was involved with working for T.V. I did several hops but that was in a light aircraft. I don't know how it will feel to fly in a large passenger airplane. I'm sure it is going to be most exciting. She smiled at the thought of being alone with Maurice. She felt a usual sensation of fun being with him. She supposed Alois trusted them being together. After all they were both in their late thirties. Was that a dangerous age? Both she and Maurice were in stable situations matrimonially speaking. Her thoughts drifted on and then suddenly they were entering the confines of the international airport. Alois parked the limousine and the three of them hurried into the airport terminal.

They were late, events in the country moved at a slower pace than the city of Paris and Alois had not realized how time was passing. Nevertheless they had arrived with three quarters of an hour to spare. Maurice and Claudine followed Alois to the travel exchange counter. He had the boarding tickets and they were duly stamped. The official behind the counter seeing Maurice with the party inquired as to the nature of the parcel containing the famous masterpiece of painting. Alois was ready for the official. He stated:

"I have an official permit for this picture to leave the country that was issued by the Department of Culture. The painting is going to be sold in America."

The official eased and scrutinized the document that Alois handed him. He pulled out another rubber stamp and franked the permit. Maurice did his best to keep the picture in its wrapping from being bumped or knocked.

In fact he lifted it expertly onto the counter. He was on tenterhooks that the airport official would ask to see what was inside the wrapping but just then they heard their flight being announced over the intercom. Claudine had read Maurice's thoughts and said quickly to the man:

"That is our flight. We had better board the aircraft while we still have time."

The next Maurice and Claudine knew was that they were walking up the aircraft steps to the cabin inside. Claudine waved goodbye to Alois in the distance while Maurice struggled with the Giotto portrait.

A friendly airhostess summed up the couple as not being usual air travelers and new to this mode of transport in fact. She looked curiously at the large tightly wadded package that Maurice had with him. She addressed him saying helpfully:

"Can I put that large parcel with the rest of the luggage in the baggage department?"

Hastily in reply Maurice stated nervously though firmly:

"No, no. I must at all costs keep this with me." He said confidingly to her:

"You see it is a valuable and famous work of art belonging to a Count from Boulougne who bought it some years ago. It is to be for sale at a gallery in New York."

Then the `plane's engine began to drown out their conversation. The airhostess checked their passenger papers for the journey and furthered her way up the aisle. Maurice had let Claudine have the window seat. He could always lean over her if she spotted any sight worth glancing at as the `plane sped on it's way through the somewhat cloudy skies, already over the Atlantic ocean.

The journey would take the whole day and the pilot came over the intercom late in the afternoon informing the passengers that they were due in at New York just before midnight after a whole day's flight. By this time Maurice and Claudine were beginning to be a little bored with one another's company. There was nothing but sea and more sea below. The pilot also announced that he was on course and proceeding normally. Claudine giggled to Maurice:

"Are you nervous?" He replied: "To tell the truth I was a bit when the aeroplane took off from Paris but I am quite used to it now. It is quite a novelty for me though, a humble artist." Claudine responded quickly to his words:

"Never mind about feeling insignificant Maurice. It is that sort of person who makes the greatest breakthrough in society in the end. All your knowledge about painting will be extended to the fore when you meet the art dealer at the Gallery that Alois has contacted. I know this for I am from humble circumstances myself as you are aware."

The passengers were shown an old cowboy movie that Maurice enjoyed rather half-heartedly while Claudine was thoroughly bored. Maurice found her quite irritating as her attention was constantly wandering from the movie and she kept asking him what was happening as horses galloped to and fro on the screen in front of the seated audience.

It was growing dark and the `plane's wing and tail lights constantly flickered into the now dimly lit cabin of the aircraft. Some of the passengers were dozing and the lighting had been turned down low. Those who were alert used their personal seat globe switches. The meals provided by the galley staff were more than palatable.

Then the excitement really began. The pilot's voice over the intercom explained that the passengers should fasten their safety belts as the 'plane would be landing in just over an hour's time in New York. There was preparation for the arrival. The airhostesses, always busy at this time during a flight were in demand. One of them informed Maurice and Claudine that they could collect their luggage at the conveyor belt in the huge air terminal.

They assumed there would be attendants to direct them to the correct place. Claudine, for all her frivolity was looking a little pale and nervous as was Maurice. They agreed on the desent onto the runway that this was not at all like home. Claudine had their tickets for the flight that were stamped and returned to her as they would be taking a return journey back to Paris. Claudine laughed when she saw all the luggage revolving on the circular conveyor belt and on recognizing their own valises grabbed them before they went hurtling on another round. Maurice was trying to be as unobtrusive as possible while holding onto the fairly large parcel containing the Giotto Madonna. This was awkward though but he had kept the picture closely protected throughout the flight. He said to Claudine:

"There should be a taxi rank outside the terminal. Let's go and see. You will have to carry our traveling cases. The Giotto is quite a difficult load for me. You don't mind?"

Out side a chaos of traffic greeted them with cars and taxis starting up from all directions. It was a huge international airport Maurice had told Claudine. There was a great variety of people all dashing to get transport into the metropolis.

The two hurried to the nearest free taxi. Alois had seen that Maurice was well provided for with traveler's cheques and the taxi driver agreed to take them to the hotel that the Count had organized for them. It was a most inhibiting experience Maurice found as the traffic on the highways of the city was terrifying. Neither Maurice nor Claudine had driver's licenses so sat at the back of the taxi in a state of near panic.

It was a long drive and the taxi driver accepted payment from Maurice on arrival at the Grand Central hotel. He waited until Maurice had extricated his curious wrapped parcel from the automobile and was on his way soon with Claudine in tow in the rush into the hotel. By now both were feeling more than a little homesick in the huge impersonal place that had been their landfall. The skyscraper buildings made them feel claustrophobic. Claudine had the papers with her in her handbag granting them the stay at the hotel until the Giotto had been disposed of.

The two entered the glass door of the hotel and stepped onto the luxuriously patterned thick carpet up to the reception desk. A bored-looking blond saw to it that they had receipts for Claudine's recompense for their stay there, a period planned for three weeks. Maurice had encompassed that they would need the full twenty-one days to negotiate the deal of the selling of Alois' Giotto masterpiece.

Alois had instructed Maurice that he should not sell it for below one hundred thousand dollars. Soft jazz was being piped through from the lounge to the dining room of the hotel where the two sat relaxing over cocktails after the flight as they were finding themselves suffering to a slight extent from jetlag. Claudine was dangling a Gaulois cigarette between her fingers and pronouncing:

"New York is full of razz-ma-tazz and stimulation, don't you think Maurice? Just the flight here and the ride in the taxi has been enough to exhaust me"

She sipped her cocktail lazily and began to take notice of the few people who were wandering in for an early meal. Mostly they kept to themselves. Claudine addressed Maurice again:

"This is not at all like home. We don't know anybody and I've noticed that the folk do not seem too friendly. I suppose one would need an introduction but probably they are all about their own business."

Maurice was half listening and idly squinting at the menu. Alois had made ample provision for their stay in New York it seemed to Maurice. He noticed that Claudine was managing their payments quite efficiently in their various circumstances whether it was the bellboy or drinks in the lounge or dinner. She never seemed to be short of travelers' cheques.

Maurice noted that Claudine received many appreciative glances from the men-folk frequenting the dining area and when they had finished there, in the lounge. He managed to steer her attention away from one or two of the men who were obviously intent on chatting her up. He said:

"It must be obvious that we are not man and wife with the interest some of the people here are showing us, especially you Claudine."

He spoke with a half-smile and almost slyly. At this Claudine pulled herself up short for she was more than aware of the effect she had on the opposite sex. She began to speak, saying:

"This is when I really do miss Alois. He is almost like a father figure, a compère to me in situations like these."

Teasingly she continued:

"Maurice, you look too innocent to survive in a place like this."

Then haltingly she added:

"Perhaps I do too. It certainly feels that way."

CHAPTER NINE

They had separate rooms in the hotel. Alois had seen to that although he was quite sure that Claudine would not take advantage of the situation between herself and Maurice in the physical sense. Anyway unbeknown to her husband it was Anzlé she was missing in these circumstances.

After dinner the two went upstairs to Claudine's hotel room. Maurice sat in an armchair while Claudine sat on the bed. They chatted quietly for a while planning their next day. Maurice promised:

"I will contact Mr. Armand the curator of the art gallery. It is he whom Alois has been in touch with regarding the Giotto Madonna. Most people of his sort are quite canny when it comes to the pricing of such paintings as this one of Alois'."

He gestured towards the wrapped painting that he had managed to transport safely without it being bumped or knocked, to the hotel. This was prior to taking it to the gallery for a price assessment by Mr. Armand. Claudine remarked:

"The streets of Manhattan here are absolutely choc-a-bloc with people, with cars and taxis tearing from one place to the next. They seem to have little thought for one another. I will have to have transport tomorrow while you are busy on the telephone with Mr. Armand.

I just cannot resist visiting some of the fashion houses that are famous here. I told Alois that it was one of the conditions that I would take the journey with you. I was only joking and the poor dear took it so seriously. So Alois gave me a handsome sum to spend on clothes."

Gradually activity in the hotel began to quieten down. Maurice bade Claudine a goodnight and left to go to his room. As he fell asleep on the luxurious bed provided by the hotel his thoughts drifted to Elize and their two children. In this vast never sleeping city he suddenly felt absolutely lost. He would need Claudine. He even began to doubt his ability to make the sale of the Giotto successfully. He told Claudine this the next morning over breakfast. He confided in her:

"I feel like a fish out of water. My chalet in the forest seems unreal to me as if it never existed. It's not that I hate Manhattan. I don't." She replied:

"I can't feel at all like that. I feel so excited about the additions to my wardrobe that I will be making."

After their meal was finished they rose, Maurice having obtained Mr. Armand's telephone number from the unexpectedly efficient Claudine. She walked over to the reception desk to arrange for Maurice's taxi.

The two met again at lunch as arranged. Maurice had a trying time getting through to Mr. Armand on the telephone. He dialed the number given to Claudine by Alois several times after breakfast. He had seen Claudine off on her shopping expedition in one of the famous yellow taxis of New York. Finally at about 11.30 a.m. a clipped voice with an American accent answered Maurice's call at the other end of the line.

"Yeah, yeah. I have been expecting you to call for a few days now. Why haven't you been in touch?"

Maurice sighed. He could tell even with the little he did know about life outside Boulougne that he had a difficult customer on his hands. He paused. Crackling over the line came Armand's voice again:

"Hullo! Hullo! Is anyone there?"

Maurice's voice came raspingly over the wire.

"Mr. Armand? Quite right. I am telephoning about Count Alois' Giotto masterpiece that I have been commissioned to set up a sale with. I would like to make this appointment to bring the picture for you to see, sometime over the next few days. We have three days left until the weekend. Will this suit you? Will you name a day and a time when we can meet? Also I will need the address of the Gallery and directions for the way there from our hotel in Manhattan. I am in New York with Count Alois' wife."

From the telephone came loud static and crackling. Then Maurice heard Mr. Armand's voice faintly again.

"Yeah, yeah. Don't rush me."

Clearly businesslike then Armand's voice continued over the line.

"We are Gallery Michaud not too far from you."

He proceeded to give both the address and directions so Maurice and Claudine could reach him by mid-morning in two day's time. This made it Thursday morning. Just as he hung up in walked Claudine loaded with elegantly boxed and wrapped parcels containing part of a new wardrobe of clothes. She did not see Maurice at first.

He stood back to view the sight of a flustered and exhausted Claudine. She just put all the boxes and parcels on the floor and stated:

"Maurice, please get me something to drink. I am also needing a cigarette. You are right. It is awful out there, terrifying in fact. The taxi driver just took matters into his own hands and had to swerve to avoid other traffic the whole way. Luckily he was an old hand at finding parking but I had to hurry at each shop."

Lazily Maurice helped her with her shopping parcels. He had not had nearly as busy a morning as Claudine. In the bedroom Maurice ordered soothing drinks for them both. It was a warm day and Claudine was too exhausted even to talk. Maurice tried her.

"What are you going to do this afternoon? After lunch I mean?" Slowly she responded:

"I think I'll flop down on the bed and have an hour's nap. I really am quite exhausted. I'll take it easy for the rest of the day and this evening." Maurice said coolly:

"Perhaps this evening we could talk about the pictures I did of you in Anzlé's barn."

Coming out of her state of exhaustion prior to their luncheon Claudine, curious now that the subject of the nude paintings, the three of them that Maurice had done of her, but flattered nevertheless, agreed.

He said sitting on a basket chair comfortably while she sat on the bed:

"Which one do you like the best?"

She narrowed her eyes each time the smoke from her Gaulois cigarette blurred her vision. What was Maurice playing at? She knew that he found her a beautiful woman but that he valued his standing as a popular figure, the artist who lived in the small community outside the town of Boulougne in France. She tried him.

"I remember most clearly the picture of myself curled up in the straw." She continued teasingly: "And Maurice, it was most uncomfortable, with the pieces of straw sticking into me all over my body."

It was sometime ago that he had done this particular painting but her shape and yes, he called to mind, her hair, that golden halo brushing the dust beneath the straw. He looked at her penetratingly once again. Suddenly she just seemed like an ordinary socialite not particularly striking in the harsh overhead lighting in the hotel room.

He came forth with a statement that made them both feel less burdened.

"The sooner that business of the Giotto with Mr. Arnaud is over the better. I don't know about you but I am longing for the forest of Boulougne and the peace and quiet of the countryside." He said this knowing she and Anzlé met regularly unknown to Alois, as lovers. Slightly nervously she pulled on her cigarette. "And what is that to you Maurice?" He answered slyly beneath the charming words:

"Only that I could tell Alois what you get up to in the forest." Claudine stamped her feet, using her hold over the artist.

"Maurice you would never do it."

He could see that she was sulking because he had teased her. He let the mood stay with her. He relished in the fact that he had the power over her psyche that he could almost control her feelings. She was such a lost forgotten waif. Only an old fool like Alois would have taken her on. Maurice despaired of having any kind of relationship with the beautiful Countess except that of being a companion to her. He could hardly call their knowing of one another a friendship. They were at it hammer and tongs from morning until night. He tried again:

"Well Claudine are we going to shelve this shopping mania of yours and get down to business? Are you coming with me to see Mr. Armand tomorrow morning or not? I telephoned him from the hotel this morning and he seemed enthralled that I have brought the Giotto safely all the way from France. I will need the Count's letter of permission for the sale to take place. This document I know you have. Will you hand it over to me before we turn in this evening?"

She answered him in humorously nasty tone of voice if that was possible.

"Of course Maurice—how would I justify this spell away from Boulougne if I didn't? I'll see that you have it later on. Have you got any ideas about lunch today? I see it's getting on for twelve midday." The answer came quickly:

"Simple my dear. All we have to do when the lunch gong sounds is drift into the dining room as if we owned the restaurant area and ask the head waiter where we will be seated."

Claudine was so impressed by this that she did not deign to answer him with an "I could have told you that." The couple lingered over cocktails produced at the drop of a hat by an ignominious waiter whom Claudine had signed to upon seeing him wandering aimlessly around the lounge. As usual not noticing what Maurice was doing she once again took control of the situation.

"Maurice look, the waiter has brought you something to drink. Now how do you suppose he knew that you wanted it?"

Maurice kept a straight face and refused to look the slightest abashed. He said:

"Let's get this over with. I will change our appointment with Mr. Armand to a time early this afternoon. I cannot bear the thought of passing the afternoon to no purpose."

"Right," she answered. "From what you told me he is just as keen to meet us."

The long yellow taxi as ordered by Maurice earlier on in the afternoon pulled up next to the waiting couple. The driver seemed quite clear about where to take them upon being given the address of the art gallery. It was apparently some distance away and soon they were experiencing again the dicing and weaving of the Manhattan traffic, around corners and up and down several motorways.

Within forty minutes they arrived outside a glass-fronted and fairly large building named just visibly "Michaud Art Gallery." Maurice asked the driver to give them until 6 p.m. in the evening and then collect the couple to return to the Grand Central Hotel. Fortunately the rather cocky taxi driver promised to do this and they had no reason not to trust him. Maurice reasoned with Claudine:

"Anyway there seem, I notice to be plenty of cabs scouring the streets for passengers." They climbed a set of stone steps and walked through a glass swing door. There was a heavily made up middle-aged women at the reception desk. She seemed to be a native New Yorker and upon being asked if they could keep their appointment with Mr. Armand, she slowly eased herself off her high stool behind the slightly cluttered desk. Lazily she showed them down a corridor with several openings into what they could see was the gallery itself.

Glimpses of colorful pictures met Maurice's eye and it was all he could do not to venture right then into the capacious gallery showroom and shelve their appointment with Mr. Armand temporarily. However after a frown from the receptionist at Maurice's obvious temptation they found themselves standing outside a large modern wooden door that was firmly shut. Maurice said to Claudine in relief:

"Just in time. The Giotto is becoming quite difficult to handle any longer."

The receptionist knocked boldly on the door and assertively made the position clear to the two:

"You'll be able to leave the portrait with Mr. Armand. It will be quite safe here. He has been a curator here for many years and has handled a variety of valuable artworks. He will be quite aware of the rarity of such a masterpiece as your seller is offering in the deal."

The door opened. Then a slight figure of a man appeared, waistcoated and with black but graying hair sleeked back over his head. He nodded a greeting to the couple. He spoke sharply to the receptionist:

"Right Mrs. Fabricius. I will take over now. He glanced to left and right outside the door and seeing no one else in sight, with talon-like fingers gestured the newcomers to enter his office. He rubbed his hands together and spat out the words:

"Ah! So the valuable Madonna has reached us. The Board of Trustees of the Gallery have given me full authority to set a price on the painting that you are offering."

At these words Maurice was a little taken aback as Alois had not made this clear to him. He immediately had his guard up and answered Mr. Armand's remark:

"Mr. Armand, I must make it quite clear to you that I and the Count's wife will put the initial price on the Giotto for you to consider. In fact just as soon as you have unwrapped the picture I will give my estimation as to its worth. Of course we will give you a few days to study the portrait. One of the first steps you will have to take is to judge for yourself its veracity as a famous artwork. From our side of the bargain we can promise that it was bought by the Count about ten years ago through a well established art dealer in Paris.

I can assure you that the portrait is quite authentic. You will want to get the feel of what the artist Giotto put into the work, the nuances of shape and color both of the arch screening the figure and the Italian country background. This scenery disappears into the distance behind the Madonna's head and shoulders. Also you will want to study the head and shoulders of the woman in the picture particularly. You will note too the typically Mediterranean atmosphere created by the artist."

"O. K., O. K. I cannot wait to set eyes on it," the dealer said and glanced shiftily and quickly from Maurice to Claudine. "May I unwrap it immediately?"

Mr. Armand picked up a pair of sturdy-looking scissors from a desk cluttered with cleaning brushes, dusting clothes and picture hanging devices, as well as square pieces of cloth for protecting artworks from being exposed to too much light. His body bobbing up and down he began snipping away at the wrapping eagerly and hurriedly. Maurice noticed the man was being quite methodical. He knew Mr. Armand would not want to damage the face of the painting in any way. As the last bits of wrapping fell to the floor Mr. Armand saw the picture for the first time. Excitedly and enthusiastically he commented:

"But this is superb. I can see at one glance that it is a absolute masterpiece." Maurice remarked casually in return:

"I am just so glad to have transported it in such a way that it has reached you safely."

Maurice was deliberately trying to create a friendly relaxed situation. This was because in the next few minutes he intended to drop the bombshell as to what he considered the portrait to be worth. Mr. Armand said:

"My office has sunlight brightening the room at this time of day. I will just open the blind so as to be able to view the portrait in natural light."

Cynically just waiting his chance Maurice waited while he placed the picture on an easel positioned at the back of the office to one side of the window. The dapper little man looked at the couple questioningly. Maurice noticed his stare and wondered which of the two parties would be the first to stake a price for the Madonna. But first came the accolades from the canny art dealer:

"Perfection, perfection by a master's hand at painting. It stirs the imagination making me wonder what it would have been like to live in those times to have such a delicate and graceful woman though outside the church's domination, as a wife and lover. Do you have any idea of the history behind this awesomely beautiful picture?'

Maurice racked his brains for an answer to Mr. Armand's question.

"I seem to remember hearing that she was the exquisite wife of one of the wealthy bankers in the early Renaissance times of the opening of the world through naval explorations. The traders who owned the early ships that were sent to the Occident, or East as we know it today were the indescribably wealthy bankers in Sienna, Genoa and Venice. They had made their millions out of the opening up of the world by ship.

Their vessels traded as far as Africa and India even to China. We know about Marco Polo the great and famous explorer. That is how the picture that I have so carefully transported by air over the Atlantic, knowing that it's worth both financially and aesthetically, fits into the historical background." Mr. Armand responded appreciatively:

"I should have known, yes I should have known. The golds and browns, more subtle than even naming those colors are as you say exquisite. The touches of green in the backdrop contrast the almost cherubic pale rose colors of the actual visage of the Madonna and show us much of the piety of that religious age.

"Now Mr. Lefèbre," he said addressing Maurice, "is it going to be you or I who is going to set up almost, I could say an auction sale for this Giotto belonging now to Count Alois Bonpierre of Boulougne in France?" Maurice responded:

"I and the Countess his wife are representing the Count he being averse to travel, and will set the initial price. The papers Claudine." Maurice snapped at her in an undertone. "We will require at least in your currency one million dollars." Mr. Armand breathed out in an almost whispered and awed tone of voice.

"A bargain! Is that final?" Maurice held up his hand and nodded affirmation. He had fallen into the temptation of making a fair amount more than the Count had asked and lining his own pocket. He was just too much of an innocent in this huge jungle of skyscrapers, cabs and cars dicing up and down the motorways and the constant flurry and bustle of people. Never before had he set eyes on such a mass of varied cultures of humanity. He was utterly a fish out of water. Fortunately Claudine did not realize what he was planning to do, that he was going to pull a fast one on the Count and Mr. Armand. His heart was pounding with what he thought he would do. Alois would never know. He did not want Claudine to be in on the actual sale so he burst out:

"Mr. Armand, will it be in order for me to make banking arrangements this afternoon and call back tomorrow for you and I to sign the final deed of sale for the Giotto portrait?" The art dealer replied:

"That will be quite suitable." Mr. Armand said and continued: "For such a large amount of money being sent out of the country you will probably have to have a personal interview with one of the large international banks in the vicinity." Maurice replied:

"Well the main purpose of this morning's visit was to let you view the painting more especially for its authenticity. There is much fraudulency in the art world of today as you will know." Mr. Arnaud nodded quickly rubbing his hands in glee.

"Of course! Of course!" He continued, "It is not every day that I have the opportunity of making such a sale. As you can imagine we have selling constantly on the go here. Many wealthy businessmen and even collectors building up new collections use my gallery. I do more than encourage the constantly changing values of the pictures I have on show in the display here. So the scene here in the art world is constantly changing. Will you set the final price for me tomorrow morning?" "Right," answered Maurice. "We will both have several documents to draw up. I know I have to hand over to you a list of all the past owners of the painting since its inception. It has a long history in which I am afraid there are some gaps. Count Alois and I have tried to fill in as much as possible. Then there is the document of authenticity to be signed by yourself. I have also got Alois' demand of the amount that we stated of the sale in writing."

Mr. Armand was affirmative. "Quite! Quite!"

Maurice considered to himself that he could make a good deal with Mr. Armand. He fluttered through the relevant papers to do with Alois' Giotto and looking sideways at the curator said:

"So I will wait until tomorrow and we will meet again and both you and I will state our prices in the bargain. You see Count Bonpierre paid roughly a little under one million dollars that is in your currency, when he bought the painting. We will have to take it from there. You can think about the amount that you want to offer today and I will be back tomorrow to hear how much you will be paying. I will make my own decision then about the sale."

Mr. Armand came out of deep thought hearing these figures and answered:

"Good, good. I am quite happy about that. I'll just see you out. The picture is quite safe overnight here in my office. We'll meet again tomorrow at ten thirty in the morning." Maurice replied:

"Yes you can tell me then the amount you are offering and we can clinch the deal. I will make arrangements with my bank in the afternoon."

As they walked down the side passage to meet their taxi, Maurice said to Mr. Armand:

"I will bring the Countess with me again tomorrow. She will witness the sale on her husband's behalf."

Maurice hailed a taxi and a yellow cab drew up smartly. After dicing through the traffic once again Maurice found himself entering the hotel. There in the foyer that evening sat Claudine dressed to kill. She said petulantly to him:

"Why have you been so long Maurice?" He answered:

"It took longer than I expected to settle a basic sale price with Mr. Armand. I'm tired now Claudine I'm going up to shower and change. I'll be down just before dinner."

He was fobbing her off as he wanted to follow up his thoughts in a scheme to benefit his own coffers in this deal. No, Claudine need not know what he was going to do. She and he had agreed that they would put a price of about four hundred dollars more on the price that Count Alois had set.

If Mr. Armand in clinching the sale set a price of above fourteen hundred dollars on the painting well and good. But to his own ends Maurice thought guiltily to himself whatever the price agreed on he would set a sale of three hundred dollars more than that and keep the profit for himself and hope Mr. Armand was agreeable to this. Should the worst came to the worst and Alois did find out he would just smooth things over and say that it was his own commission on the sale that he had taken. In her usual feminine muddle Claudine would not notice what was transpiring in the deal the next morning he was sure.

Maurice's cynicism was increasing at the thought of the kind of guile he was breeding within himself. This was on account of the idea of adding just that much more to

Alois' sale price for his Giotto Madonna and keeping it for himself and his family. His ego, on the increase now that Alois had commissioned him to paint Claudine's likeness to the Giotto Madonna, refused to let him feel guilty about what he intended to do.

He was much younger and sharp-witted than the rather jaded and apoplectic Count Alois whom he knew would turn a blind eye on any irregularity in the sale. How could it be done practically? He churned his thoughts out. That was it—he would ask Mr. Armand for a separate bill to be paid into a different account for what he would call his portion of the deal, that was for handling it for the Count.

Of course the Count had given neither Maurice nor Claudine any such instruction. Maurice would have to bluff his way with Claudine as far as the signing away of the Madonna was concerned. She was making an attempt though a poor one to keep abreast of Maurice's and Mr. Armand's transactions. The effect of the way the tide was turning in this important sale was to make Maurice rather anxious and in need of his family at home. He was still feeling somewhat of a fish out of water. He began to feel more and more worried as the evening drew on. He upset Claudine's mood of frivolity at dinner. There were several attractive and wealthy-looking American men of about her age who were not averse to giving her the eye and she of course wanted to appear a vivacious beauty. All that manifested itself were scowls and frowns from Claudine because of Maurice's attitude in the situation.

Eventually trying desperately to keep up her dignity she muttered sulkily to Maurice that it was becoming late in the evening and that they should both turn in. By this time she had imbibed more than enough wine. Maurice was feeling quite pale and strained in the evening's situation. He was not a drinker that made matters worse. Claudine had also lost sight of the fact that she had forgotten to ask the bellboy to arrange separate rooms for them.

To add to their situation Maurice had also forgotten to inform the attendant that they needed separate rooms in the hotel. In the chaos and confusion of Manhattan they had been assumed to be man and wife or at least partners of some sort. In the impersonal world of the huge American city they were just another record on the receptionist's admission journal. Claudine really needed to call it a day.

It was a warm cloying evening and outside the blinds of the windows shut now by the staff of the hotel, traffic swished unremittingly past the building. Claudine flopped exhausted onto one of the beds in the en suite bedroom not bothering to undress or remove her thick pan makeup. Her dress that was low cut clung to her voluptuous body. It was too late to change rooms now and as the night drew on Maurice found himself anxiously examining his conscience as to what he proposed to do in regard to taking a cut in the sale of the Giotto. Would Alois mind? Possibly not if it were a fait accompli and Maurice had not asked for too great a commission. He quickly thought that he would not let out his secret to Claudine. The thoughts of taking a portion of the fortune that was really due to the Count ate into his conscience and by the time three o'clock in the morning came his brain was exhausted and he threw himself onto the other bed and was soon in a deep slumber.

Not for long though. After four hours sleep the bellboy knocked firmly on the bedroom door with two espresso coffees. Claudine with her hair falling over her face with makeup running did not move. Maurice gestured that the coffee be put onto a small commode and stared at the sleeping Claudine:

"Claudine," he hissed. "You must wake up. We have business to attend to. You and I must see Mr. Armand about the painting. You know we must."

Slowly she opened one eye with mascara from the night before oozing down her cheek. She muttered:

"Don't feel well Maurice. Can't you please see Mr. Armand alone?"

This was just playing into Maurice's hands. He did need to see the curator alone. He put up a front though.

"You will be alright in an hour or so."

"No Maurice," she mumbled. It will take me hours to freshen up and have breakfast. You had better go alone. Please will you?"

This was the child in her coming out. Just as he wanted it. It seemed almost as if he had planned the course of events with Claudine who for feminine reasons was finding it impossible to accompany Maurice. Still sitting in the chair opposite the bed where he had slept Maurice seemed to have a fixed stare. He said gruffly appropriate to his guilty thoughts:

"Just as you wish Claudine. We can always finalize the sale tomorrow. You know Alois has allowed us three weeks here at the most."

Maurice's upbringing in a Catholic home that had now fallen into lapsed Catholicism caused him a sense of guilt. He did feel somehow that he just must ask for an extra amount as commission for transacting the sale of the Giotto painting successfully. The journey would have been a real waste if Mr. Armand had been a disillusioned art dealer someone who had seen it all before. No, he in his slick little way had immediately seen that the portrait was a genuine work of art and had been entranced by it. He was the curator of a small but growing art gallery with an increasingly interested and wealthy collector's clientèle.

Maurice snapped out of his trance. Even at that early hour in the morning he half wished to do a portrait of Claudine just as she was. He wondered if she knew the mess she looked. He had already showered so felt he should be on his way. He said to Claudine:

"I'll be off now. Mr. Armand is expecting at least one of us to continue negotiating the deal. If you can't make it today for goodness sake be ready to conclude the matter by signing tomorrow."

Claudine swiveled her body hardly taking in what Maurice was saying but enough to realize that Alois had asked her to be the final signatory in the sale as a member of his family. She grunted in a most unfeminine manner. Maurice embarrassed now inquired guardedly:

"Does that mean that I can go alone Claudine?" She opened both eyes and answered sleepily:

"But of course Maurice. I am feeling far to lazy to come with you today." With a double meaning he replied smoothly.

"That will suit me very well. I will look for you at lunch time."

Revived now she watched him close the door. Ah! She thought to herself. Coffee in the lounge! Perhaps after bathing and freshening up she could charm some more of these wealthy Americans who seemed to frequent this hotel. She was sure one or two of them with the typical American admiration for the aristocracy of Europe, would be entranced by the wife of a French Count, she being alone too.

Claudine clearly had her own intentions about how she was going to spend what remained of the morning. Maurice found her entertaining two affluent looking Americans over coffee in the hotel lounge. Hardly noticeably Maurice passed by her saying:

"Au revoir till this evening Claudine. I feel it my duty to Alois to put this sale underway."

Unobtrusively he exited the lounge. One of the Americans said to Claudine:

"You do have the strangest male attachments!" Claudine was a bit hipped at this remark about Maurice. She was for all her leading the high life socially an observant woman and she needed to know all Maurice's movements. They had roughly to coincide with hers as they were on this vacation to sell the Giotto Madonna together. In answer to the American's quip, wishing to get one up on the inquisitive man who was so self-absorbed that he had scarcely noticed Maurice Claudine called out as he was leaving:

"I'll finalize the sale with my signature tomorrow." Then under her breath as she swallowed down some of her espresso that was slowly waking her up that morning, she muttered:

"I am not really interested in all this boring paperwork in the Giotto masterpiece sale."

The other American who was slightly more noticing of all that was transpiring jumped at the remark made by Claudine and laughed over his cigar not wanting to be an outsider in what was apparently a momentous art deal. He began to question what was happening. The conversation went on until lunchtime. The three in the lounge began to wonder when Maurice would return.

Maurice though having taken a taxi to the little art gallery that was quite a distance away, was now haggling with Mr. Armand over the sale. Mr. Armand asserted:

"Count Bonpierre has clearly stated in this letter that the Madonna is worth a million dollars to him. We cannot change that."

Slyly with nerves taut at being alone and adrift in this huge city Maurice answered:

"Count Bonpierre gave me special permission to adjust the price according to what was being offered and the general circumstances of the sale. I do need a commission you realize."

He knew that he could pull the wool over the eyes of both Mr. Armand and Claudine. She had no patience with the documents of sale, legal requisites and banking papers. She had also found the spritely Mr. Armand to be a most uninteresting character. Ignorantly she just put aside the fascinating life the man must lead in the art world.

Chapter Ten

"*Well we will verify the* fact that my gallery will have to pay more than expected, quite substantially more." Mr. Armand said and continued:

"Perhaps we can decide this amount tomorrow when the Count's wife comes to sign for the final sale on his behalf."

Maurice, underneath his guile was quaking. This could mean that he would have to give Claudine some idea of the amount that he was seeking as commission for himself and Elize and their family. Claudine could be quite sharp on money matters. After all she had grown up in poverty in the poorer parts of Paris and had a very real sense of the value of money. She did hate the necessary paperwork that was where Maurice hoped to catch her out.

He intended to confuse the whole situation when the three of them met the next day. Money was no object to Count Alois Bonpierre and Maurice felt sure he could talk Alois round to seeing what a very valuable masterpiece it really was. It was deserving of a substantially higher sale value and by virtue of this there was a larger cut for

Maurice who was acting as agent for Count Bonpierre. Mr. Armand said:

"I don't agree with you at all Maurice. Let the Countess have the last word."

"Yes," said Maurice, "but you have admitted to the rarity and beauty of the work." Mr. Armand answered:

"Let the Countess have the final say then." Maurice replied:

"Her signing powers are only a formality. Alois gave me to understand that quite clearly. Also she is not as experienced as you or I in the valuation of such a hard to come by painting."

So with a bad atmosphere and ugly feelings between the two men Maurice left. Mr. Armand slammed the door after he had left. Maurice quailed—the man was clearly angry and matters were not looking auspicious for him especially as he would have to talk Claudine round to his point of view that evening over dinner as well as face the irate curator the next day.

A convenient taxi drew up at his lifting of his arm to stop the vehicle. The conversation at the art gallery had run on until after the lunch hour and Claudine was asleep when he returned. It was too late once again to change their sleeping arrangements. He showered for the evening and tried to relax so he could handle any female whims she might have when they talked over what price he intended to set on the following morning.

The doorman ushered Maurice into the foyer of the hotel. There was no sign of Claudine in the lounge and it was too late to get a full lunch. He arranged for a sandwich and a cappuchino to be sent up to the bedroom. When he opened the door there as he had expected lay Claudine asleep. He needed to go through the paperwork for the sale of the artwork and this seemed the ideal time. Claudine had promised to accompany him for a final business session with Mr. Arnaud much as Maurice knew she would not have the inclination to do so.

Maurice sat down at a convenient table at the side of the room. He opened his briefcase and emptied a fair number of important looking legal and financial documents onto the surface. First he glanced through the small print of the lawyers' letters regarding Alois' rights as current, that was until the next morning, owner of the Giotto. This took him some time and he slowly ate his sandwich as he tried to take in the involved instructions. No, certainly there was no clause stating a time limit to the commission he was to receive. There! There it was, the words "commission of a reasonable nature to be agreed upon by buyer and seller." He could state three hundred dollars for his own benefit quite substantially more than he knew Alois would have liked. The Count was a soft older man, Maurice had thought to himself glossing quickly over the named price and commission in the presence of first Claudine and then Alois. By sleight of hand as well as with the paperwork he could get away with it to his own advantage. This he could do amidst gossip, information, news and other pleasantries. At this point in the late afternoon Claudine slowly came awake. She muttered, eyes half open:

"What's the time Maurice? Where are we?" He answered: "In the hotel in New York you idiot." Hardly hearing his words, she saw his empty cappuchino cup standing amidst all the papers on the table and said almost in a whine:

"Maurice you could ring for a cappuchino to be sent up for me. Oh! Yours is finished. Why not order another one for yourself while you explain all these papers to me. They are to do with the Giotto painting not so?"

She was playing into his hands when she said:

"I'm not really interested in that though Maurice. I think you had best handle it. The only matter that I will understand is when you and Mr. Armand show me where to put my signature."

This suited Maurice's plans. He would briefly mention the figure he had in mind to put to Mr. Armand the next morning but it was like water off a duck's back to Claudine during the evening meal what with all the attractive men coming and going in the dining room. Maurice said to Claudine over desert:

"So you see Claudine that we are sharing an hotel room. Would you prefer me to arrange a separate room for you?" She replied:

"We won't be here much longer. Just leave it as it is."

Claudine was not drinking much that evening and was only dimly interested in the sale of the Giotto. Maurice mentioned casually:

"I am trying to get the best price that I can for Alois' painting even if I have to tell Mr. Armand that I have verbal permission to raise the written set price quite considerably.

"Yes, yes," Claudine said again in a whining tone of voice. "I am tired of the subject. I wish we could have more fun here." Maurice intoned quite humorlessly:

"You know we are here on business Claudine. Alois would be ashamed of the attitude that you are taking over this sale."

Suddenly afraid at her own lack of enthusiasm she threw him the question:

"But you'd never tell my husband about this spree I am having dear Maurice would you?" "No" said Maurice, "only if you take more interest when we visit the art gallery tomorrow morning."

They took it in turns to get ready to sleep. Soon it was morning and they were on their way through thick morning traffic to the art gallery where the sale of the painting would take place. Mr. Armand had arranged seating around his desk. Claudine pulled up her chair lazily trying to focus through her cigarette smoke. The proceedings began with Maurice saying:

"Mr. Armand, the first thing I have to state to you is that I am within my rights to set a higher price for the painting than is quoted by its owner Count Alois Bonpierre of Boulougne."

Immediately interested Claudine tapped out her ash into and already half-full ashtray on the table. Sharply she said:

"Will Alois allow this?" Maurice spoke hiding the guilt he was feeling that he was doing this for his own ends.

"He gave me the right to lower or raise the price:"

At this Mr. Armand remarked hotly:

"I was not expecting this. Another three hundred dollars! I will have to put it to the other curators of the art gallery." Claudine blew out her smoke and put in the words:

"Oh! Maurice! You could at least put the price at two hundred dollars less!"

Initially mollified Maurice held the signature document out. Mr. Armand thought that he had better sign it."

The conversation was becoming argumentative with all three parties wanting their say in the matter. As usual Maurice was the quietest in the fray. Claudine knowing least about what was needed in the transaction, as Alois' wife sought to dominate matters. She agreed:

"Mr. Armand you must listen to me. I am the most important party in the sale of the beautiful Madonna masterpiece. I have the most right to say what the price should be. It is I who is Count Bonpierre's wife. I think Maurice has set you quite a fair deal. We are the sellers. If you wish to acquire the painting for you gallery to put on the art market again you will have to accept the price Maurice has set.

Meanwhile Maurice was shuffling the legal and business documents. This was in his anger and confusion at Claudine's tirade that had been quite rightful. Gruffly Maurice said:

"Sign here Mr. Armand." Completely put out Mr. Armand scribbled his signature in the place that Maurice was indicating. He inquired sharply:

"Will you please leave me your address both here and in Boulougne?"

Before he could get these words out in the couple's presence Maurice had taken Claudine's arm and they were half way down the passage leading to the street outside. Mr. Armand had summoned the security guard and was walking rapidly after them gesticulating wildly. He ordered the guard:

"After them Mr. Perold! I am certain now that the couple you can see outside hailing a taxi are imposters. Hurry man. You must take a taxi yourself and follow them to see where they are headed:

"Doing Mr. Armand's bidding the security guard quickly managed to get a taxi to pursue Maurice and Claudine whose taxi was just drawing off. Inside the vehicle Claudine most agitated now pummeled Maurice saying:

"Maurice what is this trouble you are getting us into?" Turning backwards she said:

"You see the guard is after us. Are we in trouble Maurice?" She spoke urgently to their driver:

"Drive faster. They are following us."

The driver was quite upset at the way his passengers were behaving. He tried to ask them for a place of destination but the couple seemed more concerned about the taxi that was following them. Completely out of control with Claudine terrified, she screamed at Maurice who was grimfaced. She cried out:

What do they want with us? Their driver tried to break into the conversation continually doing his utmost to control his taxi, saying agitatedly:

"Sir, Madam where do you want me to take you?"

Claudine was almost jumping up and down in the taxi at one time telling the driver to go faster and at another almost shrieking:

"He's getting closer to us. Yes I can see it's the security guard from the art gallery in the back of the other taxi. He looks a mean customer. Maurice I hope you have not got us into trouble! What does he want, that security guard with Mr. Armand in there?" Maurice answered trying to calm Claudine down by using a soothing tone of voice:

"They want to know where in the city we are staying, that's all."

Claudine was now thoroughly upset and in need of a cigarette. The cab driver was trying to elicit from his passengers where their destination was that he was supposed to be taking them to. He was now driving most erratically and swerving from side to side. The way he was managing the car was causing other vehicles to hoot sharply at their taxicab. The poor driver made one last attempt to ask Maurice where he should go but now Maurice and Claudine were at it hammer and tongs not realizing that their driver did not have an end to the route they were following. The next thing Maurice and Claudine knew was that their taxi had slammed into a concrete wall with a billboard picture stuck onto it.

The sharp sound of breaking glass was heard from the side where Claudine was sitting. The taxi had hit the wall on the left side.

Maurice had been sitting behind the driver and after he had come right after the initial impetus of the crash he tried to see what had happened to Claudine and the driver. The latter was leaning over the steering wheel of the car. He seemed more shocked than Maurice obviously because it would mean a temporary loss to his livelihood. It was Claudine who had come off worst. She was unconscious as Maurice could see but she was breathing.

The worst of the manner in which the accident had taken her was the fact that she had received several cuts to her face. Maurice stared at her in horror as she sat there unconscious with her face bleeding. Behind them the taxi that had been following them screeched to a stop at the curbside. The siren of an approaching ambulance was heard and a traffic attendant was on the scene almost immediately. Claudine's behavior in the cab during the chase had been the cause of the smash. Maurice had come out of it merely in shock not with physical injury as had Claudine. The traffic officer took in the situation immediately and an ambulance was just pulling up. Fortunately the taxicab door could be opened at the back and the paramedics had the limp though alive body of Claudine out in a jiffy

One of the paramedics handed Maurice a slip of paper with the words:

"That is the hospital we'll be taking the young lady to sir. We'll leave you to sort matters with the traffic officer. It seems that this was an isolated accident." Maurice replied:

"Yes it was. I'll explain to the traffic official what happened. I'll be in touch with the hospital to find out how the injured passenger is doing. She had had a nasty time of it so it seems."

The paramedic in charge said goodbye, adding, "Perhaps we'll be seeing you in a few days' time when the woman's facial injuries have been assessed."

The taxi driver was busy giving his details to the other official who was inquiring about motor insurance from the taxi driver. Fortunately it seemed that the driver would take responsibility for the accident and Claudine's excitable behavior was not going to be blamed. Meanwhile the security guard from the other taxi approached Maurice and the official had moved off. The guard said to Maurice:

"This is most unfortunate. I hope you do not feel that this accident is our fault. Mr. Armand was merely wanting to know where in New York you were staying. He wanted to be sure that the price of the Giotto that you set was you last word on the deal. He is very anxious to acquire the painting for the gallery as it is a rare occasion that he gets a chance like this. But he did not want to overstep the mark financially as far as the curators of the gallery were concerned. In other words he wanted to have one last chance to knock down the price. But it seems you are adamant."

Maurice nodded firmly saying:

"You will be able to contact us at the hotel in Manhattan. Is that what you wanted to know?"

The man assented. Maurice closed the deal. He hailed another taxi to take them back to the hotel. A shaken Maurice feeling desperately lonely and anxious without his companion telephoned the hospital immediately upon arriving back. A brisk American nurse's voice came over the line.

"Yes the Countess is conscious. She is in a state of shock hardly knowing what has happened." Maurice asked:

"Can I see her tomorrow?" The same crisp voice came over the telephone.

"Visiting hours are from 7 p.m. tomorrow."

A low spirited Maurice had an early supper and fell asleep in a worried frame of mind. He refused to think that what had happened was his fault. Claudine could have controlled her behavior in the taxi before the accident, he thought

Nevertheless he and Claudine were supposed, according to Count Alois' instructions to be sticking together on this business holiday. When he woke the next morning his spirits were at an all time low. How could he have let this happen? Somehow he got through the day sometimes irritably, sometimes in despair. One thought did strike him that was that his painting, the one that Alois had commissioned him to do could be used in the restructuring of the once lovely Claudine's countenance. He had heard that there was such a procedure as plastic surgery to mend torn facial flesh. It seemed to make sense that he could help poor Claudine in this way.

He arrived at the hospital, a huge modern building not too far from the hotel at 7 p.m. promptly and was quietly ushered into Claudine's presence. Her whole face was swathed in gauze bandages. Typical of Claudine she was sitting up in the large hospital bed smoking a cigarette. On seeing Maurice she said weakly:

"They allow me to smoke in here. It is a private ward. I told the matron that my husband is a wealthy Count." Magnanimously she continued: "Maurice this has been completely an accident. My doctor says that with two or three facial surgery procedures I will be restored to my old self. He was most interested in the fact that I had a painting done of myself. I told him this when he asked if I had any photographs of myself.

It is not so essential at this stage of the operating procedures. He seems to think that once the lesions have healed in about a month we can return. I will then be admitted to a Paris hospital because at that stage there will be scars left on my face."

As she finished her cigarette she slumped down in the huge bed helplessly, continuing:

"Maurice it has been too awful. What will Alois and Anzlé say to me? We will have to explain." Maurice feeling genuinely sorry for his former model said:

"I will take the blame Claudine. I will simply tell Alois that I was trying to get the best sale of his Giotto that I could. The rest of the story you and I will keep to ourselves for your sake Claudine.

The next Maurice knew was that he was staring painfully at Claudine while saying nothing. He could not bear seeing his once beautiful model in this state. A nurse appeared from nowhere and he was lead out of the ward. The last sight of Claudine that evening was with a huge bowl of exotic flowers—from Alois of course, and a smaller but less expensive bowl of fragrant roses that he had sent her. The blooms and greenery seemed to blot out the excruciating sight of Claudine. She was now having the covers on her bed fussed over by the efficient looking nurse. Maurice noticed that it was a modern and expensive hospital. Trust Alois to give his wife the best Maurice thought wryly. A doctor halted him outside her private ward saying:

"It will be one or two months before healing for the Countess. This time period depends on whether she would like the second or follow-up operation to take place here or in her mother country. I rather think that she would prefer the latter. Her face will still show scars but a second course of plastic surgery in Paris at a later stage should leave her looking absolutely perfect of complexion once again. Tell me—it would help if her husband has a large photograph of his wife. You seem to be a close acquaintance. Would you know of anything like that?"

Maurice at first looked puzzled at the doctor's question. Then a flash of inspiration hit him. Of course! Alois was in possession of her life-size portrait that he himself had painted. Luckily the picture was almost full face. He answered:

"I do not know about a photograph but you might be pleased to know there is a painting of her at her home. I see. You will need it for a replica when the surgeon is remodeling the scar tissue. How fortunate." The doctor added:

"That is a stroke of luck then. Be sure to tell the doctors and surgeons who will be doing the final operation about this portrait. I would not mention it to the Countess but it might need another two operations to pull her completely right. I have written a letter to my Parisian counterparts that you can pass on to them."

Feeling awed and alone by what was happening Maurice walked out of the glass doors of the hospital and hailed a taxi. He was not long afterwards ensconced in a comfortable chair in the hotel lounge with a cup of strong coffee thinking what he should do over the next four weeks without Claudine.

His thoughts surrounded him as he sat in the comfortable lounge chair. Maurice was not always the most sociable of people and he in a way missed Claudine's company. He had to reply to his cable from Alois who implored him to visit his wife daily. Visiting hours were only in the early evening and Claudine was due to undergo surgery the next morning while her wounds were still fresh and the skin flaps could be sewn down by the doctor.

She had been in hospital for one whole week by the time he arrived there in the late afternoon. He was early to see her but because she was in a private ward he was allowed in to her room. It gave him cold shivers down his spine. His conscience had been nagging at him the whole day. Was it his fault that poor Claudine was in this state? She had not understood, was not aware that Maurice had annoyed Mr. Armand by setting a reasonably higher sale price for the Giotto Madonna. This was the cause of the taxi accident. Maurice had not told Mr. Armand where he was staying for the time while arranging the sale. As far as Mr. Armand was concerned too small a payment for the work had just slipped through his hands as Maurice had wanted on Alois' instructions to reset the sale price, before the bank could cash the cheque he had received.

Would he have the nerve to tell Alois the reason for the accident? They would never see that particular taxi driver again. Light dawned on him. He could tell Elize. She would never let out the secret, if indeed it was his responsibility, the state Claudine was in. These thoughts flashed through his mind and then his eyes fell on the battered Claudine. All he could see were her eyes. The rest of her face was covered with white gauze with cotton wool underneath. She blinked in recognition of Maurice.

He wondered if he should be the first to speak.

"Claudine? Claudine?" Then the nurse appeared from the side and informed him:

"She has been too stunned to speak up until now. Perhaps seeing a familiar face will brighten things up for her."

A faint murmur came from the Countess:

"Why am I here Maurice?" The nurse chipped in: "You are being very brave Countess even to try and speak to your acquaintance. There was an accident. These words obviously made her recall what had happened. Claudine just said:

"Some water to drink." Maurice could hardly hear her.

He turned away as the nurse quickly produced some water in a feeding glass. He turned back just as she had finished drinking. It was coming over cloudy and dark outside and he signed to the sister that he was ready to leave. This was because he could see that Claudine was nearly asleep. The nursing sister seeing her patient was contented for the next half hour accompanied Maurice out of the ward. She imparted some information about what procedures were to be taken in the next twenty-four hours for the Countess. She was now a pathetic sight that

Maurice had just seen, his former model Claudine as he knew her. He said on the way out:

"The Countess knows, as she was told today that she will be undergoing facial surgery tomorrow morning. It will be as the Doctor said the first of two or three operations using techniques of facial plastic surgery. She showed me a photograph in her passport of how she looked before the accident. She was a beautiful woman." Maurice agreed:

"I was acquainted with her as a model for a portrait that her husband commissioned about six months ago. She was a beauty at the peak of her womanhood."

The nurse wondered briefly what the relationship was, his and Claudine's. Seeing her look slightly puzzled he enlightened her:

"I am an artist specializing in portrait painting." She answered at his mention that he had done a painting of the Countess:

"Well that makes for a very interesting couple. You say that you have recently done a portrait of her? Where is this painting?" Maurice replied:

"It is hanging in the front hallway of the Chateau where she and her husband the Count Alois Bonpierre live." The nurse remarked dutifully:

"It could be used in follow up operations to the one she will have tomorrow by the plastic surgeon. It is fortunate that she is not alone in this city. You will visit her tomorrow evening? It will then seem like a bit of home for her I am sure. It seems as if you know her well."

"Yes," said Maurice, "I spent a few months painting her portrait so came to know her as a person" He was not committing himself further she could see.

He bade the nurse farewell and hailed a taxi. After lunch at the hotel he felt better about the whole affair and pondered how he could spend the afternoon. He wandered over to the information desk and found a couple of sight seeing brochures. On opening up the first he saw an advertisement for a display of artwork recently exhibited at the famous Metropolitan Gallery of Art. It was apparently with a French theme so he felt he would benefit from a visit there.

Maurice could do nothing more by himself regarding the sale of the Giotto Madonna that had been the reason for the journey to America. He had been told that Claudine's operation would take up to six hours. The next morning when he woke he was filled with enthusiasm to visit the famous Gallery of Art. It irritated him somewhat that Claudine had got herself and him into this mess.

He had examined his conscience a little and he felt sure that the Count would not blame him for asking a higher price in the sale. He did not think Claudine would even remember what had happened before the taxi had hit the cement wall. He dressed and shaved and was soon hailing a taxi to take him to the Gallery. According to the brochure for tourists that he had idly picked up and glanced through he noticed that there was an exhibition of nineteenth century French paintings being shown for the following few months.

He gave a faint sigh. How he would love to have even one of his now quite substantial portfolio of paintings exhibited here. It would not even have to be in so famous a place as this one, but in one of the smaller galleries in Paris perhaps!

As he lingered over an espresso in the hotel lounge after breakfast an idea came to him. He would gather together as many of his works as he could even if they had been sold already. He could surely borrow those now belonging to others. Then he could ask the owner of the newly opened bistro in the main street of the village near Boulougne to display these works of his. Plenty of tourists passed through his hometown. They might find themselves in a similar situation to what he was in with having time to kill. Someone or even perhaps more than one person might just be interested in buying one of his works.

As he meditated he became keener. He could not imagine why he had not had the idea before. This business holiday had opened up new possibilities for him. Only now was he seeing the rut he had driven himself into. Well, perhaps he would skip the visit to the Art Gallery here for today. There would be other opportunities for this.

Although frustrated by not being able to do any sketching and painting at that time, Maurice who had an ever active mind began to realize that Claudine would be out of action for a good six weeks. What he could do was to acquire a palette and an easel and wander down to Central Park to see if there was anyone interesting enough to him to be sketched. He would charge a fee naturally.

The idea of occupying himself thus gave him a lift. He had to admit to himself that Claudine's suffering as a result of the accident had depressed him quite considerably. There was no doubt about it that it had been her fault. It had been her own lack of control with regard to the taxi that was following them that had caused their vehicle to veer into the wall. It would be pointless to tell her this though. She would not understand anyway in the state she was in at present.

He left the lounge to fetch his cheque book. He had decided to set out to an art shop to buy the necessities for painting. It would be worth it he decided. He could not leave for home without her, in fact he would have to chaperone her back to Paris and Alois. The Count had sent telegram after telegram when he had heard of Claudine's plight. Maurice had no such sympathy. They could have been killed. He was not going to tell Alois the real reason behind the crash. He was also convinced Claudine would not remember any details either. He hailed a taxi that upon stopping for him he inquired of the driver:

"You surely know the city well enough to take me to an art shop?"

The man at first looked puzzled. This was an unusual request. He answered:

"Do you want to visit a picture gallery" "No," replied Maurice patiently. "More like a shop where they sell paints in bottles to use for painting pictures."

The driver still looked puzzled obviously racking his brains about the destination his client was wishing him to go to. In exasperation Maurice just got into the vehicle and ordered the driver to take him to the nearest picture gallery. He stated:

"When we are there I will get someone to direct you to such a place as an art boutique. They will be able to tell you where to go. You must know of a gallery near here?"

Suddenly the driver's wits snapped together and he drove off with screeching wheels on the tarmac. Their mission accomplished Maurice had an easel, a palette and some brushes and paints He took them up to the hotel room to gloat over them. It was too late in the day to go out painting and he would have to visit Claudine that evening so he freshened up for an early supper. On arriving at Claudine's bedside he found her far more cheerful. So she should be he considered. Alois was paying a small fortune for her treatment and stay at the hospital. She greeted him glad to see a familiar face.

"The doctor says that when all this is over I'll look the same as ever. That is true isn't it Maurice? I can believe him can't I?" She seemed a little unsure of herself and doubting matters.

The day after her operation Maurice visited her more out of pity than anything else. Still with gauze covering the cuts that had been worked on by the plastic surgeon the morning before, Claudine was feeling more cheerful and hopeful. She had apparently had a long talk with her plastic surgeon who had raised her expectations no end. She said softly though excitely to Maurice:

"The doctor said the painkillers would help me over this part of the healing process. He says I am very brave. I told him you had painted my portrait and he was impressed. He said certainly, if the Parisian surgeon could be shown that it would surely help in the final reconstruction of my face, then it should be used." Then she started sobbing.

"My face, my beautiful face Maurice. You especially are aware how I kept myself beautiful. It was for you when you were painting my portrait, and for Alois who set his young wife on such a pedestal. It was for Anzlé too when I could not resist him as a lover. What will these three feel about my looks in the interim time until the surgeons have finished with me? And Maurice are they going to be true to their word that no one would know any difference? It is terrible for me Maurice, terrible. I will have to stay here for another month apparently." Maurice replied after a few moments:

"Alois has sent in funds for your hospitalization, and to pay for the hotel where I am staying. To take your mind off yourself I have to tell you that I have bought painter's accoutrements and while waiting for your face to heal I am going to wander about in Central Park to see if there is anyone worth sketching. It will have to be someone, one of two lovers perhaps who meet on a bench at lunch hour to be together to have a bite to eat. I can tell you Claudine I am so upset by your accident that if the doctors cannot get you right I intend asking for the portrait I painted of you at Alois' request, and am going to burn it and damn the consequences.

Alois will understand I know. You see Claudine it could all have been my fault this accident. You see I put Mr. Armand's back up by asking more for the portrait than Alois had first stated. I was so sure Alois wouldn't mind, would appreciate it in fact. Now all this has happened and I am not so sure." Claudine responded weakly now:

"I don't understand Maurice."

CHAPTER ELEVEN

It was nearing the end of the visiting hour. Claudine was clearly exhausted and scarcely taking in any of the words Maurice was saying. This Maurice could see knowing her as well as he did. Perhaps he thought it would be better if she did not realize what he had spoken to her. The time was dragging now that it was Claudine's last week in hospital. Maurice was out of his home territory and could not get down to painting. He made up for this by taking long walks and watching the people who used Central Park.

He found there were never the same people there as each day went by. Therefore it was nearly impossible to settle down to one particular sketch. The benches placed in the park attracted beggars and hobos, derelicts thrown up by the rat race of society in this huge city. Maurice was actually a bit afraid to approach them. Also to these benches came the workers desperate to leave the cloying atmosphere of their offices over the lunch break. They were never the same and Maurice felt lost in a sea of unfamiliar faces.

Every evening he visited Claudine and was unexpectedly told one evening that he could fetch her at eleven the next day. He said in reply to this to the nurse:

"Do I expect to see Claudine without her bandages around her face tomorrow then?"

The brisk sister answered:

"You will be surprised. Yes, the Countess will be acceptable to the outside world again. She will only be able to see her countenance for herself tomorrow morning early when we remove the gauze from her head. Do not be shocked by what you see. The operation she underwent is only one of two operations for plastic surgery."

Maurice was puzzled but curious to set eyes on the one who had modeled for him not so long ago. He arrived at the hospital to collect Claudine as arranged. What he saw was a woman sitting in a chair her head turned towards the window on the opposite side of the wardroom. He felt his stomach turn as he cast his quick artist's eye on what was visible in her face. It just seemed that wherever there had been bleeding cuts was healed and visible scar tissue.

As his steps towards her came to her ears she turned and he could see that she was crying. The nurse appeared to facilitate the departure. She addressed a distraught Claudine:

"But you are going home Countess. Dry your eyes. Remember time will only tell about a complete healing for you. The doctor told you that didn't he?"

Maurice could see that Claudine was not satisfied with the nurse's cajoling. She obviously felt very vulnerable and was constantly and furtively looking into her hand mirror that she took from her handbag as the taxi drew off from in front of the hospital on the way back to the hotel. Maurice who was sitting on the back seat with her could see her tears. He chided her fully aware of the state of her countenance:

"Now Claudine you must pull yourself together. You know what the surgeon told you that this an interim period before you next appointment with a surgeon in Paris prior to your following operation that will leave you looking as good as new."

But Claudine could not hold back her tears and when they arrived back stunned guests at the hotel looked at the weeping battered looking woman. Some ran to her to find out what the matter was but Maurice embarrassed pushed his way with Claudine who clung to him, towards the lift. Her tears abated when she entered the now familiar bedroom suite. Claudine then dramatically flung herself onto the bed making no excuse for her tears.

Suddenly she stopped weeping. Maurice sat silently on a chair nearby wondering what to say or if she would say anything at all. He guessed that she would be the first to utter and was right. It was approaching lunch. Then Claudine spoke:

"Oh! How hungry I am. Lunch at the hospital was always earlier than now." Maurice suggested:

"Shall I ask for a meal to be sent up for us? If I explain the circumstances I am sure the waiter will do this for us."

Without waiting for her reply he picked up the telephone and ordered a meal to be brought up to the bedroom after briefly elucidating their circumstances. He said:

"After lunch I will book the soonest flight back to Paris. Will you be glad to be going home Claudine?"

Her mind was taken off her plight by Maurice's authoritative tones on the telephone. She was though in a deeply introverted frame of mind that was completely different to the old Claudine. She raised herself off the bed and fumbled in her handbag for a cigarette. This action brought back to them both some of her old nature. She said timidly, knowing that their sustenance was on it's way up:

"I won't always look like this will I Maurice? A second operation will put me right won't it?"

Maurice who had grown somewhat cynical as he grew older did not see why he should extend any comfort to her. He would not even have sympathized with Elize his wife in the situation. He waited a few moments before replying. The timid whining tone in her voice made him even more egotistical in the situation concerning the crash that they had both experienced. After all it was not he who had been the unlucky one. He said impatiently:

"Yes Claudine, the surgeon did promise that all would be put right with your complexion eventually. Remember too that Alois had my painting of you done now about six months ago, that was finished with a trace of the atmosphere created by the Giotto Masterpiece that has caused all this upset.

Apparently so, the nurse told me my portrait of you will be invaluable to the plastic surgeon who will do a final restructuring of you countenance in Paris. What we first have to do is let Alois into the circumstances so that he is up to date with what is transpiring with your medical situation. I have a letter and a doctor's report to hand over to the surgeon in Paris. Well we only have another hour of the flight to go and it will be late afternoon when we land at Le Bourget airport."

With all these facts having been made known to her Claudine comforted herself with the echo of Maurice's words. She was a person who right from her street child upbringing had never really felt loved by any one. She did know though that Alois appreciated her for the social glamour she threw his way in their life together.

Then they were making their way down the aisle of the `plane with Claudine still a little unsteady. Maurice gripped her arm. The Count had been informed of the near tragedy that had befallen his wife but he would never know the truth. Maurice was not going to let out any secrets. He considered from the point of view of his own conscience that it was no fault of his what had happened. Claudine had displayed total lack of control that had caused the accident.

Maurice soon spotted Alois. Then they were together. The responsibility and worry had caused the man who was approaching his mid fifties well over mid life to have grown a beard. This Maurice surmised must mean that the Count was taking a somewhat chauvinistic male view that it would all come right with the handling by the Paris surgeon and that Claudine's panic and angst over the whole affair was not going to get him down. With a rather unfeeling gesture Alois took Claudine by the shoulder and said:

"Just be brave may dear. I have been in touch with the hospital and it seems that they want you in right away. She burst into sobs and tried to evade this arrangement.

"Not again! Not so soon please Alois! Can't we settle in at the castle first?"

Egotistically Alois took command of the situation although underneath fuming at her loss—he had trouble keeping in mind temporarily his wife's past social graces. He addressed her: "Alright Claudine. I'll put it right with the surgeon. I have a lot of influence in this province you know."

Claudine was enraptured that although her face would eventually be put to rights by the plastic surgeon there would be some respite from the ordeal that she had undergone already. A pall of silence fell on them as they were driven to the castle. As the Count's limousine drew up to the castle moat the first face that Claudine in her sensitive state set eyes on, almost as if he were waiting for her and welcoming her, was that of Lazlé.

To her he looked kind and sympathetic unlike the reception that she had received from Maurice and Alois. Then behind Lazlé whom should she see but Anzlé. The word about her accident must have spread and the staff and surrounding folk in the area whom she felt just wanted to gawp and gossip at her disfigurement.

She pulled her shawl over her face as the car came to a halt and the door was opened for her to alight. She had averted her eyes but had to turn towards the one who spoke.

"Easy does it Claudine. You have had a tough time of it what with hospitalization in a foreign city with no relations to visit you. Though I am sure Maurice has been as kind as possible in the circumstances."

Maurice on hearing these words did not even bother to look guilty. The Count, pulled down a peg or two now back in familiar surroundings tried to hush her at her sorry sight.

Then she heard Lazlé's sympathetic voice.

"It won't be for ever, that I am sure you can believe Claudine, girl.

At this show of feeling for what she had endured she had broken into tears again. Alois said:

"Call Antoinette Lazlé." This was Claudine's personal maid. "Why is she not here waiting for us?" Lazlé answered

"When she heard the car approaching she hurried off to prepare a hot bath and a fresh bed for the poor Countess." Alois softened slightly: "You must be agonizing in you mind over the state the accident has left you in."

With his ungainly gait Lazlé her one ally in the situation shambled off to find Antoinette. Through her tears she heard him calling her. Yes, she thought she did not need these big ugly men around her. Only another woman would know how she truly felt. Where was Antoinette? The Count was feeling more and more anger about the appearance of what had happened to his wife. What he was experiencing was selfish, this because the immediacy of her situation of not being able to be seen in public at the present time was going to take him down a peg or two socially. His cronies and social partying acquaintances would have to halt their activities and it would be most embarrassing for Alois. After entering the chateau Alois fixed himself and Maurice stiff drinks. Unlike himself he snapped at Maurice before his cordial went down:

"Well, can you explain Claudine's situation?"

Maurice did not want to be caught out or blamed for what had happened. He honestly did not see it as his fault. While he waited for the large sherry that Alois had proffered him to have its initial effect he paused in what he was about to say.

"Perhaps I should explain a little of what happened while Claudine and I were away."

Alois while trying to hide the extent of his anger answered after a little while:

"I think you should." Maurice proceeded in turning the story of what had occurred in New York against it being not his fault, but Claudine's. He said, feeling his way in the circumstances:

"You see Alois I thought you would be pleased if I bargained a little with the curator at the gallery over the sale of your Giotto. That would be to make a greater profit for yourself and a humble commission for myself. You will be satisfied, most satisfied, I think when I show you now the deed of sale for the Madonna."

Out of his valise he whipped the relevant document. The Count after humming and ha-ing coughed a little after eyeing what was shown him and then exploded verbally:

"Yes! This is far more than I originally asked for the painting but I must admit the higher price suits me very well. Yes I must say, a very satisfactory deal. Very well Maurice! I'll see you have a handsome commission indeed."

Alois turned away to fill their glasses again and then continued:

"Now about the other matter. That is my wife and the appalling condition she has returned in."

Although the initial tête-a-tête had played directly into Maurice's hands with pleasing Alois in the sale of the Madonna it now seemed that Alois was becoming nasty about the whole occurrence of the accident. Maurice took a draught of sherry and began:

"Claudine did not agree with me about the increase in the price that I was setting the curator Mr. Armand. She did not understand that I was trying to make a profit for all concerned." Maurice continued:

"I think it better not to mention anything about the accident or the consequences of Claudine's injuries in front of her. We shouldn't as male acquaintances talk about it at all. The beautiful woman that she was has caused her great sensitivity in the matter of her facial scars." Alois responded to this visibly irate.

"You, Maurice are responsible for all this. I sent you with Claudine as a chaperone. It was up to you to control my wife in the time away in America. What exactly did happen?"

The Count, unusually for him, instead of brushing matters over was clearly finding it in himself to vent his anger on Maurice. He went on:

"How am I going to continue the socializing that is so necessary for the publicity of chateau? I opened the surgeon's report addressed to me that you handed me. In it is stated that there is only a seventy per sent chance that a further operation can clear her face of the marks left, though healed now of the first operation."

Maurice felt at first guilty but soon afterwards that he should stand up for himself. Moving towards the Count he looked him in the eye and began to explain the situation of the accident. He made it clear how Claudine had become aware of the taxi that had been speeding after them and how she had upset the driver of the vehicle they were traveling in. He told how she had shrieked and goaded him. He explained:

"It was almost childlike of her and it seemed at the time that she enjoyed the thrill of the chase."

He was not going to tell Alois of the other reason that he had told her prior to the accident that he had bargained with the curator of the gallery by pushing the price up for the Giotto. Somehow at the time Claudine's conscience had not been able to accept this. Her husband had stated his set price and she had found it necessary to quibble almost taking the curator's side in the deal.

There had definitely been an argument at the gallery that had caused the chase to take place. In order to calm the Count's irascibility Maurice related the facts as honestly as he could. He saw that if he did not tell the whole truth Claudine might piece what she knew of the accident together and he might really be in trouble. He breathed a quick sigh of relief when Alois stated:

"Of course I am happy that the price of the Giotto was raised higher. How silly of Claudine to doubt what you had in mind to do in the sale."

The drinking had caused him to become his usual expansive self. He went on musingly:

"Of course much depends on how the second plastic surgery operation succeeds."

Maurice said slowly and succinctly:

"I am glad that you see it my way Alois. I must tell you that I informed the surgeon who did the first treatment on Claudine's face that it might be possible to use the portrait I did of her for you as a model for the plastic surgeon's next procedure here in Paris. Of course the first operation was almost immediate, within a day of the accident. I did suggest that it might be used for the next stage of the surgeon's plan." The Count responded:

"An excellent idea Maurice. The picture is hanging at this moment in the hallway of the castle."

"Yes," answered Maurice, "I noticed as we walked in where you had it placed."

Alois then went back on his word after pausing for a minute or two, saying:

"I must say in loyalty to my wife she did try and carry out my instructions. It was not really necessary to up the price of the Giotto Madonna. However we have Claudine's likeness in the portrait you painted."

Maurice, trusting in the Count's feelings for his wife offered:

"If the surgeon here in Paris does use my portrait and the operation is a success as was promised I will be delighted."

Feeling the old sensation of guilt again he muttered under his breath:

"Alois if the second operation does not restore Claudine's looks I tell you now that I will not mind if her portrait is destroyed, burned up in fact."

The Count gave a start and said irritably:

"I am sure that will not be necessary. I would not like Claudine to know of any feelings like that you might have."

At that remark he turned and left the room. Anzlé and Maurice were left together. Anzlé broke the silence:

"It is unlike Claudine to hide her face from me. She scarcely greeted me at the entrance of the castle when Alois' limousine pulled up. She just pulled the white shawl over the side of her face opposite me and turned away."

Maurice, standing up for Claudine answered sharply:

"What would you do in her place Anzlé? She is frantically embarrassed and with the long journey back here hardly knows what has happened to her."

Anzlé looked pained. Maurice added:

"She will be upstairs with Antoinette her maid and in tears by now I am sure."

He was right. Antoinette was sympathizing with Claudine:

"Shall I ask your husband to call in the doctor Countess? You seem to have more than one worry on your hands what with your monthly flow having ceased as you tell me. Who has caused that?"

Claudine broke into a wave of sobbing:

"Do you promise not to tell Alois, Antoinette?" The little maid was quick with her reply.

"Of course I do." The little maid was hard pressed in this emotional situation.

In a fresh burst of sobbing after pausing to a attain Antoinette's confidence Claudine nearly choked in her words:

"It was Anzlé. He will be the father if as the Doctor will confirm it, and I am sure he will, that I am pregnant. You see Antoinette no one not even you my personal maid knew about our affair. Anzlé's and mine I mean. Anzlé did not want me to go to America with Maurice. He did not trust Maurice and said it could be dangerous for me. He said I was too immature. I think he suspected even before I left that something might be wrong that I might be pregnant even then. And he was right. Antoinette what can I do?"

The scatterbrained little maid tried to form priorities of what the Countess could do or what would happen in the circumstances. Firstly she thought the Count's doctor should be called in. Would she have the authority to do this? Count Alois would have to be told but just that his wife was ailing. The doctor she was sure would take matters into his confidence. Antoinette remembered suddenly that her sister had a similar occurrence but it was a failed pregnancy. Antoinette said thinking quickly:

"If you have to have another operation fairly soon . . ." Claudine stopped sobbing while her maid spoke. "I don't think they, that is the surgeon and his team will be able to do it if you have been found to be expecting a baby. The pregnancy will have to be aborted. There now Claudine does that make you feel any better? You could explain matters so that Alois need not even realize what has happened let alone Anzlé. That is unless you want Anzlé to know." Claudine burst out:

"Yes! Oh! Yes! I am in love with Anzlé and of course I want him to know."

Antoinette tried to make the situation clear to Claudine who was not it seemed thinking lucidly.

"Your position as Countess of the chateau could be saved by these circumstances. It has been doubly a shock to you poor dear but your name and reputation could be saved by timely action. And by that I mean calling the doctor in just as soon as possible. I know, I will ask Lazlé, that is Anzlé's brother to call in the goodly old doctor from the village. I will settle you for the night and tell Alois you must not be disturbed.

I will then run down to Lazlé's outhouse in the forest to gain his confidence in the matter.

It is early evening still and I think with a sedative such as I have at hand from the bathroom you will fall asleep for the night. I will look in later when I have spoken to Lazlé."

Claudine felt the comfort her maid had created around her with the perfume-scented sheets and warm blankets that rather chilly night. She was soon asleep and Antoinette was at her side when she awoke the next morning with a cup of strong coffee. The first matter on her mind came out:

"I was with Lazlé last evening and we had long conversation about your circumstances as it involves his brother. He has sworn not to let out you secret. You will have to bear the knowledge of your pregnancy and it's termination on your own. How has Anzlé been behaving towards you since you returned?"

Antoinette was being as solicitous as she could towards Claudine who answered:

"As usual he has made no approaches to me while I am with Alois. He never used to in company. I am just waiting for him to find an opportunity to be with me alone. I do feel though Antoinette that my whole personality has suffered through this dreadful accident. She began to shed more tears.

"Now, now, Claudine. You know the scars on your face might disappear forever with a second operation. You must believe that. What are you going to do this morning?" She replied:

"I will walk a little in the castle grounds and hope to be waylaid by Anzlé. I feel that now is the time to test his love for me. You told Lazlé didn't you Antoinette, what has happened?"

"Yes," the maid replied. "As you can imagine without any ill feeling towards his bother, Lazlé has told me that his heart is breaking for you both."

Claudine looked quite taken aback at this news that Antoinette had brought her. She ventured timidly wiping her eyes.

"Lazlé is concerned about me?" Antoinette responded: "Lazlé says he has always admired your beauty and charm but has never been in a position socially to speak to you. He says the only other person to know about Anzlé and your affair is Maurice. I warned him to tell Maurice to keep it a secret about your possible pregnancy as far as Anzlé is concerned."

Claudine was looking braver now and outrightly spoke:

"Yes! I want to test Anzlé's loyalty to me in this in between condition of my complexion."

Maurice who has seen me through this so far is quite ambivalent about it. If I find Anzlé sympathic I will tell him. If not I'll bear the pain of having an abortion alone."

Claudine went to bath and dress and shortly afterwards told Antoinette that she was going to get some fresh air walking in the castle gardens.

Claudine took her white woolen shawl once she had dressed warmly and attractively as was her habit. Her shapely body could just be seen beneath her warm slacks and white woolen jersey. As she walked slowly down the corridors of the castle her face mostly covered by the shawl she wondered, hoped even if she would encounter Anzlé. This had been usual for them before she had left for America with Maurice.

She summoned up her thoughts as she had remembered them to be like before her accident. Yes! She had her rights that was surely so. If she met Anzlé who she knew did not yet know the state of her disfigurement she would challenge him as to their relationship. This she would do without letting him know the state of her early pregnancy.

He would be at the little gate leading out of the castle grounds into the forest where they had met up so often in the past. He would surely be that dutiful even though she knew he could be a hard man. After all there must have been something about her other than her looks that had enamored him of her. Her body that was it, she realized then.

After the accident she had stopped indulging in the small amount of smoking that she was wont to do. So she walked slowly across the lawns holding the shawl to her face so only her beautiful eyes could be seen. They showed clearly the pain she had been through. From where she walked she could see a figure of a man approaching through the trees on the edge of the woodland.

As the couple came nearer they seemed to be walking faster and faster. Claudine's body with the stiffness of the accident having worn off began to throb. Anzlé was near and he had not forgotten their trysts. She put out her arm to greet her lover while holding the shawl firmly with her other hand. She must not shy off now she thought quickly to herself. Anzlé must face up to what she was going to show him of herself. She was determined not to let him get away with it. Then Anzlé spoke:

"Claudine—my love—so it's not as bad as they told me!"

She was half turned towards him. Then in a bold gesture she whipped the shawl from her face showing she knew all the ugly scars that it had been promised her would disappear with the second operation within the next few weeks. Anzlé stood there and his tone of voice changed. He uttered in a strained and thin voice:

"Claudine," Then he repeated her name. "Claudine! No! They'll never be able to clear those scars from you face." Claudine had a sharp tongue now, saying under her breath:

"That's not what I have been told by the plastic surgeon, Anzlé. Were you hoping by this accident and it's circumstances to absolve yourself from our relationship?"

In the insecurity of their situation Anzlé found himself changing his attitude towards her by the minute. He said slyly and almost brokenly:

"You'll never be the same to me again Claudine. I can't believe you will ever be the same as before!"

Before turning on her heel and leaving him standing there looking lost for words she spoke, a heart broken woman:

"I'll never get over the hurt your disloyalty has caused me over and above the frightening situation I find myself in."

She had only just stopped herself from telling him about the abortion that she would have to undergo as well as the plastic surgery. She opened her mouth meaning to tell Anzlé about carrying his child but in the next second closed it. Knowing her so well over the last three years of their affair he realized she was trying to come out with something mind shattering. Yes, he was certain it would be some social hiatus or gaffe that had happened in Alois' circle of acquaintances recently. What else could it be? He spoke sharply and earnestly to her. He could see it involved him.

"What is it Claudine? What were you going to say?" But Claudine just turned and walked away. Before she had stepped too far away he caught her firmly by the shoulder and swiveled her round to face him. "What has all this got to do with me Claudine?"

In her disadvantaged appearance she was just able to come out with the enigmatic words:

"You'll never know Anzlé. Can't you even imagine how I feel?"

Anzlé not understanding at all loosed his grip on her and let her go. It was no use. He would have to release her and finish their relationship. Guilt overcame him as he realized that she no longer held any attraction for him with her face full of lesions. He could not see how she could ever be herself again. Anger consumed him.

Just then he heard a step behind him and he turned. It was Maurice. The artist must have witnessed their emotional little scene. In his unprotected emotional state he broke out to Maurice whom he knew fairly well as an acquaintance.

"Its too terrible. She'll never be the same again." Maurice intoned:

"I spoke to the plastic surgeon. He assured me that with the help of my picture she modeled for the surgeon can perform miracles. You must have heard of the way older women have plastic surgery to firm up sagging facial features. Haven't you?"

Maurice was merely irritable at her lover's attitude:

"This is a true test of your love for Claudine, Anzlé." Anzlé countered:

"It only proves that I did feel for her once as a personality. You know that we were having an affair. It was not just her body that attracted me to her. Claudine was a smiling, laughing person to me full of charm and wit. I can't believe how my feelings for her have changed because of this." Maurice put in gloomily at these words of Anzlé's:

"It has been a tragedy but a true test of feelings. I never allow myself to become emotionally involved with my models. I can only hope that the surgeon can make use of the portrait that I did of Claudine so her face can be remodeled." Anzlé said gritting his teeth:

"I don't believe it." He left Maurice standing there and walked off angrily down the road back to the village where he had his home. While Anzlé fumed and raged at his own lack of tolerance towards his erstwhile lover Claudine she had found her way with tears blinding her vision, to the little chapel adjoining the chateau. She had always known where it was but had never really wondered why it was there or had ever been inside the little place of worship. There was thick overgrown foliage around the entrance. She questioned briefly why Alois had not ordered the gardener to clear the creepers there. It must be because he never came this way on the property, or very seldom. It seemed so quiet and peaceful. It must be so old she thought seeing the thick moss growing between the paving stones at the entrance. She saw clearly the old crumbling walls of the entrance as well as the stonework forming the chapel such as could be seen through the ivy growth.

Dare she open the double doors of the entrance nave? The rusted black iron bars holding the wood together looked ancient and forbidding. She tottered up to the closed entrance keeping her scarf well across her face with one hand. With the other hand she pushed at the iron framework, noticing as she did so that the metal was shaped in the form of a fleur de lis, the French national emblem.

There did not seem to be a soul in sight. Peace and quiet—that was something someone like her who had risen from the noisy Paris street life to the gossipy hum of social existence of the Provencal elite had never known. It was an atmosphere she had rarely if ever experienced.

She was in a transformed state. Looking behind her she saw no one so slipped inside the door creaking on ancient hinges behind her. She caught her breath at the solemn beauty of the interplay of colored light through the windows that were of stained glass. Quickly she went up to the front pew and sat down. She looked around her at the figures pictured in the stained glass. She could decipher on them what seemed to her to be olden day men wearing long robes some with a cross, some with a book, and some appeared to her to be shepherds with sheep and lambs and one with a shepherd's crook. The pictures in the windows began to make sense to her.

Through one window on the left the last of the day's sunlight streamed. She noticed that it was a nativity picture She could just remember what this meant from the meager and scanty schooling she had. Her drunken father had taken her out of school when she was eleven years old. Still crying she gave a start when she heard the wooden chapel door open and a gaunt old man with long, fine silver-gray hair dressed in black from top to toe entered slowly and made his way gracefully to the front of the chapel. He did not appear to be conscious of her presence.

At the sight of the elderly man of whom she had no idea who it was, never having had contact with a priest she was riveted through with fear at his ghostly appearance. There was a quiet and holy atmosphere in what was a little chapel adjoining the chateau. She felt suddenly afraid and gulped back her tears as he approached the front of the sanctuary where she had chosen to sit and ponder the situation that she found herself in. More especially this was to do with the circumstances of her relationship with Anzlé and what it had led to and the possible resulting consequences of her confirmed marriage to Count Alois

The Abbé, for that is what he was, a priest concerned with all who entered the chapel's portals, saw that her eyes were red and that she had been in tears. He felt compassion for the woman whom he recognized as the Countess of the chateau even though they had never been introduced.

Being an Abbé he was in complete innocence of the state of her affair with Anzlé and the outcome. He felt that he should extend some words of prayerful comfort to the Countess. He could not imagine what was upsetting her. He eased himself into the pew next to her and knelt down. Never having knelt in her life before let alone in a chapel Claudine was a little taken aback but felt she should take on the same posture that he did. The Abbé prayed silently by her side at first and then began murmuring more prayers. This seemed to still Claudine's weeping. The Abbé turned to her and said:

"Are you in trouble my dear child?" Claudine choked out her reply:

"Yes, Monsieur. I have no one to confide in that I can tell my terrible secret to." Then the Abbé asked:

"Would you like to make a confession then my child?" Claudine answered hoarsely not understanding at all:

"I will explain to you if you let me." The Abbé replied:

"There is a confessional box to the side of the entrance of the chapel." He nodded in the direction of the confessional.

"I will enter in and you must stand outside the metal grill so we will have no contact. I do know who you are but anything you tell me will be in complete confidence. That is what it is to make a confession. Come then my daughter let us go up to the confessional."

Claudine found herself facing the Abbé through the grill. She heard him say:

"Speak then of what is on your mind." Claudine gulped out:

"I find myself pregnant in an affair of the heart. I have been unfaithful to my husband."

Chapter Twelve

Abbé Leguire did not often have to have confession made to him only by the odd yokel of the village who had taken advantage of a village maiden, or for their part a local girl who felt she had sinned by not fulfilling her part in a domestic set-up. Then the Count Alois on some occasions when he had too much to drink burbled out a confession of which Abbé Leguire could never make head or tail.

On such occasions the Abbé stuck to his Catholic formula of requesting repentance and requiring a penance or two and granting the absolution of forgiveness. When the staff of the chateau needed their consciences cleared the Abbé was seldom as a man of God put out.

But this confession that he had heard from one whom he knew was the Countess of the chateau. He felt that he should give counsel to the poor suffering woman after hearing her story. After speaking out her sin and facing the kindly though stern Abbé whom she had never come across before in the castle grounds her chest was heaving with emotion while she told the Abbé that the doctors were not going to let her keep her child. She sobbed out the words:

"It is because the foetus inside me will not stand up to the seriousness of the operation a second one, that I will be having shortly to correct the scars on my face. The two just cannot go together." The Abbé intoned in response:

"My child although you have sinned greatly in this matter, as has the man who caused the circumstances, God is at work in your life. You would never have been able to hold your face up in society here had the birth come to full term. You would have been completely ostracized both by your immediate family and the older inhabitants of the village.

No my child, you have been lucky. As a priest I will never divulge your secret to your husband but you must do the penances of denial and promise your Father in heaven that such an event will never occur again. It will mean breaking your ties completely with your former lover." Claudine weeping promised this to the Abbé.

"Father I know now who really are loyal to me for the present while I have these hideous scars on my face. They are for one Lazlé Cordier, my lover's brother, himself deformed but never bitter. Then there is also Maurice who never blamed me for the accident in the taxi even though I confess it must have been my fault that our lives were at risk. Also there is my husband who has been more than tolerant towards me, even though he has no knowledge about my love affair."

At the end of the confession Claudine just dropped her head when the Abbé asked her to pray with him about what he sternly though kindly told her was her immoral behavior. At the end of their time together at the confessional the Abbé said:

"May the good Lord forgive you your sin. It seems as if you did not know there is a God above who loves and forgives. Now you have renounced such behavior. You shall not sin in this way again. You tell me my child that you have to face another operation on your countenance. May the good Lord shine upon you for the success of the up and coming surgery. You will be in the hands of expert doctors.

Do not fear. You will know afterwards when you see the success it has been who has really loved you and seen you through this trying time of waiting" Claudine made a motion to leave. "I bid you adieu my child. God speed now."

Claudine walked slowly down the aisle of the little chapel and when outside tripped through the stinging nettles amongst the weeds creeping through amongst the paving stones of the pathway at the entrance. She felt her spirits lifting. Everything was going to come right, the Abbé had promised her.

As she walked over the chateau lawns she thought yes, Maurice had told her that his portrait of her could be used in the remodeling of her face. She had been impressed at the uncanny likeness Maurice had managed to put into the picture. Added to that he had painted in the seraphic atmosphere he had copied from the Giotto masterpiece. She had held her head down while walking but lifted it as she reached the moat of the chateau. There to meet her was her husband Alois. He gave her a sly look saying:

"I have organized a bed for you in one of the most famous old hospitals in Paris. Don't despair my love it will all be over within two weeks." Claudine spoke low and clear:

"Thank you for your kind words Alois. Did you know what happened to cause the accident? It was Maurice's bargaining with the curator of the art gallery. That was what started the ill-feeling and bickering amongst us there. I felt that Maurice should stick to the price that you had set but he was greedy. I suppose he wanted a larger commission. Probably he thought he was doing you a good turn." Alois responded:

"All a complete misunderstanding my dear. If that is what Maurice felt about the sale who was I to change his mind in what you decided?"

Maurice was unaware that Claudine had let out his secret to the Count. Alois was not careful about money like many of his peerage acquaintances. They became bored with it becoming more interested in the latest scandal to do with mistresses and lovers. Alois had not noticed the high commission that Maurice had talked Mr. Armand into allowing for the sale of the Giotto. He had been much too taken up with the consequences of his wife's accident and the gossip it had caused in his social circle.

He felt a superficial compassion for his wife. Actually in his bombastic way he felt very sorry for her. He was more embarrassed about it for his own sake as acquaintances were constantly pestering him for news about Claudine. All he was able to say in answer was that he and his wife were hoping for a complete success in the clearing of Claudine's countenance from scars left after the first operation. He and Claudine were sitting in the lounge of the chateau an hour or so before dining. Alois had become used to the sight of the state of his wife's face and in a way sympathized with her as she sat her visage turned a little away from her husband He ventured:

"Well my dear it is only a matter of days before your operation. I don't mean to concentrate your attention on that, but remember the surgeon we consulted on our visit to Paris assured you that what with the use of Maurice's portrait of you, we would have a completely remodeled face for you."

Alois was clearly feeling a little guilty about the state he found his wife in but was not experiencing so much as Maurice was in his conscience. It was obvious that Alois had not looked closely at the documents concerning the sale of the Giotto masterpiece. If he had he would have seen that Mr. Armand had allowed Maurice an extra amount of twenty five thousand dollars in the deal.

There had been such an argument between the three of them, Claudine, he and Mr. Armand. Mr. Armand had only allowed Count Bonpierre what he had asked for in the deal but Maurice had pressed him for an additional amount. Claudine in her still shocked state but remembering Maurice's kindness to her while so far from home and in hospital began to ask why they had not seen him for a week or two. Both of them were accustomed to his dropping in to see her. Alois responded:

"I'll send a message down to his chalet that we would enjoy a visit from him. In the meantime I must really peruse the documents of the sale of my beloved Giotto that I have now parted with. But of course we have Maurice's portrait of you thank the Lord." The Count was ruffling through papers in the bedroom adjoining Claudine's chamber. She could hear him getting first irritated, muttering as he took in what must have been stated on the documents relating to the sale of the Giotto. Then he became angry and he came storming into Claudine's room grunting:

"Do you know anything about this Claudine? It seems as if Maurice has made a huge profit out of the sale of my Giotto and has either not told me yet of the sale of the picture or is keeping it all to himself. I could wring his neck. No use shaking him up at this hour I suppose though." Lying facing away from her husband she said with a start:

"You can get one of the servants to call him up to the castle tomorrow. It all comes back to me now. That was the cause of the argument he and I and Mr. Armand had at the art gallery. It was the cause of the car chase and the crash in which I was injured." Alois said angrily:

"Oh was it! Just wait until I can confront him, the scalliwag. Most probably he will slide out of the rather nasty situation that we find ourselves in and say he negotiated for a higher price for my interest's sake. But as you say he can come up to the castle tomorrow and face the music."

The next morning Alois was up early ordering one of his kitchen staff to call Maurice up to see him as soon as possible. When the servant gave him the rather unwelcome news of the Count wishing to see him, feeling as guilty as an alley cat he first sought out his wife Elize, saying:

"I have been summoned up to the castle by the Count. I have to admit to you that it is because I bid for a commission chiefly for myself, to gain in the deal in the sale of Alois' Giotto Masterpiece I told you about some time ago. What do you think? Do you think that I should slide out of any gain for myself having been intended and say that I tried for an increase in the sale for Alois' interests?"

Grandmère was rocking in her chair anxiously hoping that her son was not going to be in trouble. Sulkily Elize felt in herself that here was an occasion when Maurice was possibly involved—and it made her feel a bit better about life as it was usually herself who was the scapegoat. She said:

"Just go up to the chateau immediately and tell Alois he is mistaken if he thinks you were going to claim the extra money. Say humbly that you thought you were doing him a favor. Perhaps he will show you a sense of generosity then."

Maurice slunk out of the room having been belittled in the presence of both the women folk in the chalet.

Later for once relying on Elize his wife's advice Maurice ventured to her:

"So you think if I am adamant that I sold the picture for an extra amount of money I can press Alois in the knowledge that I did it for his benefit and that he would know that the Giotto was worth more than he was aware of." Elize responded:

"There must surely have been only one document of sale one that benefited the original owner of the painting. It should be easy to point this out to Alois. The extra money need not necessarily have been added for your personal gain. Tell him so if he becomes inquisitive." These words of his wife's sent her up in his estimation for once and he said to her:

"How foolish I have been. Of course that is the solution."

He edged his way out of the chalet again like the proverbial alley cat on his way to put matters right with Alois if he could. On his way he met one of the castle stewards sent to fetch him. Maurice saw the somber look on the man's face and intimated that he smelt a rat. The servant gave him the low down:

"The Countess has had her memory destroyed about her accident. All I can say is that Alois is furious about what she has told him and that he wants to see you immediately." Maurice put his head down, afraid of the consequences of his actions. Was it all going to be blamed on him? He must insist that what he had made of the sale was quite innocent and that naturally the whole amount would be put into Alois' coffers. By the time he had reached the chateau's ante-room where Alois was waiting for him with a glowering face he had his story about the occurrences at the art gallery and its aftermath all panned out for Alois' ears.

He entered the room and was growled at by the Count:

"Maurice please explain the reason for the excess in the price that I set for my Giotto and why there was a car chase and crash." Maurice looked slightly desperate but began to speak:

"The truth is Alois I thought that by pushing up the price of the painting both you and in a very small way myself, could make a profit in the deal with Mr. Armand at the art gallery. Claudine however wanted to stick to your original instructions. She argued about it at the gallery. When I had settled the higher price, Mr. Armand agreed at first but then thought the better of it and changed his mind. We were leaving and he did not know where we were staying so sped after us in a chase. Claudine egged on our driver in a most uncontrolled manner, hence the crash and her resultant injuries."

The Count put his head down at this blatant accusation of his wife. She was a very flighty woman he knew. Hadn't she always been to him like a piece of gossamer floating amongst the guests at their frequent socials? He would have to make some sort of judgment of the one who had always been a credit to him socially. He decided to absolve her from any blame. He just muttered to Maurice:

"Claudine is a highly strung woman. She probably thought she was doing right by urging on the taxi driver as I understand the circumstances. Hopefully it will teach Madame a lesson to control herself."

A face covered with a white scarf put its head around the door. It was Claudine. She had heard Maurice's voice talking to her husband. She knew they were both a little angry with her but were on her side, hoping the coming operation would be the final success and finish to the incident. A little shyly but trusting in the two men to realize that she would not end up with a face full of scars for ever, she ventured:

"Can I just confirm with you Alois my love that the train leaves the village station at eight in the morning in seven days time? That is a week from now?" Her husband replied:

"Yes my dear." The Count looked a little taken aback at the apparition that had appeared in the morning room. His wife it seemed. Maurice who knew her well as a person having spent nearly three months doing her portrait greeted her saying:

"If I heard aright you will be taking the train to book in at the Paris hospital where I believe the Count has arranged for top class surgeons to undertake your plastic surgery. You are being very brave about it Claudine. I admire you tremendously. There was a part of you that I never knew. Is this not so Alois?" Maurice was pandering to Alois deliberately. Alois grunted his approval. He felt that it was not necessary to accompany Claudine to the hospital and said:

"Maurice would you be kind enough to take the train journey to Paris with Claudine next week?" Maurice answered:

"Well apparently the surgeons did say that they would like to have her portrait near them during the operation." Claudine looked charmed and said confidently and cheerfully:

"That would suit me quite well Alois. After all it was Maurice and I who caused the upset." She was deliberately involving Maurice. The two of them hung their heads. Personally this suited Claudine. Then there would be nothing let out to her husband about the termination of her pregnancy. She would ask the doctors to be discreet about it too. Alois must never know this. Her husband spoke feeling she was hiding something. Alois said:

"As you know, my dear the castle is open apart from our living quarters, to the public for viewing. My family and the castle they have lived in for centuries are part of our country's history. They are a national heritage to which I am adding a decorative and curious collection of antiques. This has been a hobby of mine for some time now and I can afford the collection with the income I am paid from the French Government making my castle a site of the national heritage.

I have been invited to a museum in an adjoining province that has been suffering financially, but would like to preserve as many of it's show-items as possible in an artistic venue. The curator approached me and suggested a date that unfortunately my dear," Alois regarded Claudine's now humble appearance—"coincides with your date with the plastic surgeon." Claudine started at the reminder of this event that was now only one week away. He continued:

"Maurice would you be gracious enough to accompany my wife to the hospital in Paris? You are both of an age and I am sure you can make the train journey with Claudine more cheerful than I could. After all I do trust my wife to you as she and you have spent much time together and are of similar age."

Claudine was sitting on a setee turned slightly away from Maurice and Alois. She perked up a little and losing some of her embarrassment, thinking herself into a situation when she would not continually have to hide her face with a scarf, grasping the opportunity she said:

"Of course Alois I must not upset your official duties especially as I know how much they mean to you."

Now was her chance she thought. She would entrust Maurice with the knowledge of her incipient pregnancy and persuade him to keep the question of the abortion to himself.

Seeing to the paperwork and accounts to do with her operation Alois might want to peruse them in such a way that he might find out the truth. After all he had also kept from Alois the fact of his three drawings that he had done of her in the farm barn amongst the straw used by the animals kept there.

Alois knew nothing of this. She felt that Maurice would be a supportive ally. She added:

"Thank you Alois for suggesting that Maurice should accompany me. He and I see eye to eye on many subjects."

Her statement seemed to Maurice to be quite ambiguous but he would find out later what she meant by this. The Count rambled on as far as Claudine was concerned. He seemed to be far more interested in his growing collection of antiques. He began:

"I have been particularly interested in adorning our castle with bric-a-brac and old furniture that can be redone and redecorated. Now that the castle is a National

Heritage site for tourists this is what it is up to me to do. On a lighter side I am very interested in acquiring ceramics and pottery from surrounding antique shops or museums that are perhaps overstocked with these things, and carpets particularly with a middle eastern or Persian theme. This will warm the effect of the cold stone floors wonderfully. What we have at the moment is old and tatty. I would also like to acquire some silverware."

Maurice with his artistic flare was interested in all the Count was saying. Certainly his portrait of Claudine would now be magnificently set off with the acquisition of all these works of art. Claudine however was becoming bored by her husband's enthusiasm for what he intended. To her people mattered much more. She attempted to speak muffled through the scarf she was continually wearing to hide what she hoped against hope were only temporary disfiguring scars. She ventured:

"Alois I must be leaving you in a few minutes. So it is confirmed then that Maurice will be accompanying me to the hospital next week?" Maurice pulled himself up. The Count said:

"If that is alright with you my man I would be most grateful if you could take my limousine to transport Claudine to the Paris hospital. I have a catalogue of antiques arriving within the next few days by post and I will have my time cut out choosing what I want to buy and visiting the various museums and curio shops where these items are on sale."

"That will suit me," said Maurice adding with more consideration than her husband was showing her, indeed with a modicum of compassion considering the trouble Claudine had let him in for. Claudine said:

"I will just walk down to the gate at the end of the castle grounds with Maurice. I can then make arrangements about when we are leaving and how long the operation will take. I would like to know the length of my stay in hospital so you, Maurice will know when to fetch me again." They talked as they walked. "I will confide in you Maurice," Claudine said swallowing her words and pulling the white shawl over her face so he could only see her eyes glancing at him as she talked. He knew her face was in a pitiful state:

"I have come to realize the truth about the people I live with. Alois just sees me as one more responsibility in his life of beautiful possessions. That was, one that had been temporarily spoiled he thinks and I hope that I can be restored to my old self. Yes Maurice it was my own fault that I have landed in this mess. It could have been you whose body was mutilated in the smash. I simply lost control of myself in the taxi. I was trying to be loyal to Alois but was out of my territory being away from my own country. That caused me to behave irresponsibly by urging the taxi driver on to elude Mr. Armand's car. Maurice took a stance away from her fearing that she might burst into tears and cling to him as just another human being in her pitiful state.

She swallowed again and could clearly not continue speaking. Maurice knew that he should speak to her but for a few moments as they reached the gate to the forest he did not want to say anything. Then after a while he did speak:

"I have to admit too that I did push up the price of the Giotto with my own ends in view but I also had Alois' interests at heart. The Giotto painting is an exquisite masterpiece. I felt that Mr. Armand was taking advantage of us." He quickly looked at her bowed head. She spoke barely above a whisper:

"I have confessed to the priest of the little chapel adjoining the castle that not only did I sin with harm to myself but that I am newly pregnant too. Anzlé is the father and the doctors have told me that they cannot operate on my face as well as save the foetus. It is as if God has a plan for me Maurice."

At these words she adjusted the shawl as she turned to leave him. What he saw were dark rings under eyes luminous with pain in the situation she found herself in. Her face and partially her neck were full of the scars left by the first plastic surgery operation. Realizing that he had seen again the result of her lack of selfcontrol she tightened the scarf and walked quickly back to the chateau.

Maurice felt a sense of guilt creeping over him. No, he thought to himself. Her pregnancy is her own fault. It just makes it worse in her predicament. He thought cynically. Would the second plastic surgeon be able to smooth over her face, with the help of his portrait? That was what Alois and he knew she once was?

Strange Maurice thought as he turned to leave Claudine now that she was on her way back to the chateau, that the only person he could turn to in this crisis was his wife Elize. She would for all his arrogance towards her over the last few years while he was gaining ground or losing it in his career as an artist, be the perfect sop to his conscience. As he knew she could she would sympathize in her simple way yet also see through the complications of what had happened.

She would be grateful yes because the Count had given Maurice the wink over the higher price set by the artist who knew of the very great value of the master painter

Giotto's work. It seemed likely that Maurice too would score financially in the deal. Maurice sighed as he walked through the darkening evening in the forest on his way back home. Suddenly he felt pleased, satisfied that in all the work that he had done as a painting artist he had never allowed himself to fall physically for any of his models.

No, none were as loving, earthy, understanding and hard-working as his wife Elize. Suddenly he found himself at the door of the chalet. He had been away so long and it was good to be welcomed by the open arms of Elize. He would tell her immediately of Claudine's plight. In his forthright way having taken off his jacket he said:

"Claudine is pregnant." In her calm manner Elize put her finger to her lips. "Hush! The children are asleep and Grandmêre is nodding off in front of the fire." He said:

"I did tell you that she has to undergo another operation to save her facial beauty by plastic surgery. The doctors cannot save her pregnancy as well. Alois will never know, she asked me to keep it quiet. Suddenly a creaking voice, that of Grandmêre could be heard:

"Pregnant? Who is pregnant? Are you pregnant again Elize?" Elize went to calm the old woman as only she could. "No Grandmêre," she said. It is just one of Maurice's models." This was quite truthful and she fussed around the old lady making her more comfortable and warm and thus avoided saying any more about it. Maurice was pacing to and fro in the kitchen.

Luckily Lazlé had managed to bag another rabbit and had prepared it for Elize to cook during the early afternoon. She made a mental note to ask Lazlé if his brother knew of the situation. Lazlé would be shocked she knew. She would speak to him the next day and save him some of the rabbit stew to eat while Maurice was out at the bistros, cafés and taverns touting for business.

Claudine was now in her feminine way faced with four different attitudes from the men with whom she usually associated. Those were chiefly Alois, Maurice less often now that her portrait was done, Anzlé, importantly and quite seldom Lazlé. She met up with Anzlé who was clearly missing her as he shuffled up to the gate to Alois' property. By force of habit Claudine found herself talking to him over the last few days before leaving for the hospital with Maurice to accompany her. She reminded her former lover:

"You know I am pregnant. Six weeks gone already. I did not tell you that I will have two operations while in Paris. One is to abort the pregnancy."

Anzlé began to dither. He was at a loss as to what to say to this news. He thought that he had better pretend loyalty under the circumstances that were favorable to him socially. It would have been a chaotic situation if Claudine had borne him a child. The whole story would have had to come out. He said somewhat slyly:

"Well it is Maurice who is accompanying you to the hospital so I won't be needed."

Gathering together some spunk she answered quite bitterly:

"Yes it has so happened that things are being played your way." He snapped at her: "Not only my way Claudine— don't you realize that we are going to lose the baby?" She answered tightly: "But this the only and unavoidable way out. And it is I who will suffer. Her eyes were just visible through a gap in the shawl that she continually wore. He turned to one side noticing the grief showing in her eyes begin to stream with tears.

"Anzlé," she continued, "if I had know this could happen I would have sworn off seeing you ever again as I do now. Was this intentional on your side or was it just a mistake?" He said looking profoundly anxious:" You know I'll never tell you that Claudine:" She answered: "Then I don't want to see you again ever, Anzlé. Please keep out of my company in future." He responded: "You know that will be impossible. We are bound to brush shoulders sometime or other. We live in the same village. I'll never tell Alois you can be sure of that Claudine." She replied finally: "You are at least showing a little loyalty. I wonder what I'll feel towards you once my operations are over." "Yes," said Anzlé. "It might just all be different then."

The days grew shorter and nearer to the time when she and Maurice would set off for Paris. Finally the day before she was due in hospital she and Antoinette packed a small valise of nightwear. Claudine was behaving bravely with Antoinette cheering her along saying:

"I have heard Madame, that you will be completely your old self when the surgery is over. What did the doctor say?"

"Yes, the last scars will be gone within two weeks," answered Claudine becoming enthusiastic now. She would be the same Claudine as before the accident but a chastened one.

"There now." Antoinette snapped the valise shut saying. "Now just you get a good night's rest and your ordeal will be over in a few days time." No one at the chateau knew that she would be having two operations, not just one. She tensed as she realized that only Maurice and Anzlé knew what was being planned for her. As she and Maurice sat down in the comfortable compartment of the express train Claudine murmured:

"I suppose Alois has allowed you to book into a hotel nearby the hospital?" "Yes," Maurice responded. Then Claudine questioned him anxiously.

"How are you and the doctors going to keep the secret of my pregnancy from Alois?" He replied: "I am hoping that Alois will not have to know at all as the hospital that you are going to is a state institution."

The picturesque countryside rushed by and soon they were finished the journey and walking up the street to the hospital where Claudine was expected to book in that afternoon. Then they stood and waited in the queue at the reception desk. Maurice and Claudine were handed over to a brisk nurse who addressed Claudine:

"Countess you can come along with me." She spoke to Maurice:

"We will not need you for the next few days. You can report back here on Friday to see the Countess Claudine. The operations will be over by then." Then to Claudine she said:

"You do know you will be having two surgical procedures Countess?"

Claudine nodded keen now to co-operate all she could knowing and believing that she would be herself in looks within a short time now. She still had the scarf pulled over her face. She thought as the nurse pulled at the shawl playfully, anyone sensitive would wear a covering if in the condition she was in. Maurice had asked Alois to loan his portrait of her to the doctors who would be doing the operation and he went off to hand the picture over to the administrative staff. They would see that the surgeon doing the plastic surgery on Claudine's face would receive it.

It was quite a commotion at the village station platform where Alois was seeing off Claudine still swathed in her scarf and Maurice with her. They were starting their journey to Paris where Claudine would be hospitalized. Alois said:

"Be careful of that portrait Maurice!" "Yes," he replied, "it has a double value now both a reminder to the surgeon as to what Claudine once looked like and also the angelic nature portrayed in the picture. You told us that you had been captured by the likeness of the Giotto Madonna that I sold for you in New York."

Despite all that had happened Maurice still felt the greedy side of his nature satisfied by the bargaining he had done with Mr. Armand in New York. He was at an age when competitiveness in his world of art had got the better of him. It was just too bad what had happened to Claudine. No one seemed to be blameworthy, fortunately for him. He was actually quite curious as to the outcome of the operation.

Being a more intelligent person than most he knew Claudine was in for a devastatingly great change in her looks. He did not think that she or Alois were aware of how her appearance was shortly to be stunningly affected. Maurice held the portrait as well as Claudine's valise as she was intent on hiding her looks from all and sundry.

They had made their way down the carriage to a quiet coupé and settled in for what would be a journey of about three hours. Claudine was almost childishly dependent on her companion. Maurice spoke:

"Have you told Anzlé of your predicament? I have hardly had time to speak to you since we arrived back from New York." Desperately she answered: "Anzlé knows and I am sure that he has told his brother. That means Lazlé will have told Elize, those two are as thick as thieves. I can't imagine what Alois will do to me if he finds out the truth about it my pregnancy, I mean.

Maurice who had a good understanding of human nature realized the devastating situation that Claudine found herself in. Personally he would have thought that both Anzlé and Claudine were adult enough to have avoided Claudine finding herself in the state she was in. He said:

"Has Anzlé showed you no loyalty or sympathy in the circumstances?" She answered:

"When I told him he seemed to be shocked but did not offer to help in any way. You Maurice have been of more assistance to me than anyone. Don't think I will forget it."

Maurice clammed up then not wanting to become too close to Claudine emotionally. The train shot soothingly through the countryside and sooner than expected they arrived at the grand central station and Maurice, holding on to the painting for dear life was hailing a taxi. He felt astounded that Alois had allowed a similar situation to the one they had just come out of in New York, he and Claudine

CHAPTER THIRTEEN

As soon as Maurice and Claudine entered the private hospital where Claudine would have her operation done, a strong scent of ether came to their nostrils. Claudine began to panic but Maurice steadied her holding her arm firmly. Her shawl fell to the floor that was spic and span and shining. Maurice picked it up for her as she tried to hide her face with her hands. She grabbed the shawl and wound it again around her scarred face. A nurse approached. She seemed to know all about Claudine who said bravely:

"I am also here to have an abortion performed."

The nurse looked faintly startled but said:

"You and your escort have arrived just in time to have a consultation with the surgeons. We did not know that you needed an abortion as well but you can discuss it with the doctors." She addressed Maurice: "Are you accompanying the Countess?"

Maurice affirmed this. The nurse continued. "Just wait in the visitor's room down the passage."

Maurice went off and Claudine walked the other way with the nurse. Claudine found herself in an antiseptic-smelling side room facing three doctors. The consultation began. The leading doctor tried to put Claudine at her ease comforting her:

"You won't know yourself once we have finished with you Countess. There is apparently a portrait of you that we can have a look at." Gently he took the scarf from her face. "We'll just have a quick look at the damage. Claudine gave a start as the surgeon expertly ran his fingers over the worst of the cuts that had healed. "Yes, there is nothing showing here that is too bad for the plastic surgeon to rectify. The cuts though unpleasant enough right at present are not too deep that the surgeon cannot deal with them."

Claudine began to feel a little better. She ventured:

"I would like the operation to be done just as soon as possible. However, I will need an abortion first. I was told that you cannot do facial surgery while I am pregnant."

Not phased in any way for as a doctor he had faced many crises, he called for the nurse. An involved medical conversation ensued the result of which was that Claudine found herself in a private ward having been told she would have the abortion the next morning. She was happy that no one made any enquiries as to the reason for her pregnancy.

Meanwhile Maurice had found the clerical section of the clinic and explained to them that no mention of the abortion should be made separately on the medical bill for the two operations. He asked for the bill to be inclusive. Then Alois would not know about Claudine's pregnancy as Maurice had promised her.

Claudine lay in a sprucely cared for hospital bed letting her thoughts wander. The surgeon who was performing her operation had just left. He had told her that the doctors caring for her had quite understood her predicament and did not see any reason why her husband need know anything about the abortion.

This was a necessary part of the surgical procedure if the plastic surgeon was to operate within the following few days. As she sighed with relief there was a tentative soft knock on the door of the private ward where she lay. The door opened and Maurice's head peered around it. He whispered loudly:

"Is it alright for me to come in for a while? I have the confirmation with the clerical section of the clinic that your two operations will be put under one section. There will be no differentation." He continued sympathetically:

"Claudine—what a mess to be in!" She responded slowly as it was an emotional time to be undergoing with the abortion the next day:

"Does the plastic surgeon have the portrait you did of me? He seemed pleased to have it available if possible." Maurice nodded. Claudine said with great pain in her voice:

"I go in tomorrow morning for the first operation, that is a Tuesday isn't it Maurice?" "Right," he answered. She continued, her voice soft and seeming to float into Maurice's hearing. "Then on Thursday they said if I was strong enough to take the operation for plastic surgery I would have the second anaesthetic. Maurice I don't know how I am going to live through it all."

Encouragingly his voice came into her senses from as far away as she was in spirit at the time, from him or anyone else for that matter. "It is only an ordeal of three or four more days Claudine. I will be in to visit you every evening. I know that if Alois knew the truth he would take your part against the dilemma that has happened with the condition that Anzlé has left you in." She whispered back:

"Do you really think so Maurice? Then I don't feel so bad." Maurice was quiet, feeling a sense of the kindness that his words had meant to Claudine. She said:

"When it's all over everything will be turned upside down, my life and my relationships. I will never be able to forget my ordeal that I am going through. My whole feeling towards you, Anzlé, Alois and Lazlé too will change. I can never go back to being the thoughtless and insensitive person that I was, if the plastic surgery is a success." Maurice responded:

"But it will be and maybe in more than one sense, for the best. You can turn over a new leaf Claudine."

Maurice reliable as usual for all his artistic emotions, felt for the friendship he had with both Alois and Claudine that he should pay Claudine a visit on the evening after her first operation, the abortion. He cornered one of the younger nurses and asked:

"Is the Countess Claudine still in the same private ward?" The young woman answered: "Yes she is still very shy about her looks at present not wanting to mix with all the other patients in the more general ward. She told me that she was half expecting that you would call around to see her this evening." Maurice queried, "and how is she nurse?" "Oh!" The woman answered, "the Countess is a strong woman for her age. She has taken the surgery well and told me she was looking forward to seeing you this evening." Maurice asked, "Can I just let myself in then to her private ward? "Certainly," the little nurse answered, "just keep your visit quiet and calm."

Maurice pushed the door open. The sight of Claudine ever with her face covered with her white shawl shook even the perpetually cynical Maurice. She was not aware of him at first and was lying on her side looking out at the trees in the park outside the window at some children playing there. Then she became aware of Maurice's presence. Without waiting for him to speak first she spoke forthrightly with pain in her voice:

"Look at the children out there. I'll never have the chance to have one of my own now ever to talk to, love or play with. How angry I am with Anzlé for his disloyalty. I could have borne my child if only he had given me the support I needed. I would not have minded what attitude Alois had taken towards me then. He would have let me do as I pleased he is such a softhearted old dodderer."

Maurice was surprised at her admission to him of the inner workings of their relationship. Alois' age was telling on his behavior. He was in his late fifties and Maurice thought, far too old for someone like Claudine. However as he knew a younger husband than Alois would have had less patience with Claudine's predicament and would have been sharper on the uptake as to what she had let herself in for in her relationship with Anzlé. So Maurice said slyly:

"It would never have worked and you know it Claudine. You would both have been the talk of the town." Claudine lifted her head to nod woefully in assent to what Maurice had just said, continuing, "I have to wait three or four days more and then the surgeon will do my plastic surgery. Oh! Maurice!" she exclaimed with deep emotion. "I can't wait to be out of here. I intend to start my life again in a new and thankful, repentant way, from my heart."

Maurice was quiet for a few minutes then said: "I am glad you feel so hopeful about the result of your operation." He put in a response saying: "I also am confident of the success of the operation. Alois telephoned me from the chateau this morning. In his way he is very concerned about you." She replied: "Yes I do feel tense about tomorrow. It seems a chance that I am taking but I am so hopeful. I vow to change my whole attitude to all my friends and acquaintances. I will give my whole heart to you all who have seen me through this ordeal.

Alois has, in his bumbling way been only loyal to me though has distanced himself from my situation. He is an older man and does not quite understand the surgical procedure that I have to undergo. He will be pleased and satisfied when he sees me my old self again. Oh! Maurice! The surgeon has promised there will be no scars. It will be as if my whole life will be renewed. I do vow that I will be a better person for this pain that I have to submit to. But it was my fault I do know that now. I could have left matters as they were but I do care about what I look like Maurice you know that."

Maurice was becoming a little impatient at this female chatter from Claudine, but managed to control himself. For his own ends he hoped that he would not be blamed for the trouble Claudine found herself in. He was though genuinely glad that she was coming out of her dream world of only hoping to be her old self again. He wished she would find that in two week's time as the surgeon had promised she was nearly the spitting image of Maurice's portrait of her. That was, with a touch of the atmosphere created by his treatment of the portrait using Alois' painting, the Giotto masterpiece that he had copied.

Visiting hour was drawing to a close and Maurice got up to leave. "Good luck Claudine," he bade her. She said: "I am sad to see you go this evening. It has almost been for me that you are my good luck charm." Maurice responded:

"No luck needed in this matter. I also am anxious to see your beauty return to what it was."

Maurice walked over to the door and stood there a moment, Claudine's eyes fixed on him. "Goodbye Claudine," he said. As she went to sleep that night she thought to herself Maurice doesn't mind how I look but he at least does appreciate what my beauty could be."

Her last thoughts on the night before the operation were of Anzlé. How could he have taken such an uncaring attitude towards her? Her heart sank. The fact that the pregnancy had also been terminated for the sake of regaining her once beautiful looks had finished their relationship forever. How could she even live in the same village as he did never knowing when their paths might cross each day? Certainly Alois even Maurice and Lazlé had been more loyal to her in the period of her unsightliness.

As the deep slumber of the sleeping pill came upon her she wondered if it was human nature to be so in love with someone once there was a child in the mother's womb. Then Claudine was becoming used to the situation She was on a portable bed outside as she peered into a bare antiseptically odoured operation theatre.

Her ward nurse was wishing her luck even blowing her a kiss. Claudine summoned up courage as she was wheeled in and lifted onto the austere theatre bed. As she knew now in her third operation in three weeks the anaesthetist was approaching her right arm that was strapped down to prevent movement. She felt giddy as she knew she would and then she became unconscious. There was a team of three plastic surgeons who had spoken to her a few days ago studying her countenance all the while.

They promised an exact replica of the portrait they had studied before attempting the operation. They shaped and bent Claudine's skin into a model of what she had been, using their ointments and salves. The operation took nearly three hours and at last the surgeons were satisfied. Claudine was stirring. They wheeled her back to the ward before she came round from the anaesthetic. Her first words were:

"Finished? . . . are the doctors finished with me? It's all over . . . . I can't believe it. Is there a mirror nurse?" The nurse replied: "You will be disappointed to see the immediate result of the surgery. Only in two weeks or so will you see the change. Try not to look too much in the mirror at this stage or you will be disappointed and get depressed. Take it slowly Countess."

Claudine fell asleep soon after this exchange of words and woke to find a good strong cup of tea next to the bed and later on a nourishing lunch. She felt a yen to see Maurice knowing that he would be curious to view what was transpiring in the hospital. It was surprising the relationship that had developed between the artist and his model.

Claudine would just have loved to get her hands on a mirror but found that her pocket mirror a gift from Alois had been removed, by the nurse presumably. Carefully she lifted her right hand up to her neck and chin. Funny, with a thrill she felt nothing on her smooth skin. She wondered. Were there marks on her skin? She inched her hand further up her face. She had the same sensation. The nurse on seeing what Claudine was doing came by her bed, ostensibly to remove her teacup. She said:

"Would you like a little more tea Countess?" With her mind half on the nurse and preoccupied with the state of her face, Claudine murmured: "Yes I would. Nurse! My skin feels so smooth. Are there marks on it?" The nurse replied: "Doctor Auret wanted it to be a surprise for you. Your artist acquaintance has been told not to tell you either. It is to be a secret." Claudine said smiling for the first time since the accident:

"I don't know how I am going to bear not being able to see what I look like." The nurse spoke again:

"The surgeon wanted your hair to be cut but we nurses, knowing that it is a beauty feature of yours managed to tie it up and put a cap on your head during the procedure so you will have your full glory when the two weeks are up. You must have a generous husband to pay for the operation that you had. This is an expensive clinic."

Claudine's thoughts went to Alois. The Alois who hardly realized that she was in existence with so many tourist visitors at the chateau.

Thinking seriously her conscience pricked again even though she had made her confession to Padre d'Aguire about her affair with Anzlé and its disastrous result. She had to cover her feelings about him each time she was with him. Alois would never know that it was not he whom she loved. Also it was not Anzlé either now. She sighed. Was her heart free then? Somehow she felt it was not

Who was she in love with then? Her heart was behaving foolishly. It was not being in love that she needed, it was a friend. After confessing to the Padré she felt that she must never get into such a situation as had happened with Anzlé again. Maurice? Yes Maurice would fill in the gap in her heart for a friend. Alois was so loyal. Too loyal to be romantic. She thought to herself. Alois is like the father I never had growing up in the slums of Paris.

Maurice visited Claudine regularly every evening keen to see how his one time model protégée was improving in her looks. He had been only too glad to bring with him to the clinic the portrait he had done of her for Alois. "Yes," he said to her slowly after a week: "You are beginning to look your old beautiful self again, Claudine."

Always during these two weeks of recuperation she pestered Maurice to tell her how she was improving day by day. "Are there still scars on my face Maurice?" She asked continually. "How would you describe the marks left by the surgeon?" The ever vigilant nurse came by and heard their conversation. "Don't tell her Maurice. Let her wait out the full two weeks," the nurse chided.

When she had gone Maurice looked critically at Claudine. He said earnestly: "I am sure it would do you good if I were to tell you how your looks are improving. I'll be your mirror Claudine and whisper to you about how your face is coming on."

He dropped a couple of tones in his normally clear voice: "All I can see are what look like pieces of skin sticking down in a kind of pink color under each part of your face that the surgeons have worked on.

Each evening I come in to visit you I look anxiously to see how these marks are fast disappearing and they are too. How does that feel to you Claudine, knowing that?"

"Much happier," she answered emphatically. He continued:

"I can quite see that in six or seven days the lesions will be invisible. And the pain and suffering that you went through have left on your countenance a tremendous likeness to the Giotto Madonna that I used when doing you portrait."

At this compliment, had it been made before the accident Claudine would have simpered but now her face dropped in humble thanks that her looks had been restored to their once glamorous state. Soon Claudine was smiling gently when the surgeon who had performed the operation visited her sickbed. Claudine broke out:

"Thank you, thank you doctor! You have made my life worth living again. What you have done for me has opened up new avenues in my being."

The doctor chuckled at her obvious newfound happiness. He said:

"Tomorrow I have ordered nurse to let you have your mirror back." She did not tell him that Maurice had told her how her face was healing. He was there by her bedside the evening before her last day in hospital. He remarked, covering his enthusiasm:

"I feel I could paint your portrait all over again quite happily, Claudine."

The day dawned when the nurse and doctors were completely satisfied with the result of the plastic surgery performed on Claudine's face. She almost grabbed her hand mirror as the nurse was returning it. Claudine hissed at her benefactor:

"Where is the light best in this ward?"

The first of the sunshine crept through the window showing that it was turning out into a wonderful summer's day. Claudine, thoroughly recovered after two week's bed rest, stepped lightly out of the high hospital bed and holding the mirror walked swiftly across the ward. She pulled open the curtain of the window. It was as if the sun was shining through her face. She said unbelievingly:

"Nurse I am delighted with what I see. The operation has been a complete success as far as I can perceive. What do you suggest I use as a cleanser until my face has quite settled down to normal female facial attention?" The nurse answered, anticipating this question: "Doctor has suggested you use this tin of antiseptic cleansing pads, one twice a day." Claudine responded thoughtfully: "I must say my face has been feeling very tight since the operation, a feeling that has gradually lessened until today. Yes! Today feels like the beginning of the rest of my life. I can't wait to see Maurice this evening and Alois later tomorrow. I feel a new calmness now even though I am excited and thrilled at the transformation in my looks."

She spent the rest of the day looking into her mirror every now and again, much to her nurse's amusement. When Maurice arrived at seven that evening he too was quite taken up with her reaction. He chided her saying:

"You have many years to live out before the character of a lifetime shows on your countenance. I know this because I have painted several older women models. I do find them far more interesting subjects than younger females. You are an exception Claudine because I had to paint into my picture of you the golden aura of the Italian Renaissance using Alois' Giotto Madonna masterpiece. I can almost see the loveliness, almost holiness that has come upon your countenance."

Claudine had lost all her old worldly simpering upon being flattered about her looks. There was silence between the two.

"You see Maurice," she confided, "I have been spending time with Padré d'Aguire at the Chateau chapel. I have made confession of my affair with Anzlé and its terrible consequences, the loss of my pregnancy. I have been given absolution for my sin and will have as little to do with Anzlé in the future as possible. He has proved his disloyalty to me when he saw the once ugly condition of my face, and I have broken off our relationship altogether."

Maurice was surprised when he heard of her admittance to him of the religious divergency in her character. He remarked casually grateful, but silently that he had no part in Anzlé's and Claudine's relationship:

"So you feel nothing for Anzlé any more Claudine?" She snapped at him for the personal nature of his query:

"He is a person with a weak character. I see that now. Of course if he had really loved me he would have shown some pity or regret for what I endured that was as you know Maurice, partly for his sake. Padré d'Aguire to whom I confessed having no one else to turn to in my distress, has advised me not to let my feelings turn to despising my former lover. Because that is what he has been reduced to in my eyes. Maurice ever interested in his former model's affairs, asked:

"Has he told you he is ending the relationship?" Claudine answered bitterly:

"I told him in a few words at the gate to the castle grounds where we used to meet, to give the affair the final blow in ending it. Alois, bless his dear soul had no idea what was transpiring right under his nose. Sometimes Anzlé and I used to laugh unkindly behind the old man's back but my now frequent talks with Padré d'Aguire have made me understand how fortunate I am to be in the social position that Alois has created for me. As you know I have been dragged out of the gutter in Paris in that Alois took me on as his wife."

Both of them were quiet for a while. Claudine looked at Maurice curiously and the artist ever observant was almost reading her mind. He knew that she was wondering about his own place in her life. They were both as self-seeking as each other but there was a strange bond between them. Claudine said:

"My whole life has changed as a result of this accident and the two operations that were my ordeal. I feel a new love of people even towards Lazlé, Anzlé's twin brother. I feel pity for the dwarf in his poor disfigured shape. Anzlé used to tell me about his brother how well he gets on with Elize. Lazlé told him of his and Elize's relationship at your chalet that it didn't even matter to you. Is that because of me Maurice?"

Her old vanity since being chosen as Alois' wife was again coming to the fore. Maurice replied half seriously:

"Haven't you just told me how your life has changed since confessing to Padré d'Aguire?"

A flash of religious sentiment shadowed Claudine's face. "Yes," she said. "It is a difficult choice to make but Padré d'Aguire warned me that my life would not be easy from now on. I have changed you see Maurice, since I have seen my face healed. How ugly I looked after the accident."

It was a sudden realization, a shock to realize the interest Maurice was showing her. In his simple way he could not get over the result of the restoration of Claudine's former beauty. They both knew it had opened up a sparkling new relationship between them. She was further drawn to Maurice in that he had never thrown at her the ugliness of her disfigurement after the taxi crash.

The trauma she had undergone had caused her to forget that Maurice could probably be feeling guilty still about what had happened to cause her disfigurement even though it had been only temporary. Maurice was curious of this and knew very well that it was he who had caused the car chase by haggling and bargaining with Mr.

Armand the curator of the art gallery where the Giotto picture had been sold eventually.

Claudine suddenly came out of her dreamy state and having said nothing for a while knowing that Maurice was feasting his eyes once again on the loveliness of the Countess now restored to her former beauty. A buzzer sounded and visiting hours were over. Seeing Maurice was lost in his imagination she said sharply:

"You have to go now Maurice." "Yes, oh! Yes! Of course," he answered coming suddenly out of his daydream.

In gentler tones those brought on by her new findings about life in knowing Padré d'Aguire, she promised:

"I must see you again Maurice. I will make sure that Alois invites you to some of our social gatherings. You won't feel embarrassed to attend one or two as they come up?"

Maurice queried her thoughts on the matter:

"But why should I Claudine? I am used to any situation with models and especially you." The end had come too soon for Claudine, now in the earnest conversation that she was having with him. The nurse was chasing the visitors out. It was time for meditation and sleep for the patients. They had just been getting to the point of the memory of her modeling nude, or life postures as Maurice called them.

Without being precocious she knew that with her newly found state of mind after her confession to Padré d'Aguire that she would never again allow anyone see her naked body other than Alois. Padré d'Aguire had installed a whole new set of morals in her that included even her husband. Alois had little demand of her physically now in her newly self styled and appointed life. She was being discharged from hospital the following day and would see her husband after traveling down to Boulougne with Maurice by train the next day.

The limousine that Alois had sent from the castle to fetch her had arrived with Maurice having telephoned in to Alois the time of the train's arrival from Paris to Boulougne. It was as she had expected. Alois was not with the driver sent to collect her and Maurice. Not only did she realize that it made life more comfortable this way, but that all he needed from his wife was the social pleasantries that Claudine was so good at having studied a little acting while she had worked in television production. This made her fluent in conversation amongst Alois' friends in the aristocracy.

The only other wish he seemed to have for her was that she take on the spiritual quality on her countenance that Maurice had successfully painted into the portrait he had been commissioned to do of Claudine. This was strangely true now Alois thought to himself one evening while awaiting guests in the entertainment lounge that he had set aside for such purposes at the castle. He spoke to her:

"I see you have given up smoking Claudine. I never really approved of the habit for you. You make me very happy ma chérie. Your whole attitude to life has changed. You are quieter and more mature. But you have not lost your sparkle. You shine even more brightly for me now Claudine."

This time she did not pout or flutter her eyelids as she used to do in the past. Realizing that Alois wanted the best for her she swept her eyes downwards almost humbly, and then upwards as she had caught a glimpse of a familiar personage just entering the doorway. Yes, it was Anzlé. How could she face him? Alois obviously had not a clue as to his wife's past relationship with her lover. She did know that he was a business associate of her husband's. If Alois knew nothing of their past liaison then he also could not know anything about the result.

Maurice, she thought—as his presence came to her mind then in he walked at the entrance to the guest lounge. This was going to be a difficult situation. She would again have to play the part of the social butterfly amongst the guests slipping in and out of Maurice's and Anzlé's company. Nothing embarrassing it appeared would be revealed. The gossip regarding her and Anzlé's affair cut sharply through at Claudine amidst the conversational gibes and gaffes. It was obvious though that no one was going to embarrass her. As usual Maurice stood at a distance wondering how they both felt. It seemed that the friendships remained amongst the four people concerned, those being Alois, Claudine Anzlé and Maurice.

Claudine kept a slow conversation going with Maurice. They had spent much time together both in the studio where he had painted her portrait and also traveling to New York. There they had the horrific experience of their taxi's crashing in a car chase egged on it must be admitted by Claudine herself she not really knowing why the Art Gallery assistant of Mr. Armand had been following them.

Claudine's watchful eye could see Anzlé edging his way in the crowd coming nearer and nearer to her. She was thoroughly aware of how glamorous she was looking and tried to avoid his approach by buttonholing Maurice who was sizing up his own involvement in their situation at the current soirée being hosted by Alois. Maurice half whispered sideways to Claudine:

"I think Anzlé has something to say to you Claudine." Seeing that he was being spoken about Anzlé stopped in his tracks and began a conversation nearby Claudine and Maurice with an attractive woman who had been invited to the gathering. A femme fatale herself, Claudine sparked anger at this attempt by Anzlé to kindle jealousy in his past lover.

Maurice sought to calm the situation and began one of his ploys with women first by greeting Anzlé so joining the couple. This gave Claudine breathing space. She heard Maurice speak and smiled to herself as she sipped her cocktail:

"Yes I am an experienced artist always on the lookout for a new and unusual model. I specialize in portraits. You are new in the region?"

The conversation drifted on and Claudine lost interest for the moment as Anzlé ever attracted to her especially at that present time, drew up close to Claudine. Oh! She thought. I know all your manoevres. Our relationship is over—over! He spoke:

"Claudine!" His almost desperate tones still reaching her senses met her ears. Sharply she snapped at him in a whisper audible only to the two of them.

"What do you want with me Anzlé. You know I told you it is over. Haven't I endured enough for you sake? I think Alois suspected our affair. That is why he sent me to New York accompanied by Maurice." "Was there a baby? . . . ." Hissed Anzlé urgently. "What happened to our child?" Claudine answered:

"This is not the time or place to discuss that." She could see that Maurice was listening to their conversation. Surely as always Maurice would rescue her from this social gaffe of a situation. She was right. Maurice could not move over to the couple quickly enough. It was awkward and tense for her now as Alois had sensed that his wife was in difficulties socially. She could see that he was ending off his conversation with a neighboring farmer and anxious to come to the side of Claudine.

Anzlé was not so fast on the uptake as Maurice and Alois in coming to her rescue. Quick witted as always Maurice had heard how Anzlé was slowly letting the cat out of the bag as far as his now past affair with Claudine was concerned. Then Maurice was at her left side and taking a plunge said to Anzlé guilelessly:

"Anzlé you are the kind of person whose portrait I would be charmed to do. I do not do many paintings of men but feel you are the sort of person whose appearance I would be interested in sketching. Surely we can make an appointment to begin sometime soon?"

Anzlé was thrown off course in his persecuting of his past lover. He was flattered by what Maurice had said but was not finished with Claudine. He did not regard himself as being fully responsible for the affair.

No, he bitterly thought to himself we were just the idle rich at play. In her new guise of honest and true wife to Alois Claudine had taken onto her countenance, much to Maurice's surprise a living atmosphere of piety similar to Alois' Madonna that he had now sold. She caught her breath at the conversation between the three of them with Alois approaching, giving her the upper hand thanks to Maurice. She uttered holding back her tears:

"Anzlé I will explain everything to you tomorrow that is Sunday. I am attending a little communion service in the chapel. Wait for me outside at nine o' clock at the entrance."

At her taking the upper hand Anzlé turned on his heel and made for the door. Everyone there could see that feathers had been ruffled. Maurice just intimated to Claudine:

"I will wait outside the chapel also in case Alois is with you."

The next morning standing outside outside the old oak door of the little place of worship Maurice heard the sound of ritual chanting of prayers from inside. Then a single voice in a monotone sounded, on one note only and then afterwards silence. The door opened and a couple of farm workers and a few of the chateau staff appeared. Then a figure approached adorned with a black lace veil over her face. Beneath the lace work her eyes searched out Anzlé as he approached and as Maurice watched cynically she threw back the veil and spoke to her former lover pausing slightly first, then in almost a whisper:

"There will be no baby Anzlé. The doctors took it away. I had to sacrifice having a child for my looks. The infant inside me would not have been able to withstand the operation that I had on my face."

The nettles between the flagged stonework of the pathway were stinging her ankles Maurice could see. Anzlé felt bitterness and gall take hold of him and turned to leave. Maurice took Claudine's arm and her face turned to the newly risen sun. She and Maurice walked briskly back to the Chateau.